AF441747

Also by Joe Prosit

Machines Monsters and Maniacs Volume I

Machines Monsters and Maniacs Volume II

Bad Brains

99 Town, Book One of the "From Order" Series

7 Androids, Book Two of the "From Order" Series

Zero City, Book Three of the "From Order" Series

Look What You Made Me Do

They Come From Below

And…

The Reality Reaction Team

LOOK WHAT YOU MADE ME DO

A PYSCHOLOGICAL
SLASHER HORROR NOVEL

JOE PROSIT

**SPACE SKULL
BOOKS**

Space Skull Books
7505 Lone Oak Rd
Brainerd, MN 56401

Author Photo by Cadence Porisch, on Instagram @cadey_photography
Cover art by Jaime Coker, on Instagram @jaime.coker_artist.

Contact the author at www.JoeProsit.com or by email at joeprosit@gmail.com.

Chapter One

"Okay. Tell me everything. Everything you can remember."

Well, let me start by saying not all memories are fond. Sure, the bullshit ones are. The ones you use like paint to gloss over all the not-so-nostalgic experiences of your youth? I'll give you that. We all do it. Falsify our memories to create a version of our past that we prefer over the one we actually lived. Even those ones aren't always fair and true like fairy tale princesses. Some memories are more like brackish swamps: murky and opaque, eager to pull you in and swallow you whole the moment you dip in a toe. Mine have always been more like that than the proverbial "rose-colored" reflections of others. Never nice. Never clear.

You have no idea how much effort I've put into not remembering that night. The details slip from my mind like slick leopard frogs caught at the edge of a reedy pond. Just when I think I've pulled one free and can hold it in my hand, it kicks loose and splooshes back into the dark waters. It hurts just to think about it.

Let me ask you something. Do you think Nancy Thompson ever stopped having nightmares? What's your bet that Wendy Torrance spent one more night of her life inside a hotel? You really believe Laurie Strode grew up to be a well-balanced, high-functioning woman who sent her kids out trick or treating each October 31st?

"But you're a real woman, Taylor. They're not."

If this isn't real, then none of it matters.

I was seventeen years old. It was the summer of '99. It was late in the season. Past equinox. Days were getting shorter. Almost fall. Late at night. Way past midnight. Everything was at its twilight. The night. The summer. The decade. My youth. Everything was coming to an end. Everything was about to begin. The century was over. The year was One. I was there, where it all happened. At the cabin by the lake… In our quiet little neighborhood… Deep underneath our high school… In a sprawling, abandoned hotel… It's hard to remember which.

He wasn't one of us. I don't know why he chose us. Don't even know how he found us. It wasn't like we weren't minding our own business. But he sought us out. He watched us. We had nothing to do with him, but he came for us, from hell. And for what? I mean, I know he saw what we were doing. What we were up to.

"What were you doing?"

Just kid stuff, you know? We got some beers from somebody's older brother. There were a couple of bottles of booze. Maybe a little weed. So, yeah. Drinking. Smoking. Sex. Nothing serious. All the normal stuff kids do when they think they can get by with it, you know?

I always figured he was some religiously repressed, sheltered, middle-aged celibate, jealous of us teenagers. That's the only thing that makes sense. Not that any of it can make any real sense. That's why it's so hard to remember. Like pieces from different jigsaw puzzles, nothing fits together. There's no rationale behind it. But that had to be it, right? He hated what he never had? That had to be why he did what he did.

"What did he look like?"

I don't remember. I don't know if I ever saw his face. Or if he had a face. I don't like to think about it. I remember his eyes. Just his eyes and that permanent rictus of a teethy smile. No nose or chin or cheeks. No features besides those hollow eyes and that hungry smile. A blank canvas of a face upon which I could paint all my nightmares. But I remember those hellfire eyes, and I remember thinking, "What have they done to him? What have they done to his eyes?" They burned. When they closed, when he died and they shut for good never to open again, it felt like someone had been holding my hand inside a furnace, and I was finally able to pull it free.

It was so hot. I'll never forget how thick the air was. That late summer down by the lakeshore. In our old neighborhood. Inside that empty hotel.

In that basement boiler room. Hotter than any other summer night that came before or since then.

I left him there, dead, on the shore of the lake. The machete I used barely clung to the insides of my fingers, I was so weak. I didn't need it anymore, but I didn't know that, so I let it stay there in my hand. It was heavy, that ax. But I didn't let it drop. Even as those thick rusted nails pounded through the barrel of that Louisville Slugger dragged through the dirt and snagged on the grass, I hung onto it.

All my friends. They lay everywhere, strewn about, as lifeless and limp and empty as used condoms thrown toward but not into a bathroom garbage can. Gross to look at, worse to touch and pick up, but so recently full of excitement and energy and danger and potential and life. Everything was quiet except the distant police sirens breaking through the stiffness of the night's silence, growing louder as they approached. I staggered up the hill, away from the lake, threading between all my murdered friends, careful not to catch one of their twisted arms or legs with the head of the ax as it furrowed a line through the dirt behind me. Even as mauled and mutilated as they were, it seemed perverse to do their corpses any more harm. The machete drizzled blood in a trail as I made my way through them, so much it was as if the blade itself was bleeding from some internal waning heart. I was careful not to get any of the killer's blood on any of them.

My friends had nothing left inside.

I still did. Blood in my veins. A beat in my heart. Fire behind my eyes.

But he took something from me I can never get back. That thing inside of everybody when they're young, that belief that the world had order, that the living and the dead were two separable things, that the dead only belong in suits or fancy dresses inside of expensive, silk-lined caskets with their heads resting on lacy pillows, their hands folded, maybe twisted up with a rosary, their resting faces peacefully caked over with too much foundation, their eyes closed. That's how we're supposed to see them. That was the only way to see the dead, or so I believed. Done up, put on display, briefly exposed like nudity in an R-rated movie, only to be glanced upon and then tucked away. But that's not how it really is. Death is an interactive thing. Something we are a part of. Something I'm a part of anyway. Something I've done. Something continuously done to me.

Sometimes, it takes time to die. Sometimes it's quick.

His was quick. Too quick, really, for all that he'd done. His hands came away too clean for how much he played with death. He deserved to endure it for much longer than he had, and I deserved to savor it. But it was short.

Guess that was my fault.

Why can't I see your face?

"Where did all this take place again? You said you were by a lake."

Not by a lake. It was in our old neighborhood. Quaint, little houses all in rows twisted through the development. Elm trees hung over the street. We'd walk to school each morning. At night we'd sneak out and climb up to each other's bedroom windows. It was a good place to grow up back then, before everything happened. I've never gone back. Not since that night. We moved away. How could anyone live there after seeing all those bodies laid out in the mowed and trimmed and watered front lawns? I shut my eyes and see that morning when the sprinklers came on automatically, simultaneously, as if the neighborhood had its own desire to wash away the horrors of the previous night. But the stains wouldn't rinse away, and no amount of paint could cover all the blood splattered across our bedroom walls.

"You said you left the killer down by the lakeside."

I did. Aren't you listening? Haven't you heard a goddamn word I've said? I killed him! I took the ax he used on all of us and buried it in his brain. And I hung onto it, all the way through those twisting hallways lined with numbered doors, across the ballroom with its big windows and grand fireplace, through the lobby littered with my dead friends, toward the sound of those police cars, toward all those cameras and the reporters with their endless fucking questions. It was still dark outside. Only their flashing lights came through the front doors. It was the cusp of dawn. During that time when the sky isn't quite black anymore but before the sun breaks through the horizon. There was no sound inside that old place. No elevator music. No muffled noises coming through the walls. No drone of air conditioning. After I killed him, even as I was panting and hyperventilating, I remember noticing how suddenly calm and still everything had become. The only thing that beat was my heart. All that moved the air was my lungs. *My heart.* And *my lungs.* No one else's. Before they all came, it was only me. Just me. I had time to look at all the bodies. I had time to see our mortal nudity good and true, without the cameras cutting away, without the tracking flicking the images up, up, and up between lines of static as if someone hit the pause button on an old VHS. No. I saw it all in high-definition clarity and had time to comprehend death.

"When the police arrived, you made a statement?"

When I crawled out of the basement under our school, morning emerged too. A breeze cut through the stifling heat, chilling the sweat coating my skin. Nothing like where I'd spent the night, deep down in the sweltering dark. Down there, everything was searing metal. Steam gushed from pipes. You couldn't see far ahead of you. The furnace burned so hot you could feel it from everywhere down there in the darkness. It was so hot.

When I walked out of those front doors, it was bright and sunny. No clouds. Pure, unfiltered daylight welcomed me out of the abyss. All of the people were dressed nice. Everything was clean. The makeup was back on the corpse and the lid of the casket was sealed shut and adorned with flowers again. I was the only one who truly knew that darkness from which I came. As for all the cops, when they showed up, they brought the news vans with them, and they brought even more lights to stab into my eyes. I must have looked like something born from hell. My clothes were ripped and covered in dirt and blood. I never let go of that machete, even as they surrounded me and swallowed me and set into me with all their fangs and lights and questions.

"So, what did you say to them, as best as you can remember?"

I told them, "He's back there. The killer. He's dead. I killed him."

"And then?"

And then? Don't you remember how Sally Hardesty looked when she rode away in the pickup at the end of *The Texas Chainsaw Massacre*? Look me in the eyes and tell me that Ellen Ripley carried on with her life not checking over her shoulder with each step she took. Do you honestly believe that Sidney Prescott ever stopped screaming?

Chapter Two

The first time I really came to terms with what happened, with my past I mean, was in Doctor Hagari's office. Not that I give him any credit for it. I mean, he brought it up during our sessions. Sessions I never wanted to attend to begin with. It was a work thing. But he was no Sigmund Freud, no matter how much he wanted people to suck on his cigar. I was… directed to see him. Long story. I mean, if normal people can get through a workweek without a little help from the bottle, you'll never convince me that they're the sane ones. But yeah, I started to come to grips with what I'd been through during those counseling sessions.

The murders. The killer. How I was the one who put an end to all of it. At first, he just wanted to talk about generational substance abuse, cycles of addiction, maladaptive behaviors, and self-destructive tendencies. But eventually, inevitably, our talks switched to survivor guilt and post-traumatic stress reaction. He was always too eager whenever I opened up in the slightest. He enjoyed it too much. I think he got off on it.

He was this sort of jolly, rotund man. Before I ever heard anyone say a thing about him, I knew they'd all gush over how he was such a sweet old man. Probably had kids. Probably had grandkids. He had that favorite grandpa demeanor. Divorced, I think. Maybe widowed. White beard but mixed with red curly hair. He told this joke about how instead of salt and pepper gray, his hair was salt and cayenne pepper, because "I'm not exactly wet behind the ears, but I'm still a little spicy."

At the conclusion of our last session, he told me from behind his desk, "You've done very well, Taylor. You've progressed along quickly, and I think you have a better understanding of the world and your place in it. Remarkable, what we've managed to accomplish together," he said as he filled out the required paperwork to release me from the program.

That wasn't how it felt, by the way. As if he and I had shared some journey of spiritual awakening. As if I was his child, reborn and ready to be sent out into the world. I felt dirty whenever I was around him. Like he'd gotten the better of me without me ever knowing what his scam had been. As if by telling him everything I'd been through, I'd let him peek through my bathroom window while I undressed. But, if he filled out the paperwork saying I'd done my part, that I'd "progressed" and dealt with my issues, then that was all I needed from him.

And there he was, filling out the forms on his desk as I sat there waiting for him to release me. So I smiled and went along with it.

"Yeah. I feel… better, now that we talked," I lied.

"It's still going to take work, healing from what you've been through," Doctor Hagari said, pausing his ink pen as he talked. I watched the pen, me as eager for it to resume its scribbles as he was eager to hear about all the juicy details of my teenage tragedies. "This is a long road you're heading down, and there's many more mile markers to pass, and maybe a fair share of warning signs to heed."

"I think I'm going to lay off the bottle for a while," I said.

"That's a good start," he said. "Your family history hasn't set you up for success. And your experiences have left you with a propensity for high-risk behaviors. Drinking. Antisocial viewpoints. Nonconformist tendencies."

"I listen to pop music," I objected, biting my lips too late to stop myself. "I watch sitcoms. It's not like I'm some social deviant."

"No," Doctor Hagari said. "Externally, you present yourself as a model, professional, adult woman. Amiable. Kind. Good at her job. Funny, when it's appropriate to be funny. Reserved when it's appropriate to be reserved. You rebel inwards. Not endangering others, but often endangering yourself. Like a shaken champagne bottle, all of the chaos is inside for the longest of times, until a thumb slips off the cork. Then we have here what we had the other day. It's because, I think, sometimes you feel you don't deserve to have this nice, peaceful, successful life you've carved out for yourself. And because a part of you, during those unspeakably horrific times, overdosed on adrenaline. Like someone who's only used heroin once, you'll never forget that awful, euphoria of that solitary moment. So, you're inclined to seek out a solution for both problems at once. You seek self-destruction and excitement in equal parts."

"I don't know what—"

"Your car?" Doctor Hagari cut me off.

Her name was Ruby. She was my red hot Chevy Camaro ZL1 with a six point two liter V-8 engine. Her six hundred and fifty ponies were ready to race right through the front hood as soon as I stepped on her gas. Sharp. Speedy. Sexy. I paid extra for the super wide tires because they looked plump, voluptuous, thick, and powerful. Nothing phallic about her, but yonic, like a Georgia O'Keefe painting. Unapologetically feminine. The fact this pathetic old man called her a "car," had me holding my breath for fear of what might come out. She wasn't just a car; she was my Ruby. And she waited for me in the parking lot just like my thoughts waited behind my sealed lips: loud, fast, vengeful, and unstoppable once let off the leash.

I nodded in response.

"Stay safe. Make smart decisions. Don't take unnecessary risks with your driving, with your drinking, with your relationships," he up-spoke as if to mention my ex without mentioning my ex.

Tyler…

Tyler had called Ruby my "mid-life crisis mobile." One of many reasons why he was my ex and would remain my ex.

"You've mentioned owning weapons?" Hagari said.

"No," I said. "I mean, if I had, I lied. I don't own a gun or anything like that."

The ink pen went back to work. A thick black marble and gold thing that told everybody who looked at it that whatever was written with it must be important. When it finished swirling, Doctor Hagari set it down with a thud against his desk. He methodically folded the papers into thirds as if he was going to mail them and handed them to me.

"What we've discussed is confidential," he said. "All these forms say is that you've completed the sessions as mandated in your disciplinary plan. I've recommended a full return to your duties and responsibilities in the company."

All that just for a fucking signature. With forced patience, I held back from bolting for the door. Not too eager, I took the papers and unfolded them enough to see that he'd signed off on some paperwork from corporate. As I scanned through them, he got up from his desk and circled around me. I was distracted by what the papers may or may not have said that I let him get behind me, out of my eyesight. And of course, as soon as I couldn't see him, he set his hands on me. Two, big, heavy palms rested on my shoulders. He put weight down on them in a way that could be confused between something comforting like a hug and something constraining like the prelude to a rape. A wave of nausea radiated from where they rested.

"Remember, Taylor. None of this was your fault," he told me. "Don't forget, you're the victim here."

Doctor Hagari and I are not coworkers. That was made very clear to me when I was directed to complete the sessions with him. Being forced to complete a mandatory counseling program with a coworker who has more pay and seniority than me, who works side-by-side with my supervisor, would be a conflict of interest and bring into question the confidentiality counselors rely on to build trust with their patients. See, technically, he's not an employee of Team Next Paradigms Inc. the way I am, but an independent contractor who we just so happen to work with. Still, his office is in the same building, literally two floors up from mine. If the professionalism of all this sounds borderline… unprofessional, that's only because it was.

According to the company's slogan, Team Next Paradigms "professionally develops your team for the next paradigm challenge." We offer individual employee training, team building programs, Six Sigma evaluations, institutional culture appraisals, and as it was in my case, corrective employee retraining and rehabilitation programs. Once a company signs up with Team Next Paradigms and downloads our app, leaders can schedule team building events and small group training exercises, and their employees can access a wide spectrum of online and offline professional growth tools, from foreign language learning to mental health resources. We contract licensed psychologists, college professors, motivational speakers, mindfulness yogis, former Navy SEALS, industry leaders and more to help our clients build successful and professional individuals and teams. The way Jason, our boss, pitched Team Next Paradigms to me was, "Uber for your office," "Food Dudes for a better work environment," and "Tinder for your psychological and professional well-being." The last one kind of sounded like we were setting up mentally unstable patients with predatory providers for one-night inappropriate counselor/client relationships. But I have to admit, as a whole, the idea seemed sound. When I first joined the company, I was sure having access to all these resources would be a boon for my own mental health.

So, no. Doctor Hagari was not a coworker or colleague. But as one of our first, closest, and most recommended contractors, that line seemed more than a little blurred when I stepped into the elevator on his floor and hit the button for mine. Out of all fifty five stories of the IDS Center in downtown Minneapolis, what were the chances of our offices being right on top of each other?

The IDS Center was the highest skyscraper in Minneapolis and at seven hundred and seventy six feet tall, the city's crowning jewel. Along with the Wells Fargo Center, the Capella Tower, and a wide variety of other, lesser buildings, they chiseled an impressive skyline visible for miles in every direction. My favorite building in the city, the Foshay, was an art deco tombstone for both its creator and the glory days of the Roaring Twenties when it rose up above the surrounding pastures and farm fields. An old school four hundred and forty seven foot tall marble and concrete skyscraper, it was the tallest in the state at the time of its construction. Finished in 1929, both the tower and Wilbur Forshay, whose name it bears, were pioneers in this new Midwest metropolis, but they never saw Black Tuesday coming.

And just like the 1920s delivered the fledgling city into chaos, the 2020s weren't kind to Minneapolis either, for reasons I'm sure you read all about in the news. Racial injustice, civil unrest, a gutted police department, a global pandemic, a wavering economy, a mass exodus of office drones teleworking rather than commuting, and it was no wonder why the streets sometimes looked post-apocalyptic.

Across the street from the IDS Center is the Dayton Hudson Building where the Minnesota-based Target Corporation keeps their offices. Between the two buildings, at the corner of 7th and Nicollet, is a bronze statue of an old sitcom character, also from Minneapolis. Mary Tyler

Moore, who could "turn the world on with a smile," is frozen in time while flinging her hat into the air as the theme song sang, "You're going to make it after all!" in our heads. In the 70s, when the show was on the air, she was a national example of how a tough, witty, independent woman could break through all those glass ceilings of the white-collar business world's boy's club. If you google a picture of that statue, you'll see the windows behind the statue are all boarded up with plywood. That kind of optimism has a hard time standing up against our modern brand of jaded sarcasm. Cynicism always wins out, because cynicism is funny, right?

Right?

"Are you genuinely asking me?"

But I had a full-time job, a new little split-entry in the suburbs, and enough money left over for my red hot Camaro parked in the garage. Mary Tyler Moore should be jealous of me, right?

Right?

"Sure, Taylor. Who wouldn't be jealous of someone in your position?"

Back inside the IDS, the elevator opened on my floor. My coworkers were all in the office. That was funny too, because when we were hired, the job descriptions all said, "work remote." But the boss had a funny (there's that word again) way of calling us in to "bring the team together," "synergize," and "fight our way through this crisis as one," any chance he could get. Jason Wong was an ambitious, second-generation, Chinese American who loved to cross his arms and look out his window as if the entire city was his kingdom, but he was really just a corporate, middle manager who watched one too many TED Talks on leadership. When it came to Team Next Paradigms' gospel of shaping small group dynamics and optimizing positive workplace cultures, he'd drank the Kool-Aid. His office was in the far corner, and delivering these papers signed by the good doctor to Jason's desk was the only reason I was there. Why everyone else was here… I could only guess Jason saw some need to "gather the troops."

As for us troops?

Violetta worked behind the front reception desk, but since we were an entirely online customer-facing company, we had zero walk-in clients. Who she was supposed to receive at the reception desk was a mystery to all of us. So, she became the default secretary/office mother. And as a Puerto Rican mother of five boys, she was well-practiced at keeping the unruly in line.

"Taylor, welcome back, don't forget to unforward your phone and turn your out-of-office off, and you need to fill out your timesheet using the A Four code for your medical leave, otherwise it will be deducted from your PTO, okay?" Violetta said. Payroll. Finances. Records. PR. Building maintenance liaison. Taskmaster. You name it, Violetta did it. She was always busy. Underpaid. Overworked. Underappreciated. Eat your heart out Mary Tyler Moore.

"Yep. Okay. I will. I'll get it done right away. For sure," I re-emphasized throughout her tirade.

Then there was Robert and Roman. If you can't keep Robert and Roman straight, don't feel bad. It took me a whole month before I realized they weren't the same person. After working for Team Next Paradigms for weeks and after dozens of "team meetings" for "special projects," I finally figured them out: Robert was the slightly wider one who always whistled little songs to himself, and Roman was the taller one who never seemed to do any work, never responded to emails, never returned phone calls, but never ran out of time to bitch about someone leaving the coffee pot empty, or leaving the burner on after the pot was finished, or about how Jason liked to re-use the old grounds to brew a new batch.

As I left Violetta and plunged into the depths of our cubicle farm, Robert interrupted his off-key rendition of what I thought was Boston's "More than a Feeling," to say, "Hi, Taylor."

"Who put the decaf in the caffeinated pot?" Roman asked no one in particular from the door to the breakroom. "How many times do I have to say it, decaf goes in the pot with the orange spout. Just like at any gas station or diner you ever walk into."

"Wasn't me, Roman. I literally just walked through the door," I said and kept on for Jason's office.

"Taylor!"

And then there was Barbara. She pulled alongside me as we made our way through the cubicles and conference rooms as if we were two commuters passing freeway exit ramps. She had her own stack of papers in her hands because somehow this remote employee who worked for a cutting-edge technology company was obsessed with hardcopies. She printed out spreadsheets, emails, and calendar invites from her digital calendar just to pin them to a paper calendar hanging from her cubicle. All

I wanted was to get the few papers I held in my hands to Jason's desk so I could hop in my Camaro and get back to my real office inside my house.

She had other ideas.

"So…" she sang, shuffling through the ream of hardcopies she carried with her. "How was it with Doctor Cal?"

That was his first name, Cal. Doctor Calvin Hagari, the jolly, old, red-headed, handsy therapist.

"Barb, that's supposed to be confidential," I reminded her.

"I know, I know, I know," she waved away the notion as if it were a housefly. "But I see all the bookings that come through our database, and I couldn't help but see you had some sessions scheduled with Doctor Cal. Besides, it doesn't matter. I've been seeing him for years now, ever since my mother died. And we've always been friends, and I know you didn't mean what you said when you came in wearing your PJs the other day. So. Tell me everything."

I absolutely meant what I'd said that day, and I had no idea why my technologically-challenged coworker believed we were the best of besties, but I had a theory.

On my first in-office day at Team Next Paradigms, Barb used one of those manila envelopes with the holes punched through it and the red tie-cord at the top to "inter-office" some documents to me. During each previous day, we exchanged emails or messages from our home offices with ease. And since we sat two cubicles away from each other while we were in the building, if she needed to physically give me something, it only made sense for her to get up, walk ten feet, and hand it to me. But she stuffed that battered old shotgun envelope full of papers, put the envelope into the mail slots, and waited until Violetta came around and handed it to me.

I thought it was a gag! Why else would she go to such painstaking and archaic lengths to ask me a question? So, thinking she was giving the whole Silicon-Valley-tech-frat-boy culture a poke in the ribs, I wheeled out of my cubicle, stuffed my reply into the envelope, walked it over to the out-going mail slot, dropped it in, and maintained eye contact with her and repressed a smirk the whole time. She gave me no reaction. She deadpanned, I assumed.

In hindsight, I don't think it was a gag. But she still saw it as some kind of bonding experience as if we had tied each other friendship bracelets at summer camp.

"Barb, I'm not going to discuss my private sessions with you. You shouldn't even know I've had any sessions. When's the last time you did your HIPAA certification?"

"Isn't he great?" she carried on as undeterred as a cruise ship colliding into a codfish. "He's helped me come to terms with my grief in ways I never would have imagined. I'm so much more in touch with where I've come from and who I am. I know he can come off as a bit unorthodox or stern or forward… but if you keep seeing him, I know you'll come to appreciate him the way I do. So? Are you?"

"Am I what?" I asked.

"Going back to see him again?"

"Barb—" I stopped walking. Jason's office was right there in front of us, but I wasn't convinced she wouldn't follow me right through the door. "Has Doctor Hagari… Has he ever… I mean… Have you ever felt…" What the hell was I doing? Trying to confide in Barb? Had I gone truly and deeply insane? Clearly, she didn't share my reservations about the good doctor, and trying to explain myself to her, right there in front of my boss's office would be an embarrassing and futile waste of both of our time. I was ten steps away from dropping off the forms, completing my disciplinary plan, and being done with the whole situation for good. If she was happy with him, who was I to try to tell her different?

"Never mind, Barb," I said. "I need to talk to Jason."

Two minutes in the office and already I was tired of this Stranger in a Strange Land routine.

I smacked the papers down on Jason's desk before saying a word to him. "Can I go home and do my job now?"

The view from Jason's office should have been more impressive than it was. As high up as we were, and as flat as the surrounding land was, we should have almost been able to see Chicago. Well, maybe Wisconsin anyway. But his window faced toward the center of the city and as Jason stood, one hand on his hip and the other holding a coffee cup, posing like a boss from Hollywood's central casting because he thought that's what bosses in skyscrapers were supposed to look like, all he could really see was the other buildings. He gave it a beat for the cameras in his head to capture the shot. Then he turned to face me.

"So, no more issues of you drinking while you're on the clock?" He flipped through the papers, but only read them as much as I had.

"It was a one-time incident, Jason," I said. "You know I'm a good worker, and I get my tasks done, on time, and done right."

"True. You do," Jason said, browsing through the papers like they were a prop now. "But being on this team is about more than accomplishing tasks. We need everyone to contribute and support everyone else. When you came into the office the way you were last week–"

"I'd done my tasks for the day, clocked out, and had some wine," I explained. "How was I supposed to know you were going to call us in? This is a remote, flexible position. You can't just snap your fingers and expect everyone to be here, sober and ready to work."

"Taylor, it was noon. On a Tuesday," Jason said.

"I was going through a tough time in my relationship." The end of it actually, which, in retrospect, was the best part of the relationship.

"You came into the office wearing nothing but an NSYNC nightshirt and a pair of Crocs. You showed us all your bare bottom, made smooching sounds with your lips, and told Robert you could make better music than him by swallowing a kazoo and a can of beans. And the things you said to Barb…?"

"It was a lot of wine," I admitted.

"But that's all behind us now. You completed your sessions and according to this, Doctor Cal says you did very well. So I don't think we'll run into this issue again. Now. Speaking of bringing the team together…" Jason wasn't good with confrontation. This was him abandoning the fight on his own terms so he could move on to the next big project. "I rounded up the herd so we could be here to welcome you back, but also so we get to work on our annual retreat. I penciled in the dates already, but really all other options are on the table as far as the whens, wheres, and hows of our little work-cation. And Taylor, as our Customer Feedback Integration Specialist, I think this falls right in your wheelhouse. So, I'm handing you the reins on this one."

"You want me to plan our work retreat?" I asked, not rhetorically, because sometimes it took me a minute to translate Jason's corporate-speak back into English.

"Well, we are meeting in just a few minutes to have a little idea shower. You'll have all hands on deck for this," Jason said. "We'll touch base and get our ducks all in a row, but going forward this is going to be your baby. How's that sound?"

I held my tongue because as much as I wanted to get home, I also wanted to keep my job. The annual work retreat was maybe the most important event of Jason's year. More important than key performance indicators, customer satisfaction, corporate's bottom line, or any of those other things most bosses worry about. So, I smiled, nodded, and said, "That sounds fantastic."

Chapter Three

The best part of my workday is leaving. Ruby was waiting for me in the parking garage, pristine and sexy and eager for the road. As soon as I slid into the low driver's seat, her steering wheel and stick shift reached out for my palms. And yes, I can drive a stick. Don't be sexist. Her V8 sang an overture for our ride-to-come and drowned out all the other audio clutter of a day spent deafened by racket. Her pedals and my feet waltzed as my phone linked to her Bluetooth. When we emerged from the parking garage and into the evening sun, we were one.

"Hey Bitch," I said loud enough to be heard over Ruby's chorus and the wind coming through the open windows. "Play 'Britney Spears, Oops! I did it Again.'"

Did you know you can rename your voice assistant to whatever you want? It doesn't have to be Siri, or Alexa, or Google if you don't want it to be.

"I didn't know that."

Well, it's true. Bitch chimed back, "Playing the album: 'Oops! I Did it Again,' by Britney Spears," and by the time we were northbound on I-94, I was in my zone.

I want you to know something. That day I went into work blackout drunk and told all my coworkers what I really thought about them and all the completely unnecessary "round up the troops" call-ins? I didn't drive there. I don't drink and drive. I spent twenty bucks on an Uber and gave the driver five stars for being cool with my drunk ass, and it was worth every cent. I'd never drive Ruby drunk. There's just no way I could live with myself if I totaled her or, God forbid, ran over some kids or something. I'm not a monster.

I wanted to be present, in the moment, whenever I was with Ruby. The only problem was in order to fully appreciate her, I had to drive her fast, and the only problem with driving fast was that it made the ride go by all the quicker. There were days we'd leave the concrete jungle of Minneapolis and blow right by the suburban sprawl where we lived, and wind up someplace like Taylor's Falls along the St. Croix River. We'd park near a cliff, and I'd sit on her hood and feel her warmth as we watched the water flow south. But after getting my papers from Doctor Hagari and escaping another one of Jason's "pow-wows," which, how he got by with calling a business meeting a pow-wow in this day and age escapes me, but after that workday, I craved my quiet home. We were only halfway through the album by the time I reached my quaint little neighborhood of split-entries and townhomes. I left the tunes cranked up as we cruised through the development and past all the cul-de-sacs. Britney and Ruby harmonized their duet all the way into the garage where they reached their coda.

The music faded to silence. The rumbling settled to a stillness.

I lived by myself. No husband. No boyfriend. No pets, although I've always wanted to get a cute, waddly, flat-faced pug. Pugs are simply adorable. I can't resist how they snort through their noses and how their eyes are never looking in the same place at the same time. They're like furry little chameleons that can't breathe. I even have a name picked out for him: "Charlie," but I'd call him Chuck because pugs just look like Chucks. But I'm worried I couldn't take good enough care of it. Pet ownership is a huge responsibility. So, no. When I came upstairs from the garage, no one was there to greet me.

Did I mention that they never recovered the body from the lakeside that morning after the killings? I killed him, I know I did. But there was no one down in that basement by the time the cops arrived. Either they hauled him away and lied about it or… Why would they lie about that?

"Hey, Bitch," I called out again, and the smart speaker on my kitchen counter answered, "Yes?" to let me know she was listening. "Turn on the TV."

And with that, I dug some leftovers out of the fridge and a bottle of wine from the counter rack. Some warmed-up lentil soup with a nice chianti from the bistro downtown sounded wonderful. I put on PJs, ate day-old food, sipped red wine, dreamed about owning a dog I never had the guts to adopt, and let chaos decide what I should watch. I minded my own business. I didn't ask anything from anybody. I didn't hurt anybody.

And that was pretty much what my life was like.

But by the time there was less wine in the bottle than there was in me, I started to get the crazy idea that I should text my ex. Tyler was no good for me. He was controlling and self-centered and emotionally abusive and a general, all-around, bad boyfriend. Sure, the sex was great when we started out, but that could only carry the relationship so far. When he started moving his things piece-by-piece out of his crappy apartment and into my house? I felt the walls closing in around me. I don't like small spaces. I need room to run. And Tyler made everywhere feel smaller when he was there. It was like trying to breathe inside of a plastic grocery bag.

And I know what you're thinking: Tyler and Taylor. With names like that, we just had to be a match made in heaven. Please.

The break-up was nasty. When I asked for more space, he turned everything around on me and accused me of cheating and undermining the relationship and not giving him his freedom, as if I was the oppressive, manipulating one in the relationship. Typical gas-lighting bullshit. But you know what really made no sense? When I broke up with him, I was the one ugly-crying and feeling like no one would ever love me again. Not him. How is that supposed to work?

And still, after my "incident" in the office, after my sessions with Doctor Hagari, after putting Ruby through her paces, and talking through everything all over again with Bitch, I still opened and closed Tyler and I's chat thread over and over and over again. By the time I drained the chianti, I was typing and then deleting perfect text after perfect text that had no chance in hell of ever undoing what I'd done. And I knew it! Even if I conjured up just the right words and arranged them into the most eloquent turns of phrase, all I would get for a reward was free entry back into a toxic relationship that cramped my soul and killed my spirit.

I scrolled back up through our text history and reminded myself what I'd be getting back into.

If you leave me now you'll never get me back.

You're throwing away everything.

You bitch. You are the biggest cold hearted liar I've ever met.

Forget it. We're thru. I hope you enjoy being alone for the rest of your miserable life.

I'm the best thing that's ever happened to you.

You're going to regret ever leaving me.

I will kill to get you back. Do you understand what I'm saying?

Answer my texts! I swear to god Taylor if you don't say something soon you have no idea what I'll do to you. Text me back!

"No!" I yelled and threw my phone across the living room. It donked off the wall. No one, not my nonexistent dog, not my inanimate car, not my robot named Bitch, responded. If I did type something, if I typed anything at all, I'd be conceding to him, surrendering to his demands, and giving in to his authority over me. And then I don't know if I'd ever get out from under his thumb.

I sat on my couch, not at all feeling like the loneliest person on Earth.

The wine bottle was empty. Nothing on TV interested me. I had to work in the morning, but my commute consisted of rolling out of bed and opening a laptop. One more bottle wouldn't kill me. So, I pulled myself off my couch and waddled my drunk ass back into the kitchen. I hadn't really been watching the TV up until then. Had been fixated on my phone, doom-scrolling and coaxing myself into bad decisions. But now that my phone was in a Ficus planter, my eyes washed across the screen.

Some 80's slasher horror movie. A titular teenage girl ran and screamed and stumbled through a suburban neighborhood. Cheesy, sexist, exploitative garbage. I don't like scary movies. Never have. They're demeaning. This one was the one with Jamie Lee Curtis. A Jamie Lee Curtis young enough to play a teenager. As young as I was when I'd gone through my bad times. Young enough to be me during those bad times.

Why was I even watching that garbage? I didn't choose it. It was just something the cycling TV landed on and decided I wanted to see. But as I pulled the second bottle of wine out of the rack, my eyes fastened on the screen. Jamie Lee Curtis was inside now, running through rooms and up and down stairs and in and out of closets. She had a big glistening butcher knife.

Skipping the glass, I cracked open the wine bottle's metal screw-on cap and took a long, steady pull right from the bottle.

Doctor Hagari said something about me having weapons. About not having weapons. About how owning weapons was another unnecessary risk-taking behavior people who suffer from traumatic events resort to, the way war veterans stash assault rifles and handguns throughout their houses. But that was just him talking out of his ass. Why shouldn't I have a weapon? After everything I'd been through, why was there nothing in my house more deadly than a broom handle I could use to defend myself? And just like that, with the same urgent need to find clothes when caught naked, I had to have a weapon. Without one, I was exposed, weak, vulnerable. Anyone could do whatever they wanted to me, and I'd be helpless to stop them. Why the hell had I never bought a gun?

I had knives. A big butcher block full of them, one of them exactly like the one Jamie Lee was waving around on the TV. I ran back to the kitchen, suddenly panicked for every second that I didn't have a weapon in my hands, as composed as a five year old sprinting from her light switch to the bed covers. The wine splashed onto the carpet. I ripped the biggest knife out of the block and threw my back against the kitchen counter, brandishing the blade at the rest of the house.

My eyes panned my kitchen and living room. No dog. No roommate. No faceless murderer from my youth. No abusive live-in boyfriend. Just me and the TV.

I was freaking out for nothing. I let the stupid movie get under my skin. I let the alcohol dull my reasoning. I was being irrational.

That's what I told myself, up until I saw the bloody handprint wrapped around the chrome handle of my refrigerator. At first, I thought maybe it was my own, as if I'd soaked my hand in wine and then went digging through the fridge. Looking at my palms, I saw both were clean, and that wasn't chianti on the handle. It was bright and thick and sticky like cherry syrup. One long drip cruised down the smooth arch of the chrome handle until it reached the bottom and plopped onto the kitchen tile.

Someone had been in my house. Maybe while I was at the stupid session with Doctor Hagari or during the even stupider team meeting about Jason's ridiculous work retreat. Or more likely, with the blood as fresh as it was, someone had been here since I'd come through the front door.

While I was on my couch, zombified into my phone, someone had been inside my kitchen. Someone had opened my fridge.

I set the wine bottle down on the counter next to me. I kept the knife up and ready. There was a clean spot on the fridge's handle above the bloody print. I got a good hold of it, despite my shaking hand, and flung it open.

Inside, the milk, orange juice, and coffee creamer had been pushed to the sides of the top shelf to make room for a disembodied head, set down on the stump of its neck. It was Violetta from the office. It had been Violetta anyway. I could hardly recognize her with her eyes rolled up, her mouth frozen in an eternal scream, and with all the blood seeping from her eyes, nose, and neck. Her skin was waxy and mottled. The muscles under that blotchy and bloody layer were frozen in stretched-out terror. It was a hellish thing, the kind of thing I hadn't seen in over twenty years.

I screamed. The shape of my mouth stretched wide, matched Violetta's. Staggering back, my feet slipped on the blood covering the kitchen floor. I fell and, on the way down, flung the door shut so hard that it bounced back open again. From the floor, I aimed the knife at the interior of the fridge, as if Violetta's head could attack and do to me what had been done to it. I clambered away from it, my heels smearing red streaks across the linoleum. The door of the fridge banged off the counter and slowly crept shut again, magnetically sealing away the horrors inside.

The tip of the butcher knife shivered between my eyes and the brushed-nickel door and all the bills and birthday cards stuck to its front. Off in the living room, Jamie Lee whimpered and moaned as the killer tracked her down. My ragged breaths pumping irregularly in and out of my lungs matched hers, and in that moment, I felt we might share the same fate. After all, the victim was inside of that fridge, not the killer. I had my back to the real threat. I was distracted, just like I had been by my phone when he'd snuck inside. But I couldn't turn my attention away from what I'd found. The severed head of Violetta, Team Next in the Twin Cities' diligent receptionist, seemed as dangerous as anything else that could have ever entered my house.

My eyes flicked across the living room, to the TV, to the sliding glass door that led to the deck and the darkness outside, to the stairs leading down to the entryway and the front doors. Then back to the fridge. Then back to all those other potential sources of danger. The steel tip of the knife was like gunsights in the foreground of a soldier's point of view.

Aside from the horror movie, the house was quiet. I thought about calling out to Bitch to have her call the police or at least turn off the TV, but if the killer was in the house, did he know where I was? Surely, he'd heard me scream when I first opened the fridge, but there was no sense in giving him additional clues as to what I was up to. He'd screwed up by leaving that bloody handprint on the–

It was gone. The red impression of palm and fingers on the fridge's chrome handle wasn't there anymore. It was clean.

Scooting my butt across the bloodless kitchen floor, I came to the fridge. With a tug, the door eased open. I climbed up the shelves, knife still in hand, one by one, like a glass elevator passing floor after floor of condiments and leftovers until my eyes came above the top shelf. The milk, the orange juice, the creamer, that old jar of pickles all sat exactly where I'd left them. No head. No maw frozen in a scream. No blood. Nothing to send me into a fright.

And you probably won't understand this, but seeing nothing there terrified me more than if the head had remained. We cling to reality every day of our lives. It's what gives our world order and predictability. Reality is what feeds our responses. Without it, knowing that I'd just suffered a fully realized hallucination, or maybe that I was hallucinating now and removing that horrible image of Violetta's hacked-off head from my perception, I was a ship lost at sea, with no sense of which direction to go and no idea how to save myself.

Jamie Lee screamed from the TV again and I whirled about, still clutching that knife like a maniac.

I'd been here before. I'd done all this before. Had these reactions. Felt these emotions. Suffered these horrors before. Twenty three years ago, the same sort of stuff that was happening to Jamie Lee Curtis had happened to me. Only, it was worse, because what happened to me was real. There in my kitchen, standing in front of an open fridge, knife still clutched in my hand, my breaths went short, my vision narrowed, my whole body trembled, and that was the first time I had a full-fledged, Vietnam-Vet-style flashback.

Chapter Four

You've come along this far. You listened to me cry about my job and my ex-boyfriend and how I never had the courage to buy a dog. I guess now is when you get what you came for. Everybody wants to hear about this part. When they find out about my past, they don't want to know how I haven't been able to maintain a healthy relationship, or how me and alcohol maybe get along a little too well, or how I like to drive too fast and take unnecessary risks because my body doesn't know what to do when it's not threatened. They don't want to hear about all that shit. No. They want to hear about "that night." Well, fine.

If you want blood, you got it.

"I never said I–"

There were six of us. Three of us girls, and three boys. It was really Cheryl's friends more than my friend group. She was a year older than me, but we'd been friends since my freshman year of cross country. I think she'd watched me draw into myself over those high school years. She'd gone her way, and I'd gone my less-popular way. But in the summer before her senior year, when I was going into my junior year, I think she wanted to reconnect. Sort of wanted to share her last year of high school with me. So she invited me to spend a weekend at a cabin with her, her boyfriend Scotty, another couple named Ash and Linda, and this awkward kid named Shelton. I think me and Shelton were supposed to hook up, both of us third wheels the way we were. But, well, nothing really went as planned that weekend, now did it?

"So it happened at a cabin. Next to a lake."

While I stood in my kitchen, with my mind reliving a weekend some twenty years back, I can't describe to you how clear and concrete the details became.

"And you said this happened in the summer of 1999?"

Yeah. '99. I was seventeen.

"Do you remember what county you were in when this happened? When law enforcement arrived that morning, was it the local sheriff's department? Or maybe city police?"

I don't remember. If you go looking for it, you won't find anything. They buried the story. Can't have a serial killer taint the peaceful, picturesque profile of your little cabin and lake community, now can you?

Nobody was supposed to find out about us. Scotty learned that his uncle's cabin was going to be empty that weekend, and he knew where the key was hidden, and we all lied to our parents about being at other places. It was the perfect setup for a half dozen teenagers to do all the things that a half dozen, unsupervised teenagers aren't supposed to do, but are also sort of supposed to do. All the movies and music and stories, it was like if you didn't sneak away from home with a bunch of boys to get wasted and get laid, you didn't actually have a legit high school experience. You know how it was.

"Can you tell me their names again?"

There was my friend, Cheryl. The whole trip was her idea. And her boyfriend Scotty. They were like the cool couple, destined for future homecoming crowns and cutest couple yearbook awards. She was so pretty, she could have any boy she wanted. Scotty wasn't like a Calvin Klein model or anything, but he had this big mop of curly brown hair, and a smile like a five year old boy on Christmas morning.

Then there was Ash and Linda. Ash was one of the few black kids in our school, but he was more like Carlton from Fresh Prince than Coolio. This was rural Minnesota, remember. Anyway, Linda was a white girl, and back then it was still hip and progressive and maybe even a little edgy that they were an interracial couple. At least we wanted to think so, even if they weren't pushing any real boundaries.

Then there was Shelton. I had never met him before that weekend. Like I said, I think me and him were supposed to be an item or something, but he tried way too hard. Always telling stupid jokes. Playing games.

Messing with us. That sort of thing. I only went because Cheryl dragged me up there. I was shy and had never been away overnight with a group of boys and girls like that. If my parents knew— Well, my dad hardly knew my birthday, but my mom? She would have killed me! If she ever sobered up enough to find out.

After everything that happened, the fact that it was only us kids up there kind of blew by the wayside.

It was a really nice cabin. Like, Scotty's uncle must have been making bank. Big thick logs, but not dirty old rotten wood, like clean and polished to a honey glaze. Huge windows that looked out over the lake. A jacuzzi tub on the deck. This big, rock fireplace and a giant elk head mounted over top of it. We felt like we were millionaires on vacation, or maybe depression-era gangsters laying low at an up-north hideout.

There was a fully stocked liquor cabinet. And yeah, there were three separate bedrooms, each with big comfortable beds and thick quilts. I could see it on the boys' faces; they just knew they were going to get some action.

The Friday night when we first got there, everything was fine. I mean, I was nervous. I'd never drank before, and like I said, I'd never spent a weekend away from home, unsupervised, with boys and girls together. And there was alcohol and Scotty scored some beer and some weed from his older brother and there was a jacuzzi… Out of us three girls, I was the only one to wear a one-piece. Linda had a cute two-piece and Cheryl… She had no fear. Ever. She wore the skimpiest little string bikini I had ever seen in my life. The boys couldn't keep their eyes off her. Even Ash, whose girlfriend was like, right there. But that was Cheryl. She was the daredevil, and she made it her personal mission to bring me out of my shell.

She kept telling me, "Don't worry. Relax. Go with the flow. Live a little."

When the boys made us drinks, sticky-sweet, fruity concoctions mixed with vodka so you couldn't even taste the alcohol, I was sipping mine ultra slow. But Cheryl was like, "Bottoms up, girl! If it's safe for the rest of us, it's safe for you too."

We all got super wasted. But nothing happened. I mean, I guess I shouldn't say nothing happened. The boys wanted to scare us. Throughout the day, Scotty played some horror movie on the TV, and Shelton kept telling me about some mental hospital a few miles away and how some of the patients had escaped and were still on the lam. To this day, I don't know if that was true or not. But at the end of the night, Shelton slept on the couch. Maybe because I threw up over the side of the jacuzzi. But I bet he would have still had sex with me if I'd let him. Boys don't care about stuff like that.

Before blacking out, I remember wandering down to the lakeside. There was a small dock there, leading out over the water, but no boat. Overlooking the lake and the dock was a firepit surrounded by some chairs and a pile of split wood. An ax was wedged into a stump where all the splitting was done. I didn't remember much after the jacuzzi and all those fruity drinks and throwing up in front of everybody, but I remembered that ax. It gleamed in the moonlight. Most axes don't do that, I noticed since then. Not in real life. In movies, sure. But in real life? The blades are painted, and the metal is only exposed near the edge, and that's usually scraped to a dull matte finish and covered in sap and crud. This one shined silver moonlight back into my eyes like midnight fireworks. I remembered that ax, and I remembered walking out to the very lip of the dock. I'd only gone out there to clear my head of all the alcohol, but standing there I felt the danger of falling in and sinking all the way to the bottom.

I think I went to bed after that.

If you believe me so far, here comes the part where people start to look at me like I'm making up stories.

"I believe you."

The next morning, I wandered out of one of those big bedrooms wrapped in a plaid quilt meant for two. Shelton had spent the night snoring on the couch in front of the fireplace and under the big elk head, but he was gone that morning. I paid it no mind. Under my mounded-up rat's nest of hair, my head spun like a Tilt-a-whirl, so I went right for the kitchen sink to drink straight from the tap. Cheryl must have heard me open and shut the bedroom door because she followed me into the kitchen. She was wearing nothing but Scotty's Nirvana t-shirt. It was that one with the black and white photo of Cobain from MTV Unplugged. They only sold them after he blew his head off. You remember that one, right?

"Yeah, I think I know the one you're talking about."

Well, she came out wearing the shirt he wore the day before, and that kind of tells you how they'd ended their night. I didn't say anything. If you want to be cool, you have to not say things most of the time. And I was really trying to be cool that weekend. So, I gave her a glance, pretended that I wasn't still wearing my own clothes and the kid I was supposed to hook up with hadn't dipped before the morning light, and I said, "Hey."

"Hey," she said and went about working the coffee machine. Because of course she knew how to make coffee and could drink it black but preferred espresso and cappuccino and all those other fancy kinds I knew nothing about. Starbucks wasn't a thing back then, at least not in Minnesota. But of course, she knew all about coffee because she was older, and she was cool. As the machine whirled and steamed, she drew out a big butcher knife from the knife set, checked out the sheen of the blade, and shucked it back into place. Even the way she did that, pulling the knife out, toying with the handle, and setting it back into the block, seemed mature and cool and sexy. I waited for her to leave the kitchen before I stuck my head under the faucet and sucked in water like a cow at a trough.

My lips were about to touch water when her wineglass-shattering scream sent my head backward into the basin of the sink. Stars exploded in my vision as her throat dragged out the sound like nails ripping through flesh.

Scotty burst out of the bedroom door wearing just his boxer shorts. Cheryl stood stiff as a board in front of the fireplace. Inches from her nose was that ax from the splitting stump. Someone had swung it right into one of the log beams next to the fireplace and buried the head halfway into the wood. It still glimmered, now reflecting the sunrise off its chrome finish. Its handle stuck out at an angle, ready for Cheryl to walk right into. Neither of us had noticed it when we first wandered out, but we all saw it now, and we understood what it meant: Someone had come into the cabin while we were all passed out. Someone who could have done whatever they wanted to us while we slept. Someone who wanted to send us a message.

The three of us stood around it, staring, sorting it out in our minds.

"Hey, some people are trying to sleep up here!" Ash called from behind the upstairs bedroom door.

It didn't cut the tension.

Shelton jumped out from around the corner, brandishing the big fork from the barbeque grill, snarling, and wearing a mask that was just holes where the eyes were and a big wide smile full of teeth. No nose. No ears. No shape to the cheeks or chin, just a blank face with deep, deep eyes and a maniac's smile. We all jumped. I jumped anyway. But he didn't scare us. We could see his clothes and his body shape and knew it was him immediately after he sent our hearts into overdrive. I smacked his shoulder as hard as I could. Cheryl stormed off swearing and bitching. Scotty caught the bottom of the mask and flipped it off his head. Shelton was laughing. Scotty was not.

And Shelton, unmasked and repressing his laughter after finally reading the room, was saying, "What? What? It was just a joke!"

Then Scotty pointed to the giant ax chopped into the wall, too pissed to express it in words.

"Holy shit!" Shelton said. "Hey, man, I swear! I didn't do that shit!"

And Scotty was like, "My uncle is going to notice shit like a giant fucking ax chopped into the wall of his cabin!"

And Shelton was like, "I swear to God, bro. I didn't do that! I just wanted to give you guys a thrill is all. Jesus, man. Cut me some slack!"

Scotty worked the ax, rocking it back and forth out of the timber, until it pulled loose. Then he stood there, holding it like an unhinged lumberjack. "Not fucking funny, bro," he said.

"Okay! Alright! Sorry!" Shelton backed away, picked up the mask from the floor, and tossed it onto the dining room table. "Sorry, I tried to get a rise out of ya. But I'm telling you, I didn't put that ax there like that."

"Oh, I suppose it was the escaped insane asylum convicts, then," Scotty said, but was already calming down.

"It's too early for that shit, man," Cheryl said, holding a freshly brewed cup of coffee now. "You gotta give us a little time to wake up first."

But that was Shelton. He tried, but he really didn't get social cues. Then there was me, backed up to that big dining room table with nothing to say and my fists clenching the quilt up to my chin, my nerves still in knots. And I kind of related with him in that moment. Somebody trying to fit in and making all the wrong turns along the way. Even if he never admitted to putting that ax there.

Later, after we'd eaten a bunch of eggs and pancakes the boys had cooked up with their rudimentary kitchen skills, we sat on patio chairs on the deck. Our headaches faded into a general, not-all-that-unpleasant numbness. The night before I got too drunk too quick to benefit from any euphoria or ease in inhibitions. But at some point that morning, I found a balance between still drunk and hungover that let me forget all the social awkwardness and insecurities. After all, it was Shelton who'd made an ass of himself. Not me. And God dammit if that didn't draw him to me.

The view helped mellow our moods. There was this valley made up of the boughs of pine trees between the deck and the lake. The waves shined thousands of starbursts into our eyes. The sun warmed our bodies. We talked a lot, the six of us, but we also spent a lot of time not talking. Just chilling. Taking in a day so perfect we would have only realized its perfection in our memories. If things had gone different. If they'd have lived long enough to reminisce. This was 1999, so of course, none of us had cell phones. I mean, Alicia Silverstone had one in Clueless, but none of us. And even if one of us did have a cell, there was no way we would have gotten a single bar of reception up there by that lake. No towers. And cell phones in those days? There were no games to play, or things to post, or videos to watch. No digital distractions whatsoever. So we just hung out.

At some point, one of the boys, maybe Shelton, maybe Scott or Ash, brought out some weed. My hangover from the night before was long gone, but the inhibition still resided. If it wasn't for that, there's no way I would have tried it. I'd never drank before. I'd never smoked weed. I'd never been with a boy. It was a whole weekend full of firsts.

And that first hit of weed? I didn't regret it. For once, it felt like I was at the right place, with the right people, doing the right things. All of life's sharp edges softened. All the abrasive textures turned to silk. All of the universe's out-of-tune sounds harmonized into a chorus. All the angst and anxiety burned away and drifted off with the gentle breeze. Maybe it's nostalgia, but I've never had a better high than what I got from that first toke. Never really went back to smoking weed since then. Nothing could match that first hit. Or maybe it's just something I associate with everything that followed it.

"Sorry about scaring you this morning," Shelton said to me as my eyes soaked in and simultaneously squinted against the sparkling water. "And about all the mental hospital stuff."

"It's cool," I said. But I was high, so everything was cool. But he really was cool. Like, for the first time since I'd met him, he wasn't trying so hard and was just, you know, being cool.

"Nah, I was being a dick. You've been chill though," he said. "How is it you're always so smooth, even when everybody else isn't?"

Was that how he interpreted my introverted sheepishness? As being chill? All I knew was that I was blushing, like, so much I thought he'd notice my big rosy cheeks and understand that I had never been cool from the word "Go." I tried to swallow my fluster, tried to be as smooth as he thought I was and failed. He was cute.

"You're pretty smooth yourself," I said, and then it was his turn to blush and turn away.

And that was it. That slippery, fragile, fleeting, perfect moment. If I could take a single moment of my life and capture it in a bottle and only open it when all the worst parts of my life dragged me down so I could escape and go back to a better time, me calling him smooth and watching him blush, that'd be it. We didn't know what we had, there on that deck with a gorgeous cabin behind us, a serene glistening lake in front of us, a sweet mellow high in our heads, and a warm excited beat inside our hearts. We had no idea how rare those moments were. How short-lived they'd become. How much pain would follow after them. You have no idea how many times I've wished we could have never left that place. How, if it were possible, I'd pause life right there and live every day with my heart balanced on that razor's edge between fear and hope, my innocence tipping me optimistically off balance.

But the sun sank below the trees, and that firepit down by the lake was waiting for us to strike a match.

"Okay," Cheryl said, spreading her fingertips toward the other five of us, telling us we should pay attention. "You guys have played 'Never Have I Ever,' right?"

Scotty cracked a big smile as he prodded at the fire with a big cast iron poker. He knew his girlfriend and knew she was up to something. Cheryl was always up to something. The boys and Linda all said they had played as if they had a hundred times before. It was a drinking game, so of course I hadn't, but I nodded along just like the rest of them.

"So you all know the rules," Cheryl said, "But I got a twist to it. You guys wanna play?"

There was a bottle of Fireball whiskey we were passing around the fire, so we all agreed without question. It was totally dark out by then. The pure blue sky had dissolved to a black jeweler's cloth littered with diamonds. The fire cracked and popped. That ax was behind us, cleaved back into the stump where it belonged, forgotten.

"I'll start," Cheryl said. "Never have I ever… been naked with a member of the opposite sex."

"Pass the bottle," Ash said, his hand stuck out to receive the Fireball.

See, the rules, in case you didn't know, are that if somebody says something that you have done, you have to drink.

"Wait!" Cheryl stopped Scotty just as he was about to hand over the Fireball to Ash. "I said there was a twist, and all y'all agreed to play so…"

"What's the twist?" Ash asked.

"Instead of drinking, you gotta strip. One piece of clothes! And socks and shoes and hats do NOT count!"

And that got a rise out of everybody. The boys, of course, loved the idea. Linda yelled, "Cheryl, you are such a fucking slut!" but said it in a way that was all affection and appreciation. I sat there with my mouth open, because despite all the cinnamon whiskey and sweet weed, I still wasn't ready to start taking my clothes off in front of these people.

The boys were quick to yank their shirts off over their heads, throwing them aside, inside-out as if their moms were going to come by and pick up their dirty laundry. And then, to my horror, Cheryl and Linda both followed suit. Linda, at least, had a normal, boring, old, skin-tone, padded bra on. Cheryl wore something silky and lacey and red.

"Taylor?" she said to me. "You've honestly never been naked around a boy before?"

"No!" I objected. "I mean, when I was a little kid, my grandma would put me in the bath with my cousin but not like–"

"That counts!" Scotty announced and pointed that fire poker at me.

"Now might be a good time to mention I'm not wearing underwear," Shelton said, half to himself.

"He was my cousin!" I shot back. "I was three!"

"Doesn't matter!" Scotty argued. "What she said was, 'Never have I ever been naked around a member of the opposite sex.' Your cousin totally counts."

"She did say 'ever,'" Ash said and tipped back the Fireball.

I looked to Cheryl and thought about mentioning that she'd lied. That she said never-had-she-ever when she clearly had just last night. Leave it to her to bend the rules in her favor. But she had peeled off her shirt and gave me this look that said so much while not saying anything at all. It said, if you want to get along, you gotta go along. If you want to have this kind of fun with these cool kids, you gotta play the game. It said be smooth. Be chill. What do you really have to lose?

And so, I reached my hands down to the hem of my cute and trendy, Hypercolor, long-sleeved t-shirt and pulled it over my head and set it down on the grass next to my chair. There I was with all eyes on me, my belly and shoulders and most of my chest exposed, and my flat chest only hidden by a boring, plain-white, sports bra. I tracked the boys' eyes as they spotted my belly muffin-topping over my pants, the ache where the bra straps rubbed my skin, the crooks of my armpits where unshaved stub lurked, but also the tops of my breasts where the sports bra pressed them together enough to create a meager amount of cleavage. And they gave me a little cheer and some whoops and hollers, and I hid a smile, and the better part of me believed it was for my bravery and not just for my skin.

Naive, right?

"I'm in no place to say."

Well, the game didn't end there. Next, it was Scotty's turn, and if you ask me, he really cheated.

"Never have I ever… kissed a dude," he said.

He had a beer in his hand. Ash still had that plastic bottle of Fireball. They clunked them together as if it were a toast. Cheryl swore. Linda threw a fist full of Doritos at Scott. I clamped my eyes shut and tried to pretend like I hadn't heard. Sure, I'd kissed a boy before. I wasn't that much of a sheltered prude. Kevin Campbell, at the bus stop, when we were both in fifth grade. When I opened my eyes, Cheryl and Linda were both undoing the flies of their jeans and working them down their hips. Remember how your mom or your grandma is always supposed to tell you to wear clean underwear in case you get in an accident? That's what I was thinking about as I shimmed out of my oh-so-stylish-for-the-90s baggy cargo shorts down to my plain white cotton undies. Clean, but not at all sexy, just like grandma would have wanted.

And then us ladies were there in our underwear, and we were all thinking about how unfair the male-dominated world was, but also sort of okay with how we could use our bodies to manipulate those males that supposedly dominated our worlds.

We didn't notice Shelton dropping trow until his bare ass was next to my face.

Linda screamed when she spotted his genitals shining in the firelight in front of all of us. Then I noticed, and as was my way, said, "Oh," and nothing more. Cheryl cackled like a witch from MacBeth.

His penis dangled there, limp and wagging under a cloud of dark pubes, like a toy waiting for a cat to bat at. I couldn't stop looking at it. I wanted to stop. I was embarrassed that I ever started looking, but now that I had, I couldn't pull my eyes away. This was nothing like taking a bath with my cousin when I was three.

"What? I told you guys I wasn't wearing underwear!" Shelton said.

"Wait. You kissed a *dude*?" Ash yelled. As progressive and hip as we thought we were, the idea of one of our friends being gay was still lightyears away.

"Like, not for real! It was a gag!" Shelton expounded to all of us. "Me and Jake Savini made twenty bucks around the lunch table on that dare. Just for a little peck. No tongue! I swear!"

Cheryl hadn't wrangled her laughter under control, and only took time between gasps of air to yell, "It looks like an elephant's floppy nose!"

"Go ahead! Be jealous! I…" he said, letting his announcement hang just like his dick. "…am getting some bug spray."

And that was the funniest joke of the whole night. But it didn't stop the game. After we watched Shelton's full moon bounce back to the cabin to save his skin from the encroaching mosquitos, caught our breaths, and wiped the tears from our eyes, we carried on. It was Linda's turn.

"Never have I ever…" she said and let her eyes search the sky for the next barnburner, "made myself cum."

Everybody laughed good and long at that. Scotty and Ash gave each other one hardly-ashamed look and undid their belts and their flies. Cheryl cried, "Whatever!" and then reached around her back for the clasps of her bra.

My stomach had dropped. Because I'd gone along with everything so far. I'd played fair. I hadn't lied. I hadn't cheated. So far. But had I had my own private moment? Behind my locked bedroom door? If I hadn't, how would any of these people ever know? But I was already leaning forward in the chair, my own arms twisting to undo the little two-hook clasp holding together my boring and practical sports bra. When I looked up, Linda wasn't taking off her bra. And as for Cheryl?

That thin lacey excuse for a bra was already gone. She bared her chest as proudly as a porn star. Her perfect breasts were golden in the firelight. There could have been a hundred paparazzi photographs popping off their flashes and she couldn't have been less unabashed. She was a queen. As for Scotty and Ash, she held them both in the palm of her hand.

She dangled her little piece of Victorious Secrets lingerie from a fingertip and when the boys unglued their eyes from her nipples and shifted them to her bra, she flung it into the blazing fire.

"Eat your heart out, boys," she said, as bold and bare as a Greek goddess.

I was frozen, equally a statue, with my hands awkwardly turned backward around my torso, my own less-than-statuesque chest still hidden behind that K-mart sports bra.

"Oh my god, Cheryl," Linda said, her eyes fixed on the flames as they consumed the lace and silk. "That was so expensive!"

"Well?" Cheryl said, showing no concern for the money she was burning and not taking one ounce of precaution to hide herself from us. "Have you?"

Only then did Linda notice me. "You pervs," Linda said, judging us both.

"No," I said when I realized the gazes had shifted my way. "I haven't. Not that. Ever. I was itching. There was a bug."

"Oh, come on," Scotty said, down to those same boxer shorts I saw him in that morning when the ax was lodged into the wall next to the fireplace. "There's no shame if you have. Look at us!"

"I–" I false-started.

"You know you have," Ash said, cool like Coolio instead of Carlton now.

"I…" I what? I hadn't polished my pearl while paging through Seventeen's spread of Jason Priestley? Because I had, and by now, I'd basically told everyone around that fire as much. There was no lying my way out of it. Not with any amount of conviction.

"I need some bug spray," I told them and abandoned my Hypercolor shirt and my cargo shorts there in the grass.

I swear, I wasn't crying out of fear as I ran back to the cabin, thinking about my gym bag in the bedroom that had my warm and comfortable PJs in it waiting for me. I was fully composed. Cross my heart and hope to die, I swear, I was not an absolute wreck.

God, how I wish for the problems I used to have.

As I wiped tears away with my bare forearm, I hoped I wouldn't run into Shelton, him being completely nude and me just in my underwear. When I slipped back inside through the deck door and found the house completely still, a part of me was relieved. Another part of me, the part still riding on the thrill of flirting and smoking and drinking and being seen in my underwear, the part that was jealous of Cheryl's brashness, was a little letdown. Surprising that I even noticed that the mask Shelton had scared us with that morning was missing from the dining room table. It had been there all day, ever since he'd tossed it there. Strange that it was suddenly gone.

I came into the cabin with my arms crossed over my chest, hiding what little cleavage I had exposed. But finding it empty and my fear retreating from me, I let my arms fall and moved further into the cabin. Tip-toeing, eyes up, I searched the place for where Shelton might have gone. If I found him in the bedroom where I set my duffel bag, if it was just the two of us, and if he was cool and kind like how he'd been on the deck that afternoon, if he would have consoled me, would I have let him lie me down on that big bed with all the flannel quilts? It's hard to say after all these years. But, yeah, probably.

It wasn't until I kicked the barbeque tongs with my bare toes that I noticed it. The noise of it scattering against the hardwood floor shocked my nerves. The pain had me biting off a curse word. The big spatula that had been hanging on the grill next to the tongs was also lying on the floor, but the big fork that completed the set was nowhere to be seen.

So was that what I was going to walk into? Another one of Shelton's gags? I stepped over the barbeque tools and ducked into the rear bedroom for my duffel bag and some clothes.

It was dark in there, but I closed the door behind me anyway, eager to shut out any unwanted eyes or pranks. A few seconds ticked by as my hand groped for the double light switch in the dark. I clacked both switches up. The overhead lights popped to life and the ceiling fan began to slowly spin. And there was Shelton, still completely nude, but not like I expected him.

Instead of standing in front of the bed, ready to hold me in a warm and soothing embrace, he hung from the ceiling fan by a length of fibrous rope. The barbeque fork from the grill set was stabbed through his chest. His slack face hung down. His eyes fell in my general direction. The fan turned and rotated his body around like he was a piece of artwork on display. Blood that had been pooling into a soggy puddle on the blankets now drizzled in a circle all over the bed and the floor.

Instead of screaming, I tried to suck in air, but the room was like a vacuum. I gasped but didn't take in any oxygen. I stumbled backward against the door, and when my back hit the wood, it knocked out what little air I had in my lungs. I'd found Shelton. We were finally alone together. But no amount of weed or booze could have prepared me for this.

Outside the door, big heavy boots plodded against the hardwood floor. It was the killer. I didn't need to peek into the living room or wait for an explanation to understand that whoever had done this to Shelton, wasn't finished yet. He'd do the same to me without a thought. Not making a noise, I reached and turned off the lights so the shine wouldn't be seen under the door. And so I wouldn't have to see what had become of my afternoon crush. Then I twisted the lock in the knob as quietly as I could and prayed the tiny mechanisms hadn't clicked too loudly.

Chapter Five

"You said earlier that the details were hard to remember."

I know, I know. They were until I had that… reaction in my kitchen. The night I got drunk on wine and watched Halloween with Jamie Lee Curtis on the TV and thought I found Violetta's head in my fridge? It all came back to me crystal clear as if I was watching my own horror movie play out right in front of my eyes.

"You also said you don't like scary movies."

I know. I don't. But, I mean, I have seen them. Like, all of them. I don't remember when or why. I think… I think maybe Doctor Hagari showed me some, as a sort of exposure therapy. To inoculate me from the fear I'd experienced. I remember even less of our sessions than I do of what happened when I was younger. He… I didn't like going to those sessions.

"But you were telling me something about a school's basement, or a suburban neighborhood where you'd all sneak out after dark. Or an abandoned hotel?"

That was before. When I had that flashback, when everything came back to me, my vision became as clean as a mountain stream. I was in my kitchen. I'd blacked out. When I woke up, I was lying on my back, staring up at my recessed lighting. My little pug Chuck was next to me, slurping up the red wine I'd spilled all over the floor when I'd passed out. And as small as he is? Um, no. He should not have been drinking that much wine.

I should know. So, I shooed him away and bit by bit, limb by limb, I picked myself off the kitchen floor.

"But you said–"

From there, I kind of sorted myself out. I mopped up the blood– I mean, the wine, double-checked the fridge for any decapitated coworkers' heads, and finding none, wandered back into the living room. Some other horror movie was on by then. I didn't know the name of it. The one with the doll that's possessed by a demon. The cute doll though, not the other one with the ugly doll. That probably doesn't narrow it down, huh? It's the one—

"Tell me more about your sessions with Doctor Hagari. Why didn't you like them?"

Because he was a stinking, smegma discharge. Is that a good enough reason for you? No? Okay. Well, like I said, I think he made me watch some of those movies. All of those movies, even. It's foggy, but I remember being laid back in a chair like at a dentist's office with one of those TVs on a big arm put directly in front of my face so I couldn't turn away. And he was behind me, like just out of eyesight, and he was saying things to me like, "Do you remember being there, Taylor?"

And, "Put yourself back in that place. Back when you were a teenager with your friends."

And "Don't avoid it. Don't run away from it."

And "Stay in that place, Taylor. Inside of that fear. Remember when you were the victim of all those terrors."

He was a serious creep.

"Doctor Hagari was an accredited psychologist with a long and successful career."

Look, I already reported what he did to HR. They should have everything on record already.

"I'd like you to tell me."

Why? Are you actually going to do something about it?

"And, what, at this point, would you have me do?"

He put his hands on me. He groped me. While he was saying those things to me. Everything is fuzzy. I can't remember it like I should, but shit like that, you don't just make up things like that in your head. And you don't forget it. Those movies were playing, and he was saying those things to me, and his hands were on my chest and on my crotch and… I think he may have drugged me.

"You were prescribed some fairly significant narcotics, but nothing that isn't commonly used for psychiatric treatment."

I couldn't move. I wanted to get up and leave but I couldn't.

"Why couldn't you move?"

I don't know! I felt like a turtle, trapped on its back under the hot sun. I wanted to leave so bad, but I couldn't.

"Why couldn't you move, Taylor?"

I told you, I don't know, and I don't want to talk about it anymore. I'm done with him. Honestly, I'd rather talk about the night I started having my flashbacks. Or that night up at the cabin when everything happened. I'm not talking about Doctor Hagari anymore. Got it?

"Okay. Tell me what happened when you came to after your flashback."

I don't even know why I woke up. Maybe it was my dog, slurping up that wine and licking my face like he wanted to play. But the TV was still playing the horror movie with the doll, and I had no patience for any of that. Not after reliving everything like I had. See, the thing is, sure, I've seen all those movies about the innocent teen, or the group of stupid friends who always want to split up, or the demon-possessed doll or little girl, or the haunted mansion that drives the occupants insane. The thing is, I was different than all of them. I'm stronger than all of them. I survived. And look at everything I've done since then.

I found the remote and changed the channel.

That old movie, the one where the guy's dancing through some street in London and swinging from the light posts? It was that one that came on next. I plopped my drunk ass on the couch with the open wine bottle still in my hand and tipped it back for a good long pull. Three or four bubbles worth went down the hatch. My eyes went crossed, then back uncrossed and focused on the screen. And it was the weirdest thing in the world, that old musical with all the corny songs pushed me right back into the flashback.

Chapter Six

I was alone in the dark with a corpse, which felt infinitely more lonely than being in a room without a corpse. When I hit the switch, I only killed the lights. The other switch, the one that operated the ceiling fan, I'd somehow left on. Which meant Shelton's body was still slowly rotating around in the dark. And the bed wasn't exactly centered in the room, so as his body bled out, he dribbled sometimes on the blankets, making a fat thwap thwap thwapping sound, and occasionally on the hardwood floor, creating sharp crack! crack! cracking noises like a drumstick on a snare.

And all I could do was wait and listen to it on rotation like it was a scratched record.

This was the room where I was supposed to lose my virginity. I'd known it from the start. It was something I'd been lying to myself about not wanting. It didn't matter that much who Shelton was, although he was kind of cute and funny and kind and not always insufferable. What mattered was, I was ready, and the cabin and the back bedroom were just right for it, and we flirted on the deck, and I'd already seen his penis, and he's already seen me in my underwear. It had become inevitable.

But now? It was as if someone had taken something beautiful, froze it into glass, and shattered it into a million bloody pieces like the windshield of a fatal car wreck.

And the thing that had destroyed my naive, cute, sexy-to-me, little dream was right outside the door. I could hear him breathing. It was… healthy. Not raspy or struggled or labored or irregular. Strong. Steady.

Even. Paced like a yoga instructor's. And somehow that was far more disturbing than if I'd heard Darth fucking Vader huh-purring outside the door. It was so controlled!

It was not as if I'd met any murderers before, but none of my assumptions about them led me down a road of calm, cool, methodical minds. All the same, that's what was waiting for me on the other side of the knotty pine door.

I tried to make my own lungs as obedient to my super-ego as his. They failed. My short, rapid breaths hitched and bucked and worked around the fear welling up inside of me. I stayed still, sitting with my back against the door, needing to remain absolutely silent, but fighting my own body.

The doorknob rattled against the lock. There was no deadbolt. No chain I could latch. Just that tiny little switch in the center of the round knob that up until that moment, I wasn't even sure worked. But a big heavy hand was twisting the knob from the other side, and the lock held. He twisted it again, and the knob threatened to break right off its screws. He was trying to get in. The lock wouldn't hold for long. There was no place to hide and no other door through which to leave.

I went for the window first, as quietly as possible, still holding my ungovernable breath, because I was on the ground floor and that was the most obvious escape route. When Shelton's still-warm foot swung in its circle and smacked my hip, I repressed a whimper behind tight lips and tip-toed on to the window. It was one of those old ones that was supposed to slide up the wooden frame, but decades of rain and snow and ice had waterlogged the wood until it swelled so fat, the window wouldn't move an inch. Breaking it, with what I never got around to figuring out, would have been loud, and would have given the maniac on the other side of the door all the motivation he'd need to kick down the door and splinter that little locking mechanism to shards.

There was no way back outside.

But there was a laundry chute. Across the room. They don't put laundry chutes in modern houses anymore. It was one of those eccentricities of older houses that fell out of fashion. A cabinet door in the wall opened to a small chute that started in the upstairs bedroom and went down to the basement laundry room. I found it when I first set my duffel bag at the foot of the bed. It fed down into the basement, where I hadn't been before, but it was somewhere other than here. From down there, I could find another way out and get back to Cheryl and Scotty and Ash and Linda and they could help. We could get to a phone and call the cops. This didn't have to end with me dead!

Having a plan helped me control my breathing. Slowly, I moved my bare feet across the cold floor. I could still hear him breathing, as steady as a sleeping baby. I traipsed around the bed and Shelton's still-rotating body. I almost kicked my duffel bag sitting at the end of the bed. A hoodie sat right on top, and maybe it was silly of me, but the thought of having a shirt to wear made me feel so much safer. It would take no additional time and cause no additional noise. Meanwhile, the fan continued to turn Shelton in circles and Shelton continued to bleed one, two, three thumps of blood on the thick flannel blankets, and then four, five, six splats on the floor.

The hoodie slipped over my head. My hands found their way through the big loose arms. It was on. Now all I had to do was make it to the chute. I took another step, and my foot came down on a wet and slimy section of the floor. I'd stepped in blood. Shelton's blood. But I didn't slip. I could ignore it. Only, when I continued my creep, my wet heel squeaked against the wood.

Something huge and heavy slammed against the door. The killer's boot maybe, or his shoulder. The door nearly buckled out of its frame. The tiny lock, against all odds, held against the mass, but it wouldn't last long. The killer collided against the door again, and I could hear metal breaking.

I bolted for the chute and threw open the cabinet door. If it was dark in the bedroom, it was a collapsed mine shaft inside the chute. I couldn't see the bottom, but I didn't have time to change my mind or come up with another plan.

A third impact finally busted the tiny little lock in the knob. Pieces of it clattered across the room as the door swung open. A silhouette, backlit by the living room chandelier, stood in the doorway. I couldn't see his face or what clothes he wore, but his black outline nearly filled up the entire door frame. He was massive.

There was no time to carefully shimmy down the pitch-black, narrow, laundry chute. I plunged in, headfirst. Only, it wasn't wide enough for me to just dive through it, and I hadn't taken the time to make myself thin like a pencil. My arm holding open the cabinet door trailed behind me. My shoulders twisted and dragged against the unfinished wooden walls of the chute, wedging me half in and half.

A palm, smooth and not at all calloused but impossibly strong, landed on my ankle and squeezed it tight. He'd reached me. Even as I screamed and kicked and writhed, I could still hear his clockwork breathing. A massive force pulled me back toward the bedroom, but my hands pressed hard against the wooden walls of the chute, clamping me in place. Back inside that room, there was only darkness, blood, and death. Anywhere was better than in there.

I cried out for help, as loud as I could. My voice came out in a panicked shrill. There was no way anyone could mistake this for some joke or a gag. I needed help and I needed it desperately and immediately. But my friends were out at the fire, and I was screaming into the basement. The man behind me yanked again, hard enough for the tendons in my hip to turn to fire. I couldn't let go of the sidewalls of the chute, but I still had one foot free.

I sent my heel out and back, pumping like a piston in an engine, making contact with the man's torso. But there was too much mass there, too much body for my strikes to matter, and I couldn't see back up the chute to spot his groin and kick him where it counted. And his fingers were groping for my free ankle too. They grazed my skin as I flailed. If I didn't get loose from him, quick, my strength would give out, and I'd be hauled back into that chamber of black murder. I needed one good kick; this one I aimed for where his hand was latched onto my captured ankle. I dodged his grasp and wound up. The ball of my heel went straight into the spot where his thumb connected to his palm. It must have hurt because that robotic breathing halted for a moment. Only for a moment. The kick hurt me. Kicking his wrist almost broke my ankle, but it was worth it. The bear trap clamp released. I shoved myself downward for whatever waited for me below. Hopefully something soft.

I slid down, out of the bedroom, and out of the killer's reach, but just as my head cleared the chute and just before I could be dumped out of the tunnel, my hoodie snagged on a nailhead, twisted me up again inside the narrow space, and wedged me tight in the narrow confines.

Above me, I heard the cabinet door slam shut. That even-keel breathing became agitated, huffing and exhaling, not out of exhaustion, but frustration. Then I heard those heavy footfalls thunder across the floor and the bedroom door slam open against the wall.

Was he coming down into the basement to wrench me loose by my dangling hair just to murder me there? Or just swing whatever blunt instrument he found at my head like I was a pinata? I squirmed again, trying to find the nail head that had caught my shirt and twisted me up. Using my arm dangling out of the chute to pull myself the rest of the way out only bound me up more, and there wasn't enough room for me to free my trailing arm. The chute was so narrow, I could only slide down if I was perfectly straight, and with one arm caught by my hip and one over my head, my spine was twisted up. The weight of my pelvis and legs pushed down on it, binding it even further.

I couldn't move. Not one inch.

Stupid. So stupid. How could I be so stupid as to wedge myself there like that? The blood rushed to my head. I still couldn't see anything, the basement was just as dark as the bedroom had been, but now phosphenes swirled in my vision. All my senses reported vertigo and nothing else.

Until someone opened the deck door upstairs.

"Taylor?" It was Linda, come in from the fire.

"Baby, I told you she's fine. Just give her some space." That was Ash's voice. They'd come in to check on me and make sure I was okay. And now they were in a house with a madman.

"Run!" I screamed as loud as I could. "Shelton! He killed Shelton! Run!"

I heard confusion in their voices but couldn't make out words. And then only chaotic commotion. A storm of weighted footfalls. Cursing. Linda screamed. A struggle.

"Run! Run away!" I screamed even louder.

I don't like small places. I don't like not being able to move fast.

I thrashed inside the laundry chute, hoping to solve my conundrum with sheer violence, but nothing gave an inch.

More indecipherable noises came from upstairs. Loud thumps. More of Linda's screams. More thunderous footfalls. Whatever was happening up there, I was powerless to help. It didn't last long. The pounding steps grew more distant and the sounds of struggle even more incomprehensible. Had they fought the killer off? Were they running away? I heard Linda scream one more time, and then another burst of thumps and bangs and rattling.

Then everything was quiet.

"Oh god…" I whimpered to myself, fearing that silence meant the worst.

I was crying again, but hanging upside down the way I was, my tears streamed up over my brow and down to the basement below. When they landed, they didn't make that sharp snap, but more of a dull thump. Like Shelton's blood landing on the bed rather than the hardwood floor. That meant there was something soft underneath me. Something I could land in, and with any luck, not break my neck.

Upstairs, a door slowly swung on its hinges and latched shut. Was that the killer leaving? Or maybe the wind just blowing shut the door Linda and Ash had left open?

None of it mattered if I couldn't get myself free of the chute. I tried again to pull myself free with my one arm, but the angle was all wrong. The more I pulled, the more the nail head ripped into my hoodie and the more wedged I became. And I still couldn't free my other arm. My legs were uselessly aimed upwards, unable to push off anything to add to the pull of my arm. Like a Chinese finger trap, the more I strained, the more stuck I became.

And that was the solution. Just like a finger trap, if I could push back up, maybe I could unhook my shirt from the nail, straighten my spine and shoulders, and slip free. With only one arm free, it wasn't an easy task to push my whole body weight back up the chute, but it was my only shot. I squirmed to get a better position. My knees pinned my legs in place, alleviating some of the weight off my torso. I wiggled just right, then pushed myself back up with every bit of strength I had.

I heard fabric rip. The clamp of the chute walls eased off my shoulders. I twisted again, aligning everything straight, and released the pressure my knees exerted against the chute walls.

I slipped right out, as easy as a fish going over a dam. An old wicker hamper softened my fall. That, and some musty towels thrown down the chute and forgotten a long time ago. I was free, and I hadn't broken my neck. Now all I had to do was pick myself up and greet what horrors waited for me above.

Chapter Seven

That weekend was the first time I'd ever stepped foot into that cabin. I had never been into that cobweb-laced, unfinished basement with its furnace, water heater, and laundry machines. But now my mind was busy mapping every twist and turn of its floor plan. The fall left me completely disoriented and it took time to find the dim, red lights of a smoke detector and an overloaded power strip. Like distant lighthouses, I used them to navigate to the base of the stairs. And once I set my hand on the railing? I had my bearings again.

The basement stairs were directly under the staircase that led to the upstairs loft and Linda and Ash's bedroom. They u-turned once on the way up before reaching the entryway and kitchen. And you know what was waiting for me, right there on the wall of the kitchen?

"A telephone?"

God damn right! An old school telephone. A landline. It even had buttons, instead of the old spinning dial that would have taken forever to even dial Nine One One. A phone! Right at the top of the stairs.

I crept up, testing each tread for squeaks before putting down my full weight. One creaked. The rest were quiet. So was the rest of the house. There was no door at the top of the steps, and as soon as I put my foot on the floor, I was reaching for that old phone on the wall.

When I picked up the receiver, the buttons lit up in an off-lemon-yellow glow. I hammered Nine One One.

It rang.

An operator asked me what my emergency was.

"There's been a murder. The killer is still here," I said and read off the address. "I can't stay. Come quick."

Hanging up the phone felt like unbuckling from the seat of a race car, but I couldn't stay tethered to its cord. I had to keep moving.

I left the sanctuary of the dim corner of the entryway and kitchen. Maybe you're thinking, why didn't you run out the front door? You could have been down the road and off to the neighbors, no problem. Well, two things about that. One: your head never works that clearly when you're in a situation like that, and Two: I had to find my friends.

The cabin's main level, with its big open floor plan comprised of the kitchen, dining room, and living room with the big fireplace, was quiet. Still, I took my time stepping into it. I saw nothing.

No killer. No bodies. A couple of chairs around the dining room table were knocked over. The rug by the deck door was crumpled up. There had been a struggle. I hadn't hallucinated that. But the participants were conspicuously absent. And what did that mean? Had Linda and Ash made it out safe?

As I stepped before that giant rock fireplace, I heard a noise that was becoming disturbingly familiar. Not that thick fat sound of a kicker landing on a bass drum, but that crack! crack! crack! of a wood stick on the tight head of a snare. Blood dripping on a hard surface. Looking down in front of the hearth, I saw a growing puddle. Looking up, I saw Linda. Thrown from the upstairs balcony, she had landed face up, into the antlers of that massive elk. She was impaled there, halfway up the vaulted cabin wall, but was also cradled like a fainted woman in the arms of a large man, held up by too many arms and fingers. Still dressed in just her underwear, I saw where the elk's tines had gored into her back and through her chest and stomach. With the multiple puncture wounds, there wasn't just one stream of dripping blood, but an irregular waterfall fueling that puddle on the floor.

Forgive me if I come off as some stupid girl in one of those slasher flicks, but that image destroyed my mind. All higher-functioning brain activity shut down. I screamed, barbaric and animalistic. My feet led me backward, away from the gruesomeness before me. My ass bumped into the loosely latched deck door and knocked it open. I staggered through it. Out there on the deck, the living room chandelier painted orange rectangles on the boards. At the far end of one of those rectangles, I found Ash.

The butcher knife Cheryl had been playing with that morning while waiting for her coffee to brew was buried up to the hilt in Ash's face. It had gone through bone, and I couldn't help but think of the force that drove that blade into place. It was just below his right eye, and now that eye was all full of blood and other yellowish, unknown fluids from inside of him. He was still wearing just his jeans, no shirt: an after-effect of that stupid game we were all playing around the fire.

The fire. Cheryl and Scotty. They were still down there. Looking that way, I saw the flames devouring split logs and warming up the night. I stumbled away from Ash's mauled face, around the jacuzzi, and toward the stairs leading down to the backyard.

"Cheryl!" I called my best friend's name from the deck. I couldn't see them down by the fire. Maybe it was stupid of me to call out, to let the murderer know exactly where I was, but I was thinking about her. About warning her. About saving her. When there was no response, I screamed her name again. "Cheryl!"

Before I could stop myself, I was trampling down the steps to the backyard. When my bare feet hit the dew-wet lawn, my toes dug into the grass as I sprinted toward the firepit. Three strides later, my feet were out front under me. My back slammed flat against the ground and my blurred eyes were staring up at the stars. I hadn't expected the wet grass to be that slick against my bare heels. I hadn't expected a lot of things that happened that night.

Turning myself over to get my legs back underneath me, I saw a dark shape a few feet away, lying still in the shadows.

"Scotty?" I said to him softly. Something about his stillness demanded reverence. I crawled on all fours over to him. It was him. I could tell by his mop of curly brown hair, bare chest, and blue jeans. The cast iron rod he'd been using to prod the fire was next to him too. Only, there was something wrong with his chest. It was ragged and dark where it should have been smooth and pale. "Scott?"

That was when I made the mistake of putting my hand on his chest. I didn't know what I was thinking, maybe that he'd spilled something on himself, or maybe it was his wadded-up t-shirt, or he'd grown a forest of chest hair, or... I don't know. Instead of any of that, my hand sunk into a mess of blood and flesh. His torso seemed to swallow my entire hand. There was no structural integrity to it. His ribs and sternum had been broken apart and his chest cavity had been opened by some crude instrument.

Screaming, I pushed myself away as if his blood was raw electricity. I hated that I had screamed so much that night. So stupid and useless. But my mind had taken a permanent vacation, and without it, I had nothing left but screeching and crying and running. I think I was yelling Cheryl's name, over and over again, as if calling out to her could keep her alive. By then, I had no reason to believe anything quite so hopeful. I scrambled toward the fire pit, still slipping across the dew-soaked grass, but eventually making it down to the still-burning fire where we'd all sat so happy and innocent and mischievous and confident and scared and daring just a few minutes ago.

We had been all of those things, all at once. What were we now?

I skidded to a stop next to the pile of split wood and the chopping stump. The ax was gone. I fully intended to pry it from the stump and take it with me, but with it missing… I knew then what had been used to destroy Scotty's chest.

"Taylor," a weak voice called my name from beyond the glow of the firelight.

I spun. My best friend was there, lying in the grass, belly down, only wearing the bottoms of that red lacy underwear set, her head barely able to lift off the ground to meet my eyes. She was alive, but something had been done to her to keep her there on the ground as if paralyzed. Cheryl raised up one hand, reaching out to me with splayed fingers. Blood leaked from the corner of her mouth.

"Help me," she begged.

That massive figure emerged from the darkness. The featureless mask Shelton had worn that morning for his little prank stared me down. The killer clutched that glistening ax across his chest like a soldier carrying a rifle at port arms. The blade was darkened with blood. His machine-like breathing raised and lowered his shoulders like the slow waves of an ocean, rhythmically pushing in and pulling out.

"Cheryl!" I called.

Her own name was the last thing she heard.

The giant took one step, hefted the ax over his shoulder, and brought it down hard and fast, right into the middle of my friend's back. The ax head cleaved through her spine and shot electrical impulses to each of her limbs as if it were a bolt of lightning. But one strike wasn't enough. The maniac ripped the ax loose from bone and flesh just to bring it down again, chopping this girl apart as if she were timber.

There was nothing I could do. You understand that, right? I had no tools or weapons. I couldn't have reached the man or the ax in time to stop him, as if I even had the brute strength to interrupt that monster. All I could do was watch as he murdered her. I don't know how many swings he took, but by the time he was satisfied, she was more than dead. Cheryl, my bold, brash, brazen best friend was nothing but biowaste.

He stepped around her, toward me. The only non-black piece of his attire, that faceless mask, was splattered red.

I ran.

Only I couldn't run. Not with the grass as wet as it was and my bare feet with no traction. I scrambled away from him, slowly climbing and pulling myself back toward the cabin. I had no plan. I think my primal brain just associated the lights inside with safety. But I couldn't move fast enough to escape him. If I'd been on dry ground, or if I had shoes that could have gripped the soil, I know I could have outrun him. I was young and in shape and could do the four hundred meter dash in a minute ten flat. But I just couldn't make any headway. Every time my heels pushed hard off the grass, I found my hands holding me off the ground.

I don't like not being able to go fast.

That in and out tide-like breathing of the murderer at my back persisted, and all my screams and cries and slips and trips weren't doing a damn thing to get me further away from him. I wanted to let my brain go and rely on my legs and lungs, but that wasn't working. I silenced my fright, if only for just a few ticks of a clock, and forced myself to think. All the while he breathed and marched, as steady as an army. I needed a plan. One that didn't rely on my speed.

The man behind me wasn't running. He was taking big, long paces, not rushed, but still gaining on me all the same. Steady strides. Evenly placed steps. That was how I was going to move if I was going to be able to move at all. His breathing quickened, ever so slightly, and I knew he was getting ready to deliver another killing blow. I hastened my strides, knowing exactly what would happen. My feet went out from underneath me. My body spilled down into the grass, sprawled out for a perfect target. The killer's lungs sucked in. I could almost see that ax blade reflecting moonlight as he raised it up.

My hands gripped the fire pit poker. I landed on it, intentionally, knowing he'd suspect nothing and be too eager to not take advantage of what he must have thought was another stupid girl stumbling and slipping and tripping to her own death. I twisted around and raised up the heavy, cast-iron shank. The ax was already coming down for my head. I slipped my head sideways and jabbed the poker toward the stars. The ax blade sang through the cool night air and submerged into the soft dirt next to my head. The tip of the poker sunk through the murderer's throat.

He made the strangest noise, something between a groan and a question. Not a scream or a roar or anything to indicate pain. Only slight annoyance and perhaps a bit of confusion. It wasn't much, but I'd finally, *finally*, made that son of a bitch do something other than breathe.

His weight rode the poker deeper into himself. The handle sank firmly into the ground, and there was no more need for me to hold it. I slipped out from underneath him. When he stood up, the cast-iron rod came up with him, the point of it protruding from the back of his neck. Both of his hands gripped it tight to rip it loose, which left the ax stuck in the dirt. I snatched it up quick, and having never chopped wood in my life, swung it like a softball bat.

The ax hit him square in the head, but sideways, smacking him instead of cleaving into him. But it struck with enough force to send him staggering backward.

The memories grow hazy again after that. Or maybe it was just my mind going into a rage. People in car accidents often say they never remember the crash, just everything before and after it. I couldn't tell you, but I remember this much. I readjusted the grip so the next swing would lead with the edge. While he still fought to pull the fire poker out of his throat, I wound up, skip-stepped, swung, and sent the gleaming edge straight through the side of his head. I nailed that fucker. Homerun.

Chapter Eight

And that was how I survived. All my friends were dead. I was the only one left standing. The cops came eventually, too late to actually do anything, but in time to find me standing amongst all those bodies, covered in blood, and clutching the murder weapon tight in my hands.

Why can't I see your face?

"You said they never found the killer's body?"

That's what they told me. I know he was dead. I killed him. Otherwise, he would have come back and done it again, right?

"I think, by now, you know the answer to that question, Taylor."

What nobody understands is what I've had to live with every day of my life since that night. Not just the memories of my past, but the possibilities of my worst imaginable future. Because I can imagine such terrible things now. I don't want to ever experience anything like that again. I don't ever want to go to a cabin by a lake ever again, even though that's what everybody else in this entire state seems to be compelled to do every weekend. I don't like campfires. I don't like scary movies. I don't like being caught in my underwear. I don't like confined places. I don't like going slow. And I don't like to think about my past.

That doesn't mean I can escape it. That night lingers with me still, in the most mundane and boring times and places. Still, I'm expected to show up to work and smile and get along and answer emails and sit through meetings and meet deadlines and be excited about a new project the boss gives me even when it is entirely out of my scope. Nowhere in my job description does it say anything about being a fucking party planner. But the morning after that flashback or panic attack or whatever you want to call it, you know where I was?

In front of my desk in my home office, logged in, fresh cup of coffee in hand, hair brushed, make-up on, wearing a clean, professional blouse and my favorite comfy pair of pajama pants, the white ones with the little glasses of wine all over them, ready to work.

And guess who else was logged on already? Good ol' Barbara. She video-chatted me early, right off the bat, because in her words, we needed our "girl time."

"So, what are your big ideas for the retreat? Last year we didn't even do one because, you know, COVID, and the year before that… well that was COVID too. But I think it was three years ago? Yeah. Three years ago, we did it at this conference center by the Mall of America and then went out to some comedy show as a group and Jason was going to sign us all up with this improv troupe to help us team build?" She said that last statement like a question, as if it were too ridiculous to be reality, which, in this case, I agreed with her. "Anyway, I guess that went alright. But, please, girl. Don't let Jason sign us up for any improv classes. I do not do comedy!"

"Clearly," I said, but my attention wasn't on her. I had a bit of my bagel left and normally, I'd feed it to Chuck the Pug, but he either hadn't woken up yet that morning or was hiding from me, which probably meant he'd made a mess somewhere.

"Hey, I'm sorry to bring it up. I mean by-gones are by-gone and water under a bridge and all that but… What you said about me, the day before you went to see Doctor Cal, you didn't mean any of that, right? Just 'cause, I always thought we were good. We're good, you and I, right?"

"Golden," I said. What had I said about her that day? Whatever it was, must have been a doozy.

"Okay. Great. Like I said, I'm sorry to bring it up. Just thought we should clear the air. Anyway… Jason wants us all to pitch ideas at this morning's nine o'clock," Barbara carried on, paging through sheet after sheet of things she'd printed off. "And I'm going to suggest something away from the Cities. Like, we should head up north. There's so many resorts we could check out."

"Hold on, Barb," I paused her. "Keep talking, but I gotta step away from my desk for a minute. Keep talking though. I can still hear you."

And let me tell you, she did. Meanwhile, I went looking for Chuck with a bagel bite in hand.

"I know it's your project and Jason gave you the lead on it, so I'm not trying to step on your toes, but there's this place up in Bemidji I think you should check out. Here. I'll chat you the link. Their Yelp reviews are, like, all five stars. There. It should be in the thread now."

"Chuck," I called through my empty house. I liked my house empty, understand. Without the intrusions. But I was missing my puppers. "Heeerrreee Chucky. Want to play?"

When I came to the kitchen, I saw my big butcher knife out on the counter, out of the knife block where it belonged. Of course, I took it out from its spot last night after finding what I'd found in the fridge. But I never noticed until that morning how similar it was to the one at Scotty's uncle's cabin. Same shape. Same size. Same slot in the block. Same block of knives too. It wasn't just similar. It was identical. Why had I ever bought something for my kitchen that so closely resembled the tool used to murder Ash?

When I closed my eyes, I saw that blade buried in his face with just the hilt left outside of his head, just under his right eye.

The chunk of bagel slipped to the floor. My hands shivered. My heart skipped second and third gear and ground the transmission right into overdrive. I knew it was my knife. I knew I'd left it there. I knew everything was just fine. But those sorts of reactions, you can't control them. You can't just rationalize and think them away. When my phone buzzed from over by my potted plant, I jumped.

Barb's voice playing came back into focus. As I gathered my senses, I collected my phone from behind the plant and picked up the half-empty coffee cup from my desk. She hadn't stopped her tirade the entire time.

"Mostly I just ignore the one star reviews, because, seriously, who takes the time out of their day to leave one star reviews? Bitches, that's who."

"Yes?" Bitch answered her call.

"Shut up, Bitch," I said.

"Okay," the speaker said.

There was an unread text message on my phone. From Tyler. I read it but didn't respond.

We should be together, you and I. Text me.

Fucking prick. I buried the phone in my pajama pants pocket, dumped the rest of my coffee down the kitchen sink, and filled it half full of the warm chardonnay I'd also left out from last night. I love chardonnay because it pairs perfectly with not giving a fuck. I'll run it off later, I promised myself.

"Are you okay?" Barbara said as I sat back at my desk, my wine inconspicuously hidden in my oversized coffee cup. I held it as if it warmed my hands.

"Yeah. I'm great. I'm fine. It's fine. Everything's wine," I said. "Fine, I mean."

"Anyway…" Barb said. "You never told me about you and Doctor Cal."

"Barb," I sighed and took a sip. A gulp. "I really shouldn't–"

"I know, I know. HIPAA this, patient confidentiality that. I know the rules," Barb said as if she actually did. "I just hope you go back to him. Even though you're done with your program. Otherwise, you'll regret it. Trust me."

"You're not even supposed to know I was in a program," I reminded her.

"Oh please! After that day in the office? And then all of a sudden you were gone? Everybody else assumed you were fired. I mean, everybody besides Jason of course, and Violetta because she does all the HR stuff, and me cause I saw you booked with Doctor Cal, and I think Robert knew too because otherwise your workload would have been shifted to him, but regardless. We were all happy to see you back in the office yesterday. I think Jason's having another in-person later this week."

"Barb, I gotta let you go," I told her. "I gotta prep for this nine o'clock."

"Okay, but I'm going to get it out of you yet. I kind of have a knack for prying out all the juice details. But you do you!"

"Yep. Okay. Right," I said, my cursor hovering over the "End Meeting" button. "See you at nine."

"At nine. And check out that link I–"

Click.

The nine o'clock turned out to just be a meeting to plan another meeting, in which we'd make a plan to plan the retreat. No input required from me. No decisions from Jason. The conference was only a week away, and we still hadn't booked anything, and that didn't seem to be an issue of concern for anybody really. The only thing was, it was my ass on the line for this stupid thing, and if I waited on a committee to make a decision all of the venues would be booked out and of course, it would be no one's fault but mine. So, I clicked on the link Barb had sent me, and, sight unseen, booked a block of rooms and a conference hall. I could always cancel later.

There. I'd completed a task. I'd accomplished more than the rest of the team would for the rest of the day. Now I just had to hire a caterer, come up with an itinerary, maybe book a guest speaker… you know, everything else. But I promised myself a run, and after polishing off a coffee cup of red before noon, I stuck with it. Because self-care is the best care.

I like to go fast. On my feet. In my car. Wherever.

I played softball when I was younger. Before I found my true love. Once I hit high school, I ran in long distance track and cross country, and although my distances have decreased and my times have increased, I've never stopped. At least three times a week, rain or shine, I get out and get in my miles. It's as much a mental health benefit as a physical one. And if I sound insufferable, sorry-not-sorry. I do it for me. Not for anyone else. If my legs look good in yoga pants because of it, that's just a bonus. I do it to outrun my demons, and to be able to outrun them again if they ever reappear.

Plus, if I just so happened to catch a little pre-lunch buzz from my "coffee," it helped to reel me back in. I'd refilled my mug all the way up to the brim after our pointless nine o'clock and had it empty and in the kitchen sink by eleven.

So, when I stepped out of my front door, pulling up each of my feet in turn to limber up, the neighborhood swirled in my vision ever so slightly. But with my phone strapped to my arm, earbuds in, athletic wear cool under the sun, and hair in a pony, I felt good and confident. Not showy, but not ashamed. It was going to be a good run.

Bitch narrated my run, and five seconds after pressing start, she told me in a reassuring voice, "Start workout." The downslope of my short driveway gave me a good propulsion into my pace. Kate Perry replaced Bitch in my ears. I curved to the right and I was off.

My neighborhood is nice. A development full of ramblers and split-entries. You can make all the "little houses made of ticky-tacky" sarcastic comments you want. The houses were new and in good shape. The yards were all maintained. No graffiti. No meth labs. No rusted-out old cars sitting in tall grass. The roads were smooth but rarely busy. Traffic rolled by slow. Wide sidewalks wove through the houses and connected to trails in various directions. There were mature shade trees. I didn't like my neighbors, but I had no reason to dislike them either. They were present but never interactive. We minded our own business. This wasn't a community. It was just a place to live, and that's all I wanted out of it. They knew how to keep an appropriate distance. For example, if I was running on the shoulder of the street, passing drivers would give me a wide berth and a little wave that consisted of two fingers lifted off the steering wheel. If I was on the sidewalk, they ignored me, or at least waited till I was in the side mirror before trying to check out my ass.

At an intersection, I veered right into an older neighborhood, built before the modern era of vinyl siding, split-entries, and subprime mortgages. Down this street, the sidewalk narrowed, and the mature tree branches stretched from either side of the street, almost touching in the middle. I hadn't made a cognitive decision to turn this way. My restless mind just demanded new scenery, and I hadn't been this way before. New scenery, but really, it was old scenery. I grew up on a street like this one. The houses were all flat-faced, two-story ranch homes or single-story ramblers with plenty of brickwork around the bottom. The one at the corner wasn't all that different than where I'd grown up.

But that was miles from here. And a long time ago.

In a flash as fast as a subliminal message, I saw Shelton's naked corpse hanging out of my teenage bedroom window. His abdomen had been shredded by the broken glass and spilled a red waterfall down the white, stucco exterior.

I had to pause at the corner, with the image of my old house and the first boy I'd ever had in my bedroom bleeding out of its window at the edge of my peripheral vision. I locked my eyes forward.

"Wait. You just told me you met Shelton for the first time at the cabin and—"

I know what I said. I know what I remembered happening at that cabin. And I know what I saw. Or imagined. Or hallucinated. I told myself that's all it was even as I waited for the traffic to clear from the intersection. A trick my mind was playing on me. Not a memory. It happened at Scotty's uncle's cabin, up north on the lakefront.

At the intersection, I jogged in place as a big, black, pickup truck pulled up to the crosswalk. The driver, hidden behind tinted glass, held up at the stop sign to wave me by. Polite, but if he'd gone first, he and I could have both been through the intersection quicker and without interfering with each other's day. Typical Minnesota Nice.

I jogged on.

Bitch interrupted Beyonce to tell me, "Time: Nine minutes, ten seconds. Distance: One mile. Split pace: Nine minutes, ten seconds." Thanks, Bitch.

I found a trail that wound away from the street, around a playground, and between a row of backyards and drainage ponds. The backyards had big, plastic, kid toys, decks, and sporting equipment littered inside their chain-link perimeters. There was an old wooden baseball bat tipped against a shed: a Louisville Slugger, I recognized by that iconic burned-in oval logo. As I ran by, my eyes dragged behind. Because, sure, at first all I saw was an old bat. That was until I noticed the giant nails driven through the barrel so the points stuck a good two or three inches out the other side.

I found that I was whispering to myself, "It was an ax. He used an ax, a polished chrome splitting ax. Not a spiked Louisville Slugger. With something like that... I could have gotten him on the first swing instead of having to take two hits like I did with the ax. But I got him with that ax anyway."

The trail intersected with another road. I had a crosswalk, but I never trusted drivers to pay attention to it. Covered in a full sheen of sweat, pumping air in and out of healthy lungs, the chardonnay long gone from my bloodstream, my mind a mess of misremembered murders, I slowed up to the curb and checked both ways like a good girl should. No traffic. I stepped out and double-checked my left.

That same big black truck was slow-rolling up to the stop sign. I shouldn't have looked too long. I shouldn't have let him know that I saw him. If it was the same truck. If it had anything to do with me. But Tyler had a big pickup, all black and star-spangled chrome. Maybe he finally got fed up with me ignoring his texts. Or maybe it was the killer from my youth, back from the dead to finish me off.

That's how my hair-trigger works now days, and it fucking sucks. You ever had a perfectly, nice, sunny day, and then something as simple as a truck or an errand bit of imagination turns it as gray and cold as winter? Do you know what it's like to have your anxiety waiting behind every bush and every door, even when you have no reason to get upset? Ever have something as stupid as a plain old bedroom window, or sporting goods, or a random truck set you off? No?

"Let's keep this about you, shall we?"

Sure. We called it "hyper-vigilance," in sessions. But am I really the weird one? Am I hyper-vigilant or is everyone else just oblivious?

I crossed the crosswalk, as cool as a cucumber in the crisper.

Half a block down, workers were remodeling a house. The backyard was littered with sheets of plywood, two-by-fours, scraps, and tools. The men doing the work wore cut-off t-shirts from rock concerts and backward baseball caps. Not professionals then. Buddies building a deck on their off time. I steeled myself for the cat calls all the same. But that's not what got me. I could handle a whistle or a rude comment. That's old hat. You know what got me?

"Tell me."

One of them set a circular saw into a piece of wood, and that whirl and whine and screech? I'd run past them by then, so I only heard the sound of it, but that was all it took. It was worse than the hiss of a cat or the rattle of a snake. I jumped, I knew I jumped, setting my pace off rhythm. Then my mind jumped back to my childhood neighborhood. And while I was there, in that flashback, I forgot all about any cabin by any lake. It had happened in a place just like this. And my killer? The giant who breathed like a metronome? He'd used a circular saw to dismember Ash and Linda both, while I hid behind a hedge between our backyards.

"Time: Eighteen minutes, fifty five seconds," Bitch said with Ariana Grande fading into the background. "Distance: Two miles. Split pace: Nine minutes, forty five seconds."

I was slowing down. I had to keep my pace. Slowing down equaled death. Not just in a sense of trying to outrun some masked psychopath, never mind that for once, but also in the boring way most people think about death. If I couldn't keep up with myself, it meant high blood pressure, heart disease, and muscle atrophy. It meant I was aging, getting older, deteriorating, dying. Death is a carriage driver, and we are his horses, and the only way to keep from being run down is to keep pulling him along. There's a moment in your life, and for women it's younger than men, when you don't run to get faster; you run so you don't get slower. It happens sooner than you might think. It happens without informing you or asking for permission. Ignore running for a week, and the times only get longer and the distances shorter. It was a constant chase, and I was consistently losing ground. Everybody does. I just knew what it meant to get caught.

I sped up.

In a bad way, I've thought about how the bad guys make us better. Hagari called this "maladaptive thinking," but I couldn't care less. If it wasn't for our bullies, we'd never get stronger. If it wasn't for our nightmares, we wouldn't guard our dreams. If it wasn't for the monsters, we'd never be heroes. Hell makes life worth living, especially if you know that's where you're inevitably going. If it wasn't for that black pickup truck and the memories of my youth, whether faithful or false, my pace would have slipped. I would have grown weak. I would have grown older. I would have let myself die. I should thank my tormentors for making me who I am. I should be grateful for all the suffering they've inflicted. For all the nightmares. For the half-seen hallucinations. For the hyper-vigilance. For the sharpness of my teeth and the steel in my spine. If it wasn't for them, I could never give them more than they'd given me.

I ran faster.

Funny, how I can hold onto the memory of what happened to me at that cabin up north while simultaneously having memories of the slaughter in my own neighborhood. But I closed my eyes and saw Shelton hanging out of a window, and Ash and Linda being cut apart like two-by-fours, their bodies spitting out blood instead of sawdust in surreal vivid detail.

Funny. To you maybe. Funny too, how I lost my place in a neighborhood I had known like the back of my hand.

"Time: Thirty minutes, fifty four seconds," Bitch said in my ears. "Distance: Three miles. Split pace: Eight minutes, fifty nine seconds."

Good. I was going faster. I was going longer. More speed. More space. That was good.

I bolted across a street without looking. There was never traffic. In my peripheral, a big black pickup truck rolled out of a cul-de-sac. I was through the intersection and running along a street-side path back toward my house. My pace wasn't sustainable, not after three miles. Maybe not after one mile. But I had to keep going. I had to go faster if I was going to outrun the carriage driver's whip.

The street widened around me. The shadows of those elm trees pulled back and let the sun beat on my back. That truck was behind me. My abuser's truck. The killer's truck. The cops never found his body. After he'd murdered Scotty and Cheryl, I got the jump on him. While he was hacking apart my best friend with a machete, I pulled that spike Louisville Slugger out of Scotty's bloody mess of a torso, and it only took me one swing. I heard his skull crack, just like an up-the-gut-fastball sent back to the fences. Those long metal nails sunk right into his brain. No way he survived. Only, somehow, he had. In some inexplicable, inhuman way, he lived. Of course, he'd lived if the cops never found his body. Who else would have dragged the body from Cheryl's front lawn if not the killer himself? Who else would have the dedication to track me down twenty three years later and stalk me on my run?

When my house was just two blocks down, I sped up again. The music and Bitch's reports on my distance and pace were distant background noise. My own uncontrolled, gasping, wheezing breaths drowned out the rest. My arms pumped. My lungs burned. My legs churned. The soles of my feet were hot, absorbing the heat and energy through the asphalt and my shoes. My mid-day alcoholic blur had been replaced by endorphin sobriety, followed quickly by fear-fueled adrenaline. I burst across the last crosswalk between me and my house, ignoring the neighbors and their lawns, in a full sprint now. When I reached my own lawn, I cut across the grass for the front door, vaulted over my pretty little conformist flower bed onto the front stoop, and crashed into the front door.

My eyes flirted between the number coded lock on my front door and either direction of my street. I hammered in 1-4-2-8 and the deadbolt clacked open. A moment later, I was through the door and into the dark safety of my house. The deadbolt resealed, and I was safe inside.

Chapter Nine

When one unsettling thing entered my life, all the rest followed. Even inside my front door with my lungs working like bellows to normalize and oxygenate my blood and with my eyes readjusting from the bright, midday sun, things inside of my house seemed strange. Even the sensation of strangeness was strange. There was no immediate reason for it. As far as I could tell, everything was in order inside the house, but at the same time, things were ever so slightly out of place.

In hindsight, it made sense. Why should the physical things in my life stay in place when I couldn't even keep my memories straight?

Don't answer that. That was rhetorical.

Still catching my breath, I moved up the split entry and into the dim cool of my kitchen and dining room. The sink was dripping slowly into the basin. Had it been doing that before? The butcher knife was still out on the counter. Is that where I'd left it? I didn't touch it. It was evidence now, in my mind, of someone either having been here since I left or not, and whether what had been done to me happened at a cabin or in a neighborhood all too similar to this. The empty bottle of chardonnay stood next to the butcher knife. Had I really finished off the bottle before noon? The refrigerator stood where it always stood, possibly containing a disembodied head and possibly not, as if Dahmer and Schrodinger were splitting rent. I moved through my kitchen, not touching a thing.

A flicker of light across the house caught my eye. My TV was on, muted, but playing some movie all the same. A horror movie. The old black and white one with the black guy protagonist surrounded by the racist white people all trapped in a house together. I know I hadn't left that on. And even if I had turned it on, I know I wouldn't have started playing some old zombie movie.

"Bitch?" I said.

"Yes?" she answered dutifully.

"Turn off the TV," I said.

"Okay," she said, and the screen winked out.

And the house became even stranger when the flashing was gone. Too still now. Too quiet. The mail on the counter was half an inch too far to the left. The TV remote was on the couch cushions instead of on the coffee table. The door to my bedroom was open only a crack. I never left doors partially open. Always all the way open so I could see inside, or closed and latched to trap whatever was beyond it. Someone had been here; I was certain of it. Someone had gone into my house and moved things ever so slightly.

If any question remained, when I stepped into my dining room/home office, all doubt was removed. In the wall, just to the upper left of my computer monitors, a splitting ax was lodged into the wall. Not a spike Louisville Slugger. Not a circular saw either. It was the ax. It had always been the ax. An unfinished, long, ergonomic, wooden handle and a bare, metal head polished to a shine. The very one I'd used to split open that maniac's head outside the cabin by the lake. And now it was here, in my house, chopped into my drywall, just like it had been that morning next to the fireplace.

"What about your ex? The black truck? What about Tyler?"

I never told Tyler about what I went through when I was a teenager. Never trusted him enough with that information, so even if it was him in the pickup truck, how would he know to put that ax there, just like we found it that morning in the cabin? I never gave Tyler a moment of thought. You want to know who I was worried about? My dog.

Oh my god, my dog. Chuck was nowhere to be seen. I was so busy worrying about the TV, the kitchen knife, and my stupid junk mail, I forgot all about my beautiful little pug. Usually, he came waddling right up to me, his tags jiggling like sleigh bells as soon as I came through the front door. But the whole house was as still as a painting. Maybe that was what had set me off as soon as I'd gotten back home. Not what was here or what was moved, but what was not here and what was not moving.

"Chucky!" I called out, my voice sounding more scared than I wanted. "Come here, baby! Mommies home!"

Dear god, what if the killer was still here? What if he did something to my dog? What if he was still waiting for me in the basement or in the back bedroom, just behind that almost-closed door? With a firm tug, I yanked the ax from my drywall. Chunks of gypsum and white dust fell on my keyboard. Doctor Hagari said I shouldn't possess any weapons. Well, the good doctor can lick my ass.

Not wanting anything to encumber my swing, I unvelcroed the strap of my phone case and dropped it to the workstation. Then I crept toward the bedroom door.

The living room looked in order. The remote sat on the couch cushion. The TV was off. The little jar of potpourri sat centered on the coffee table, precisely where it should. I held the ax cocked-back over my right shoulder, elbows up, just like any good lead-off batter. My eyelids fell and I saw Shelton dangling… dangling out of my bedroom window. No! He'd been dangling from a ceiling fan with a barbeque fork stabbed through his chest and leaking a circle of blood half on and half off my bed.

Behind me, my phone rattled against my desk.

"Incoming call from: Fuckface Pencildick," Bitch announced. You know you can rename your contacts in your phone to whatever you want, right?

"Bitch, not now, you stupid wad of wires and–" I groaned through tight teeth.

"Answering call from: Fuckface Pencildick," she replied.

"No! Hang up, hang up, hang up!"

Too late. "Baby?" Tyler's voice came through Bitch's speaker. "Is everything okay? You sound upset."

"It's not a good time, Tyler," I said, still clutching the ax and staring down my bedroom door.

"You haven't been answering any of my texts. I need to talk to you. If not now, when is it ever a good time, Taylor?" Tyler said.

See how quickly the whole Taylor/Tyler thing becomes downright obnoxious?

"It's *really* not a good time right now," I emphasized because, with Tyler, you had to draw it for him in crayons.

"Taylor," he summed up his courage as if he'd ever had a daring thought germinate inside of that barren skull of his. "I think we should get back together."

Meanwhile, I pounced through my bedroom door. My closet doors were wide open, and all the drawers of my dresser were pulled out. The bedding was a mess. Dirty clothes covered the floor. A wine glass lay sideways on the nightstand over a small, red stain. Everything as I'd left it. "Have you been inside of my house?" I demanded.

"Taylor, what are you talking about? We lived together," he said, like an idiot.

"Today," I said. And now I was coming back to the kitchen, brandishing the ax at the sound of his voice, as if I could get rid of him by murdering Bitch. "Did you come into my house today? You know when I like to go for my runs. And you know the route I like to go on. Was that you following me through the neighborhood during my run?"

"You're talking like a crazy person, Taylor. See, this is why we should be together. Not just for me but for your own good. I can help stabilize your life. You need me around to help you with your issues."

"My issues? You're my issue, Tyler," I snapped. "Wait. What have I told you about my issues? What have I told you about axes?"

"Exes? Taylor, we agreed we'd never bring up past relationships or worry about—"

"Not exes! Axes! Like a baseball bat with a blade on the end! What have I told you about axes?"

"That's it. You need my help. You need me, Taylor. I'm coming over," he said.

I leered over Bitch with my hands tight like two nooses around the ax's neck. "You come over here and I will gut you like a fish, understand?"

Bitch stood silent on the kitchen counter. No response from Tyler on that.

"I mean, I'll call the cops. I'll dial Nine One One and have them put a restraining order against you. How would you like that?"

A pause in the quiet house. Then, unconvinced and undeterred, Tyler answered. "We belong together, Taylor. You're going to regret ever saying that. You'll regret ever leaving me."

"Call ended," Bitch told me.

Only, the threat wasn't over. My killer wasn't dead. The danger had never left. But I was expected to continue on and do all the little things a successful aspiring Mary Tyler Moore was supposed to do. I went through every room in the house with that ax, kicking open doors and tossing closets. But I didn't find the killer, and I didn't find Chuck. When I came back to my desk, I took a good swing and buried the chrome ax head in the wall just to the right of my monitor, back in the hole where I'd plucked it from. Then I logged back in and made my two o'clock team sync with Team Next Paradigms.

Chapter Ten

That meeting, I don't know if I can describe it. There was nothing special about it. Nothing unique. It was exactly like every other meeting I'd ever attended. I had to check my calendar just to see what it was about, and after reading my calendar, and reading the calendar invite, I still had no idea what it was we were all supposed to be discussing. Still, they talked.

"Admittedly, it's a bit of a problem-management problem, looking at it from my foxhole," Jason said.

"Sure, but if we give it the time and space it deserves, I think we can workshop through it and find a resolution," Robert said, talking over Roman who was going on about, "Instead of rushing to failure, let's table it for now, set up a meeting specifically about the issue, and bring solutions instead of just problems to that juncture." To which Robert added, "We should crack the nut then instead of trying to do it here and now."

"We have multiple, viable options right in front of us," Violetta, head still firmly attached to her body, chipped in but wasn't heard. "If you want my recommendation–"

"No. Robert. I think you said it best," Jason said. "Let's not boil the ocean on this. We'll take it offline for now and circle back on it when we have the bandwidth. For now, I'll block out a touch base and ping you on your calendars. Good?"

Everybody concurred, feeling satisfied as if they'd actually accomplished something more than kicking a can down the road.

Meanwhile, my eyes danced between the wooden handle of the ax, just out of view of my camera but well within reach, and the rest of my house. The entrances and exits mostly. I couldn't see my front door, down the steps in the entryway as it was, but anyone coming through that door would have to come up the stairs first. And having the high ground was always an advantage. As for the sliding glass door, anyone could creep up the stairs to the deck and remain out of sight until they were right on the other side of the glass. The curtains were drawn closed; my thought being it was better if they couldn't see in even if I couldn't see out.

I wished I had a gun. God, why had I never bought a gun? It would make all of this so much easier. I could even get one of those little cute ones with pink hand grips that I could fit in a fanny pack and keep with me during my runs. What the hell had I been thinking all these years?

A chat message pinged from my computer speakers. Barb. Again.

We need to talk.

Did we really? I doubted it. Another message popped up.

Are you hearing what they're saying?

I mean, I heard it. I didn't know what any of it meant. I wasn't sure they even knew what they were talking about, but yeah, the sound of their flapping gums had entered my ears. I typed back to her.

What's up?

Barb messaged back.

I'll call you after the meeting. I can't believe this.

What the hell was in her craw now? Whatever. I didn't have the headspace to deal with her drama. I had to keep a watch on my windows and doors. I had to buy a gun. I had to find my dog. Where the hell was my poor pooch? I should have been out stapling LOST flyers to all the telephone poles in the neighborhood. How could he have gotten out?

Because someone else had gotten in.

I spent years trying to figure out who the man was who invaded our little teenage pleasure dome back in '99 and murdered us one by one. What drove him to us that night? Was he really some random, insane, asylum escapee who happened upon us? Or did he know us? Had he been watching us smoke our smokes and drink our drinks and play our stupid little game? What set him off? I didn't care if his mommy never loved him or if he mutilated small animals as a child. I wanted to know, why *us*? He was only in our lives for maybe a few hours, and then he was gone. At the very end of five of our lives, and really only near the beginning of mine. Why were our lives so important to him that he had to spend his to end ours?

Of course, there was no real explanation for any of it. And the randomness of it all only made him more dangerous. If we'd desecrated some Indian burial ground, or read passages out of some ancient Satanic text, or allowed the death of some innocent kid through our own negligence, then all I had to do is not do that thing and I had nothing to worry about. But that wasn't the case. Since there was nothing we did to bring about his wraith, there was nothing I could do to prevent it. He just chose us and then went about killing us. And he, or anyone else, could choose me again, just the same.

God damn it, why didn't I have a security system? How had I been so careless all this time? I should go through the house again, just in case I missed something the first time through. A closet. A corner. A crawlspace. Someone could still be in there with me. How the hell was I supposed to sit through another one of these bullshit meetings while a killer might be creeping up behind me?

"Oh, sorry, everybody!" Barbara interrupted the endless ramblings. There was a little two year old boy climbing up on her lap and into the view of the camera. He had a big head of bright, red, curly hair and a stranglehold on some plastic toy covered in slobber. "Guess my little guy needed some of mom's attention. This is mommy's work time, okay? You run off and play."

"Alright, gang," Jason said in a way that told me we were finishing up. "I think we made some sausage today. Real value-added. Let's socialize this a bit more, identify all the moving parts, think through the second and third-order effects, and hit the ground running with a good holistic approach next time we meet on this. As always, I appreciate everyone's input. We have a great team here! And if anything comes up, don't be afraid to hit me up one-to-one. My door is always open."

And at that, the team departed, one by one and chime by chime, out of the meeting. No sooner had I clicked out, did my phone buzz. It was Barbara. I pushed back my chair, snatched up my phone, and threw in an earbud so I could be hands-free.

"Yeah, Barb, what is it?" I said and began pacing through my house.

"Can you believe this shit?" she started right in. "I'm going directly to Jason about this. This is absolute horseshit. I can't believe he's folding like a sheet of paper on this."

"Yeah. I couldn't believe it either," I said, not having a damn clue what she was going on about. There was still a feeling of someone else present in the house. That someone was watching me. And that riddle of who our killer had been still boiled inside my head. I yanked the ax out of the wall and brought it with me as I patrolled my own house.

"Taylor, can't you read between the lines?" Barb said. "'A Problem Management problem?' 'Personnel realignment?' 'Constructive dismissal?' Were you not listening to the meeting?"

"Yeah, I was listening," I said. She didn't seem that upset then, playing with her little redhead while everyone else blathered on. But she was only talking about work bullshit. Not about anything that mattered. Not about what happened to me and my friends. My attention was back to my house's exterior. I peeked around the deck door curtains. I swear something moved out there.

"Taylor, they fired Doctor Cal!" Barb finally spat.

I paused on my way toward the front door, but only briefly. Both doors were locked, heavy deadbolts set in place.

"Barb, he's not an employee," I said.

"How can you play semantics at a time like this? Team Next cut his contract. He's on administrative leave. He's under investigation!" Barb said.

"Holy shit," I said, not because I was upset by the good doctor's misfortune, but because I was shocked they'd actually done something about his behavior.

"I know! Absolute horseshit, right?" Barb said. "And without him being a contracted provider of Team Next… I can't see him!"

I'd filed the complaint. After he touched me when I told him not to. Repeatedly. After he kept fondling me. I filed the complaint and beyond all expectations, someone actually did something about it.

"Holy shit," I said, doing my best to hide the joy in my voice. This was the best news I'd heard in weeks. This was... This was *justice*! Finally!

"I'm going to Jason about it, in person, and I think you should too," Barb said. "He needs us. I need him. I– Hold on a second, Taylor. My husband Wes just walked in."

Back in my living room, I tossed the ax onto the couch along with the TV remote. I was still in shock. Nothing like this had happened to me before. There was a cause and an effect. There was action and then a result. Someone, somewhere, in that giant, senseless hivemind of corporate, had listened to what I had to say and done something about it.

"Hi, honey. Yep. Just on the phone with a friend from work. Kind of private though," Barb was saying to her husband on the other end. Her voice was sugary sweet but distant. Then she redirected to me and became hushed and conspiratorial. "Sorry. That was Wes. Don't worry about him. Now, like I was saying. I'm going to Jason, in person, as soon as possible. I checked his schedule, and he's going to be in the office first thing tomorrow. I think it'd send him a message if we went together."

"Barb, I can't. This is a remote position and–"

A lifeless clunk from across the house yanked me out of my euphoria. Something had fallen to the kitchen floor. Only, no one was over there to knock anything down. All that ecstasy of a fair world drained away like the blood from my face. Slowly, quietly, I stalked that way from my living room.

"We need solidarity here, Taylor," Barb was a distant whine in the background of my sudden paranoia. "We are both patients of Doctor Cal, and if he's not a contracted provider of the company, we can't see him."

"Yeah, I know, it's just I can't go driving–" I stopped myself when I reached the kitchen and saw what had fallen. It was the butcher knife. The big triangle-shaped sheet of mirrored metal had fallen from the counter and was now stuck tip down into the linoleum. The smallest vibration still remained in the flex of the metal.

"Doctor Cal has done so much for me. For both of us. And right now, he needs us as much as we need him," Barb said firmly.

Mostly ignoring her, I was bent down and building up the courage to dislodge the blade from my kitchen floor when the TV snapped to life. Shooting up, looking across my house, I saw another horror movie playing out on the big screen. This one was that creep fest with the kid pedaling his Big Wheel through a maze of hallways covered in bad 70s carpet. The drone of the plastic wheels against muffled carpet, then echoing on hardwood, then back to the carpet, filled my pleasant suburban home.

Completely aware that I'd abandoned the ax on the couch in front of the TV, I got a good hold of the butcher knife and plucked it free from my kitchen floor.

"Barb, I gotta go," I said into my earbud.

"Will you be there tomorrow morning? Don't flake out on me with this, Taylor," Barb said. "I know you can be a bit… flighty… but I need you with me. He needs you. *We* need you. Tell me you'll be there."

"I don't know. It's a remote position," I said. "I have to be here. For my dog."

"Since when do you–" she started, but I pulled the bud from my ear and Bitch ended the call.

I held the knife up by my ear, its tip and my elbow pointed forward, ready to stab anything that came my way. And that was how I crept back across my home, past my workstation where, I suppose, I should have been sitting and toiling away. But I had to see what had turned on the TV. I had to see if the remote was still where I left it, on the cushions next to the ax. Meanwhile, that kid continued to roll through hallway after hallway on his big plastic trike.

The remote sat exactly where I'd left it. The ax was gone.

The kid on the Big Wheel rolled up on some bloody murder scene. I'd seen it all before. And someone could have turned the TV on from outside the house, aiming another remote programmed to my TV through a window, or via an app. It was a smart TV and it had an app. That was how I'd connected it to Bitch. Through Bitch, anyone could have turned it on from anywhere. It could be the Russians as much as anyone inside of the house. But the ax…

I spun. The door to my back bedroom was cracked open again, not wide enough to see into, but wide enough for someone to move in and out of it unheard. It was quiet back there, as quiet as the rest of the house. My mind spun as to how someone might have made their way inside while I sat at my desk or wandered about the house. I'd checked the whole house after I came back from my run. I'd watched the entrances and exits. I'd stayed vigilant.

The ax had hung from my wall next to my monitor all afternoon. I distinctly remembered pulling it loose and carrying it with me until I threw it right there, on the couch, next to the remote. There was no way it moved by itself. Maybe I'd left the kitchen knife on the edge of the counter and gravity finally got the better of it, but the ax, even if it had fallen, should have been laying there on the floor right between the couch and the coffee table. Someone took it. Someone who had a desire to use it.

"Bitch," I called across the empty house.

"I'm here," she said back.

"Call the cops," I said, because I was a lot of things, but I wasn't stupid.

"Calling: Nine One One," Bitch informed me, and the ringtone replaced the soundtrack of a small boy losing his mind.

When the dispatcher answered, she rattled off the familiar spiel. I didn't wait for her to finish.

"Someone is in my house," I said. "Someone was following me on my run today, and they came into my house, and moved my things around, and they left something… They left an ax, and now the ax is gone, and I think they mean to hurt me."

"Is the person in the house with you?" the dispatcher asked.

"Yes. They turned on my TV, and they took an ax, and they opened my bedroom door," I said the evidence of panic growing in my voice.

"Okay. We have a unit nearby I'm sending to your address. Stay calm and stay on the line," the dispatcher said in a voice that was on the surface calm, but I could hear the tension underneath, and the sound of that woman's fear validated and vamped up my own.

"I can't," I said, knowing from my past how I couldn't just stay there on the phone like a sitting duck. I had to be able to move. "I—"

My doorbell rang. Way too soon for it to be a cop at my front door. There was no internet connection to the doorbell. It wasn't smart. Just a button hardwired to the electric chimes in my living room. Why hadn't I got a ringer with a camera and a connection to Bitch so I could see the front stoop? Regardless, it wasn't some hacker in Russia manipulating it through an app. Someone was out there.

"I have to go. Bitch, hang up," I said, and she did.

Enough hiding. Enough running away. Enough games. I milked the blade of the butcher knife, getting a good grip on it through my sweat. Moving slow to the top of the steps, I glared through the vertical frosted glass next to the front door. Nothing but daylight, but that meant nothing. I took one second to wrestle my courage into place, but no more than that.

Racing down the stairs, I came upon the door already at a run. The deadbolt and handle twisted one after the other, and then I rushed out of my front door screaming as loud and as maddened as I could with the blade raised up, ready to stab. Nothing on the front stoop. No one on my front walk. I charged out to the middle of my driveway, knife still ready over my right shoulder, still screaming like a banshee.

It was an ordinary fall afternoon, an idyllic Indian summer day only made unique by its pleasantness. The sun shined and emerald leaves danced in the breeze. Down the block, a school bus was emptying out the neighborhood kids. Across the street, a man let his push mower sputter to a stop as he slowly slipped the earmuffs off his head. Panting, covered in sweat, brandishing a kitchen knife, my eyes swung to my left and right.

No threats. No maniac killer. No evidence of the suburban massacre that haunted my memories. Nothing. No one.

Over my shoulder, my front door stood wide open, just waiting for someone to slip in or out behind me. I couldn't have that.

Back inside, I relatched the deadbolt.

The horror movie was playing again on the TV. In my foyer, there were two directions to go: upstairs to my living room, home office, and kitchen, or downstairs to the unfinished basement. I kept my back against the wall and worked my way upstairs. By the time I reached the top and I could see the TV again, my lungs were hyperventilating. My vision fixed on the screen, and it drew me in as if I was falling down a bottomless hole with the movie at the far end. Fading, I braced myself against the kitchen counter but came down with the knife. It sank deep through the laminate countertop but stabilized me and kept me upright until the sound of shattering glass brought me immediately out of my fugue.

The big sliding glass door next to my desk. Someone had thrown a rock straight through it, leaving a jagged but circular hole the size of a grapefruit in the middle. Bits of glass covered the floor, but I still had my running shoes on, and I still had the knife.

The blade yanked free from the kitchen counter without much effort. The glass crunched under my running shoes. I threw open the broken sliding glass door and stormed onto the deck. From there my backyard and a half dozen other backyards to either side and beyond my property laid out before me. I should have been able to see him. I should have been able to hear him. No doubt he could hear me.

"Come and get me, motherfucker! Come and get me, and I'll kill you all over again, you cocksucker!" I cried out to the whole god damn, nice, neat, little, well-adjusted housing development.

The doorbell rang. The chimes sounded soft coming from inside the house, but the threat wasn't inside the house. It was back around the front, waiting for me again. But I knew better this time.

My running shoes were soft on the wooden deck stairs. My steps propelled me forward almost at the rate of falling until I reached the soft grass of the backyard. It was dry enough not to slip but moist enough not to make a sound as I sprinted around the side of the house, through the fence gate, around my garage, and onto my driveway from the flank. And as soon as I turned the corner, I came around not screaming, but roaring like a primal huntress, knife raised up, ready to end this son of a bitch.

A blacked-out sedan sat at the end of my driveway, and standing a short distance from my front door was a man in tan khakis and a black polo with a radio and a gun hanging from a thick leather belt. A cop, I recognized perhaps a second slower than I should have, but the moment I began my roar, it was too late to cut it off. That animalistic noise erupted out of me, and I was powerless to stop it.

The cop, all instinct and muscle-memory training, sunk his shoulders, drew his sidearm, and backpedaled his black leather boots through my begonias. The gun was up in a flash and the barrel was aimed straight for my face.

"Drop it!" he yelled. "Drop the knife, lady! Drop it now or I'll shoot!"

My roar cut. My shoes screeched to a halt against the asphalt as soon as I saw the gun. And then I was backpedaling. "Don't shoot! It's not me! I'm not the killer!"

"Drop the knife, lady!" he ordered again.

I threw it. The steel clanged against the pavement.

"I called! I'm the one who called the cops! I live here!"

"Keep your hands up! Keep 'em up!" the cop said, his gun still pointed in my direction, but lowered to shoot me in the gut rather than the face. "Lay down on the ground! Face down! No quick movements."

I listened, knife far from me and the killer nowhere to be found. The cop called something over his radio, something calm and de-escalating, and I put my hands behind my back and waited for the cuffs. With my cheek against the asphalt, I looked out across my neighborhood. The school kids pointed. The lawnmower man watched with his hands on his hip. The leaves danced without interruption.

Wonderful.

Chapter Eleven

Later, we sat down on opposite ends of my conspicuously ax-free couch, me still rubbing the red handcuff marks from my wrists, and the cop with a little, spiral notepad flipped open to take "a statement."

"I guess if I was a black kid, I'd be dead," I told him.

"You can't say that," Officer Hansen said. "That's not true."

He was about my age, with strong arms and a familiar but striking face that could somehow be serious and strong one moment, but playful the next. His skin was chiseled from marble and polished to a soapy-smooth shine. His handsomeness washed away the circumstance that had brought the two of us together to share a couch. It's always hard to explain why you find someone attractive, even to yourself, but this one, he hit me just right. Furtive eyes and a demure smile told me this was maybe, just maybe, a two-way street.

Still, I couldn't let him off that easy.

"I've seen the news. It's called 'unconscious bias.' I'm a middle-aged white woman. If it had been a young, black, teenage boy come screaming around the corner with a knife, it'd be a different story," I said.

"I do not have unconscious bias," he said.

"Okay, but how would you know?" I asked, maybe because I wanted to play with him rather than go on with the normal business of reporting a home intruder.

"Because I'm black," Officer Hansen said. "I *was* a young black kid not that long ago. I wouldn't have shot me, and I wasn't going to shoot you."

"It's called *'unconscious* bias' for a reason," I muttered.

"Listen. Miss Mosley. You, a white woman, do not get to tell me, a black man, that I'm racist against other black men. That's just not how it works," he said. He could have backed down on the issue if he wanted to, but he didn't come off as someone who'd back down on much of anything. I liked that about him.

"So," he re-started, the pen in his hand yet to land on the spiral notebook. "You told the dispatcher someone was in your house."

"I thought– I mean, someone definitely came in here," I said.

"But you thought I was the intruder when I rang your door from the front step," he stated.

"Yeah, and someone also clearly threw a rock through my deck door," I said. The rock, a fist-sized chunk of granite, sat on the coffee table next to the pot-potpourri. He'd set it there after assuring me that no, he couldn't get fingerprints off it. "That right there, that's evidence of a crime."

"No, I understand that," Officer Hansen said. "There's a hole in your door, glass on your floor, and a rock right here. You've definitely been vandalized."

The way he said that made it sound so aggressive but welcoming all at the same time. If only he had been the vandal. My god, when was the last time I'd been truly, thoroughly, and properly vandalized?

"But what I'm trying to ascertain is if the threat is currently present," Officer Hansen said. "Do you have any reason to believe there's still someone currently, at this time, in this house?"

"No," I said and truly believed it. "I think, maybe, you must have scared him away. I mean, obviously, he had to be outside to throw the rock through my glass and to ring my doorbell so…"

"Did you see the intruder inside the house?" he asked, still having not written anything down on that notebook.

"No, but he took things. He moved things around," I explained. Then suddenly I remembered, "My dog is missing."

"Do you know why anyone might have done these things?" he asked.

Terrific question. Did I know why that maniac slaughtered my friends when I was seventeen? Did every crime come with a motive?

"I… Where do I start? I have… a history," I said, not the most alluring thing to mention to the most attractive guy to have ever sat on my couch, but the words were out of my mouth now. "What I mean is, yes, I have this ex who's not exactly taking our breakup well, but there's also this thing that happened back when I was in high school." I stopped. Because, yes, this man sitting on my couch was drop-dead gorgeous, but there was something else about him too. "I'm sorry. What did you say your name is again?"

"Officer Hansen," he pointed to the embroidered name sewn into his shirt just below the embroidered badge.

"No. I mean, I think I might know you from somewhere. What's your first name?" I asked.

"Stephen," he said, dismissively, but this wasn't the first time I've had to work through a guy's defenses.

"Steve," I pseudo-repeated. "So, why aren't you wearing a normal police uniform? You know, the dark blue pants and button-up shirt and bullet-proof vest and all that?"

"Well, I'm a detective," he said. "I don't spend a lot of time on the highway handing out tickets anymore. I just happened to be in the area when your call came in."

"Detective Steve Hansen," I said. "What year did you graduate? I'm sorry, you just look really familiar."

"Two Thousand. Anoka High School," he said.

And with his affirmation, it all came flooding back to me. His name, his face, his polite and firm mannerisms were like a rope thrown to a passenger fallen over the rails of a cruise liner. I clutched onto this thing, this tangible part of my past as if it— he— was the only thing I could be certain of.

"Steve Hansen from Anoka High School? Class of Two Thousand? I remember you!" I said, maybe a little too exuberant.

"No shit," he said, genuinely. See? His icy layer of professionalism wasn't that thick. He'd been a cool customer back when we were in high school too, having to deal with the ubiquitous racial jabs of being a black kid in a school chock full of white kids in the late nineties. It had to have been tough wading through all that bullshit, but he made it look easy. He evaded most of the stereotypes of being "the black kid," listening to rap, playing basketball, sagging his pants… until he wanted to lean into the cliches and turn the jokes back on the jokesters. Through it all, he managed to find his way to the upper hand.

"We never really met, but we were in Mister DiMaggio's journalism class together," I reminded him. I stuck out my hand and re-introduced myself now that we were more than just cop and victim. "Taylor Moseley. I ran track and cross country. Played softball when I was younger. Not that I was, like, in the jock clique. I was kind of an oddball back in school."

"Okay," he said, giving my hand a shake. Strong grip but measured. Skin not abrasive. "I can relate to that. And yeah, I remember you. Taylor Moseley…" he tasted my name in his mouth.

"So you remember then? What happened?"

"Like you said, we never really met. We ran in different circles. It was all a long time ago," he said.

"Well, look me up in your yearbook when you get home," I said.

"Yeah, so you were saying something about your past," he said. "Something happened?"

"You have to know what I'm talking about. I mean it was between our junior and senior year but… Cheryl, Linda, Scotty, Ash, Shelton…" I led him, and when he didn't take the bait, "You have to remember."

The smile didn't fall from his lips, but he did this thing where his chin turned a little to the side and his eyebrows tightened. A way of asking a question without verbalizing it.

"Anyway," I said. "There was an ax, right here on my couch. And it wasn't even my ax. I went for a run this afternoon and somebody in a big black pickup truck, I swear, was following me around the neighborhood. And when I came back, the ax was lodged right above my work desk."

"And the ax is gone now?" Steve said.

"And my dog! I haven't seen him for like a whole day now. And he's a little pug. He doesn't run off. It's not like he's some hound dog who will smell a steak on the grill three miles away and just take off after it. He can hardly breathe!"

"You had a dog here?" Steve said. "Can you show me his food dish?"

"What does that have to do with anything? Steve. Listen."

"Stephen," he said. "With the P and the H."

"Stephen, someone broke into my house, chopped a fucking ax into my wall, took my dog, or at least let him out, and then came back, rang my doorbell, and threw a rock through my window," I explained to him in the clearest way I could.

"Okay. Yes. And you think the person who did this is your ex? You didn't say his name," Stephen said.

"His name is Tyler, but I don't think–"

"Last name?" Stephen said.

"Haig. Tyler Haig," I said. "He's always been a pain in my ass, but this isn't about him. I… Don't you remember? I survived a mass murder. Back in '99. The summer before we graduated. Cheryl? Scotty? Shelton? Ash? Linda? You have to remember. There was a candlelight vigil and the whole deal. The whole student body attended. Anyway, my friends, they didn't make it, but I did. There was this guy. He wore a mask without a face, and he attacked us. He killed them. All of them. But not me. I took a fucking ax to his brain… or maybe it was a baseball bat with nails at the end… or a machete… Whatever. When the cops showed up, I was still alive. No one else but me."

"This man who attacked you…" Stephen led me.

"The cops never found his body. They never arrested anyone in connection with the murders. They had no idea who he might have been. I was sure I'd killed him that night. I split his head wide open. But now?" I said. "I think he's back. Back to finish what he started."

"Killing you?" Stephen asked.

I nodded. "I think the local police did everything they could to hide the story. It didn't happen in Anoka or anywhere around here. We were up north at a cabin."

Stephen nodded as he wrote, acknowledging the importance of what I was telling him. "If it wasn't inside of city limits, it would have been a sheriff's department that would have responded. What county did this take place in?"

"I don't really know. That's not the kind of thing you think about as a kid," I said.

"Well, what was the nearest city?"

"I don't know. Maybe Duluth? Bemidji? I think there was a mental hospital nearby."

"That doesn't really narrow it down, believe it or not," Stephen said, but dutifully took his notes all the same. "Well, keep in mind that it could have been anyone who threw that rock and rang your doorbell. I'd put the neighborhood kids at the top of my list of suspects. And maybe your ex as Number Two. But I'll look into these killings you mentioned. See if there's anything there. In the meantime, your house insurance should cover the broken glass."

"So what? That's it?" I asked, a little shocked when he stood up from the couch. "Steve– Stephen, I mean. We sort of know each other, having gone to Anoka together, Class of 2000 Tornados and all. I mean, what if he comes back?"

"You did the right thing. Call Nine One One, and I'll be right back. In the meantime, keep your doors locked and maybe run with a friend. Use the buddy system," he said.

"You'll come back," I repeated his words. "If something happens, and I call Nine One One…"

"Calling: Nine One One," Bitch piped in.

"Bitch, no!" I shouted to the speaker.

"Canceling call to: Nine One One," Bitch said.

"Listen, I am a victim here," I told Stephen. "Something happened today. Someone was here, in my house. I can prove it to you."

"Ma'am–"

"Taylor. Please, call me Taylor," I said, and then realized I'd let myself get too excited. I dusted off my best smile. "I'm sorry. I just need you to believe me. I need someone to take me seriously. I can't show you the ax, but the hole in the wall is right over there, and the hole in my deck door, and the rock…"

"Taylor," he said my name and took ahold of both my elbows. His eyes were infinite swirling pools of rich melted chocolate. "I believe you. We'll have a patrol car stay in the area. If anything happens, you can call us."

"If I have to call," I said to Stephen, "you'll come?"

"Yeah. Of course. You don't have anything to worry about," Stephen said. And the way he said it, I believed him. Now, I just had to make him believe me.

Chapter Twelve

It wasn't just the neighborhood kids playing ding-dong-ditch. No way. For one, they hadn't gotten off the school bus yet. For two, kids just didn't do that anymore. They all just sat inside and played video games. And for three, there was another, far more dangerous thing after me. A towering thing. A thing with a big glistening ax. A thing without a face. And if I was going to prove to Stephen it was real, I needed to drag that thing back out into the light.

"You didn't think it was–"

It was the killer from my youth. I had no doubt about it.

I blew off work for the rest of the day. They could plan their own god damn work retreat. This was so much more important than their endless, stupid, petty bullshit. I was still wearing my running gear, yoga pants, sports bra, and running shoes, which suited me just fine for what I had in mind, but I threw on a thin athletic hoodie to give me a little more coverage up top. Taking an Amazon delivery box from the recycling bin, I covered the hole in my deck door with cardboard and tape. My vacuum ate up the bits of broken glass off the floor. Then I set out a Tupperware dish of water and another dish of some chopped up hotdogs on my front stoop and called Chuck's name across the neighborhood. Nothing. But he'd come back. He loved hotdogs and he loved his momma too much not too. I grabbed that big butcher knife from the kitchen and the keys to my ZL1 Camaro from my nightstand.

Ruby waited in the garage like a dragon sleeping on her horde of gold, dangerous and easily aroused. One press of the unlock button on the fob and all the orange lights flashed like she blinked her fiery eyes awake.

Dusk was sinking down over my quiet little neighborhood, giving it the blood red hue it deserved. Neighborhood kids, Stephen had said. There was so much more out there than stupid punk kids. I'd show him that. Ruby warmed up her voice, loud inside the enclosed garage until she idled out to the curb.

There were two things, in particular, I was looking for: the cop car patrolling nearby that Stephen had promised, and that big, black pickup that had followed me around that afternoon. The cop car, if I spotted it, would only serve to reinforce my trust in Stephen. I didn't really need some random, bumbling, beat cop hanging around. The killer's big, black, pickup truck on the other hand, that I needed.

I'd done this before, beaten the killer at his own game, and if I'd learned anything that night, it was this: feign fear, feign cowardice, feign vulnerability, and just when he feels the most confident, turn on him and attack. I'd convinced Stephen to give me his phone number before he left. Not just the number to his station, but his direct line. And he gave it to me without much arm-twisting. Maybe because it was a work phone and that's what it was for, or maybe because he wanted me, Taylor, the pretty girl from his old high school, to have it. I already added it to my favorites so I could find it fast and call him with a single command to Bitch or a few taps on Ruby's touchscreen.

She hummed her way into second gear as we headed out into the evening to hunt down a killer. I kept her RPMs low and quiet. Let them believe this car was just a show car. Nothing under the hood. Nothing dangerous inside.

See, I was only wearing the mask of a damsel in distress, as the weak and vulnerable "woman out at night all by herself." Everything about me said I'm a pretty and harmless thing. Come and get me. I'm a cat with no claws. I'm a rose with no thorns. Pet me. Pluck me. Take me. Play your games with me. I won't fight back. The butcher knife fit nicely in the gap between the center console and the passenger seat, point down, handle up, out of sight, but as accessible as the shifter and the parking brake.

We spotted the cop car maybe a mile from the house. He was parked behind some trees, nose out, so eager to hand out speeding tickets like the beat cop he was, just like Stephen wasn't. Stephen was a detective. I kept it under the speed limit as we rolled by. I tried to eye him, to see if he was paying particular attention to the girl in the bright red Camaro, as he should have been, or if he was sleeping on the job. There was too much glare on the windshield to tell. It didn't matter.

I purposefully put distance between me and the cop. After all, my stalker wouldn't want to be anywhere near a law enforcement officer, detective or otherwise. I drove back into my neighborhood, past my house, and off in the opposite direction.

This was eternal suburbia without beginning or ending or declination between one place and another aside from city limit signs. But I stayed off the freeways and kept looping away from and then back to my neighborhood, like a fisherman dangling bait through the water. And it didn't take long for my fish to come swimming by.

At first, I couldn't be certain if it was the big, black, pickup truck when it pulled up behind me. I was at a stop sign, idling for longer than I needed when it emerged from the gloom with those overly bright, cold headlamps illuminating the back of Ruby's headrests and reflecting too bright in her rearview mirror. As dark as it was, and as bright as those lights were, I couldn't see the shape or color of the vehicle. By the width and height and cold brightness, I could tell it was big, and by my intuition, I suspected it was the same truck, so much so that pure distilled fear replaced all the blood in my veins.

But I'd sought this out. This was what I wanted. I had to draw him out, no matter the cost.

When I took a right turn, without using my signal, he followed. On this wider, four-lane street, I goosed Ruby's accelerator and pulled out of the glare of his headlights. I switched into the middle lane, and for one, brief moment, we were at an angle to each other, and he was under the streetlamps. The pickup was just as big and black as it had been that afternoon. He switched lanes and closed the distance between us.

I tapped on Ruby's touchscreen. The phone app was at the ready. Stephen was one touch away. But I couldn't. Not yet. I needed to let my stalker strike first. Then, and only then could I capture him in my web and descend upon him like a black widow on a thread with my fangs dripping in venom.

But was I feigning vulnerability or feigning courage? As the light ahead of us turned red, the fear in my veins boiled. I knew what I had to do, but knowing and having the grit to carry it out were two different things. Still, Ruby and I eased up to the red light. The big black truck rolled right up to our rear bumper. The tall headlights shined through the back window, into the rearview mirror, and into my eyes. If he got out, I wasn't sure I'd spot him before he was at my door, ripping me out of Ruby by a fist full of hair. But if I ran the light, would he follow? The fly was approaching the web, but he hadn't landed yet.

My hands shook on the steering wheel. I pushed out one, long exhale through pursed lips. It was time to commit to the plan. It was time to wrap the fly into the web.

The light flipped green. I buried my foot into Ruby's gas pedal. Her engine belted out. Her tires smoked. She pinned me into the seat and was through the intersection before I could rack her transmission into second gear. She begged for third, then fourth, then fifth gear. We were over sixty miles per hour, and I let her stretch her legs into overdrive. The next intersection came and went with a flash of its green light splashing over the hood. Ruby was no princess to be put on display. She was pure power.

The truck was still in my rearview mirror, coming after us. He'd taken the bait. I had him stuck to the web, but he wasn't wrapped up yet. I couldn't expose myself too soon or he'd escape. Ruby could outrun this son of a bitch no problem, but that wasn't what I needed. I only wanted him to think I was trying to get away. At eighty miles per hour, I eased up on her accelerator, and the pickup crept up my back. Ruby climbed up to ninety with ease. The truck churned along after us through another green light.

Ahead of us, the lights turned red, but we couldn't stop now. Not until he was thoroughly tangled in my net.

"And where would that have been? What exactly was your plan that night?"

I didn't know. Not yet. But I knew I had to bring him to a place where I'd have the advantage. As a woman, I'd always had the plan to drive straight to a police station if I ever found myself in this situation. I knew where it was, and it wasn't far. But if I went to Stephen now, I knew the black truck would slip from my grasp and cruise right on by, and I'd have nothing to show for it.

The light was still red ahead of me. I swung into the right lane, no pretenses of turn signals now. This was a chase. I knew it and he knew it. He just didn't know who was in charge. The traffic was clear, so I hooked a sharp right turn while keeping Ruby in third gear. The truck followed, again, slower and much less agile. He had no idea just how fast Ruby could go.

And then I recognized the neighborhood and remembered what was ahead. Anoka High School, home of the Tornados, had been renovated several times between now and when I'd last wandered the halls back in 2000, but I still knew the place like the back of my hand. And I bet they still left that door back by the dumpsters unlocked. On foot, on dry ground, in my running shoes, I was just as uncatchable as Ruby was on the road.

Already back up to seventy miles per hour, I had to stand on the brakes to make the turn. The truck came rushing up behind us as I did and probably would have plowed straight into us if I hadn't cut the wheel and raced into the high school parking lot.

He followed, every step of the way further tangling himself in my silk.

Ruby wove around the twists and turns of curbed medians, driveways, empty lots, and sparse streetlights, to the side of the school and down into the back lot where delivery trucks backed up to loading ramps and the grunge kids snuck out to skip class and smoke cigarettes. As a part of my role, as a part of the dance, as soon as I saw the truck's headlights turn the corner into the back parking lot, I let Ruby's engine rage. We coursed in a big curve around the lot and when I hit the brakes, I let the back wheels slide around sideways, leaving four, big, thick, black, skid marks on the pavement. We stopped only a short distance from the always unlocked back door.

The big black truck nosed to a stop, right next to Ruby.

I spilled out and stared at the blinding headlights. I didn't have to feign fear as part of the act. That came all too naturally. But I kept my hand on the hilt of the big kitchen knife inside of my hoodie's kangaroo pouch. Then I ran.

But not as fast as I could. Much slower than I could have. Just like I'd kept Ruby on her leash. I had to keep him unsuspecting and confident in his dominance, even now as he crawled closer and closer to the center of the web. I heard his truck door open and his boots scuffing against the blacktop, and I knew he was after me. And it was only then I realized just how much I was gambling on the hunch that this door would be unlocked just like it had been all those years ago. Back then, Columbine had just gone down, and everyone figured it was a one-off tragedy, not the first in a long string of massacres that would forever change schools into locked-down, active shooter-ready bunkers. There was no way the janitors could get by with leaving a door unlocked twenty four seven just so they didn't have to fight with keys whenever they went to haul out the garbage. No way this door was going to be unlocked. I was about to run straight into it and fight with the handle for a few seconds, just for my killer to catch me out in the open, pin me against a wall, and finish what he'd started. Did he have the ax? Would he use its long handle to sink it into my back while staying well out of knife range?

I reached the door. My trembling hands fell on the latch. I pulled and it came open. A deep, dark maw waited for me to enter. To the sounds of a murderer chasing me down, I ran inside.

Chapter Thirteen

I told you before what happened to me happened at Scotty's uncle's cabin up north by a lake. Hell, I told Stephen that's where it happened. And honest to God, up until the moment I stepped back into Anoka High School, I believed that's where it happened.

"So in your old neighborhood then?"

No. That was… That was just some malfunction of my faulty memory.

"And not at the cabin either?"

No. But I only knew that after I went into the high school. It's strange. How my memory works. Like I told you, as soon as I think I have all the details down just right, everything slips away like a frog back into the swamp, and when my hand plunges into the brackish mud, what I pull out of my past is something completely different. I can't… I can't seem to get it straight. Each time I retell it, my memories shift and move through opaque waters. But here? Now? With you sitting across from me? I can tell you with a hundred percent certainty that what happened back in '99 didn't happen in my old neighborhood or at a cabin up north by a lake.

It happened there, in our high school, down in the basement where us kids should have never been. He lured us down there, one by one, and murdered us each in turn. I was the last one, so I was lucky enough to find each of my murdered friends. But I got the best of him then, and I was going to get the best of him now. Just like he lured us down there all those years ago, now I was luring him.

As soon as I ran into that school, the very moment I slipped through that unlocked door, all the memories of that night flooded over me. I wished the door had never budged and that I would have been forced to face him there in the parking lot. What happened down there back in '99, it was a fucking nightmare.

And he was coming after me.

I ran. After all these years, I could still run much faster than him. But here it didn't do me any good. I sprinted over the waxed tile floors reflecting the red light of the EXIT signs, taking a hundred strides as he marched and covered as much ground in a dozen paces. As if in a trance, my feet, lighter and quicker than his, brought me to the staircase that led down into the basement. I twisted around the railing to take the metal steps into the hot glow below. I saw him through the railings: a huge man, painted in black shadows, his face shielded behind a featureless, white slate. My feet flew down the steps.

"Why? Why go into the basement?"

It had to be in the basement. That was where he'd killed us, so that was where I needed to kill him. It wouldn't have worked anywhere else. I knew that as I raced down those steps, but at the same time it was like I'd forgotten it, and I wasn't luring him. I was just running as if I'd forgotten my plan, to tangle him into my web and take him out with the butcher knife. My mind left me, and I hated myself for it. I was right back in that night twenty some years ago, transported there against my will, all my defenses and plans and fangs left behind.

The basement of the high school seemed infinitely bigger than it needed to be. You know how you revisit a place from your childhood, and everything seems so much smaller and pushed together than you remembered it being? This was the opposite of that. The basement was expansive and cavernous. You figure a high school needs to have a boiler room, right? And maybe a place for water heaters and maybe a backup generator and shit? Well, this place was like that, only there was no end to it. An eternal maze of metal catwalks, dripping pipes, and burning furnaces. Everything was hot. Everything was wet. Everything was red.

And as soon as I was down there, the stairs leading up from that place were gone.

Around the first corner, I found the first of my murdered friends. Shelton met me, close enough to plant that kiss we never shared. He was the first one of us to be lured away from the group on that night back in '99. Now he was tied at his wrists and ankles, stretched spreadeagle across the width of the gangway. His head hung limp. His stomach was opened up like a slit sack of grain. His bowels hung from his abdomen all the way to the ground.

Dead.

And to get around him, to keep running from the killer, I had to slip through the gap between his torso and the rows of super-heated pipes that ran along the wall. His arms and legs were pulled taunt and left little give for me to shove his torso to make room for me to get through. I seared my palm on a hot pipe.

"Shelton's body was there? Just a short while ago when you went back to the school to run from your stalker? Shelton's body was there?"

No. Of course not. He died in 1999. But I was back in 1999 too. It was like I was in the present and in the past all at the same time. Memories bleed into the moment. There was no border between my senses and reminiscence. It was a flashback, just like I'd had in my kitchen, only this time I was reliving my trauma in the very place where it happened. The only thing I can't explain to you is exactly how terrifying that was.

I ran, and when the killer got to Shelton's body, he hacked him down like he was a cheap shower curtain. He had a machete. It was broad and thick and long enough to almost drag on the metal grate as he walked. And now it dribbled blood from its tip. My little kitchen knife seemed like nothing in comparison.

I came upon Linda next. She was impaled on one of the vertical pipes as if she was slid down over it, through her crotch, up her body, and out of her mouth. The top and bottom of the pipe were greased in her blood. I ducked around her and kept running.

When the walkway opened into a room, I found the rest of my friends. I slammed into Scotty first and found myself pinballing between him and Ash and Cheryl. They hung from long chains on huge metal hooks like sides of beef in a meat locker. Those steel hooks ran right through their chests. The sharp upturned points stabbed out of their sternums. They twisted on those hooks so when I knocked into them, they turned to face me with their slack, blood-drooling mouths and their unlit, open eyes. Cheryl's face was frozen in a scream. Tiny brooks of blood trailed from the corners of her eyes and blended with her makeup.

They were still wearing what they'd been in when I'd last seen them: cute, trendy outfits that made them cooler than most other kids, myself included, even if it was only posthumously now. Blood rained down from all of their mouths, from their Wu-Tang, Porn for Pyros, and Big Johnson shirts, from their wounds, down to their Airwalks, Doc Marten combat boots, and platform Filas, and onto the floor.

And still, the killer came. Not running. Having no need to run. This was a dead end. He had me trapped. Just when I thought I had him, he'd turned the tables on me.

"Did you recognize him?"

I swear to Christ, he was wearing that mask again. The mask without a face or features. Only eyes and a small smile full of teeth. It was like looking in a fogged-over mirror. The details were there, but unavailable to me.

"So you didn't recognize him when you saw him down there in the basement?"

Oh, I recognized him. He was the same man who killed my friends back when I was seventeen. Part of me knew I was hallucinating seeing my friends there again. A small part of my brain that was drowned by the sheer horror around me knew they weren't real. But *he* was.

"What did you do?"

The only thing I could do. I hid.

There was a row of lockers along one wall. The kind you might find in a worker's changing room. Tall ones with a metal hasp for a padlock and vents near the top. Six of them. I picked one in the middle of the row and ducked inside, pulling the door shut behind me just as he stepped into the room.

Through the narrow gaps in the vents, I watched him. He moved through the hanging bodies of my friends the way an animal stalks through the trees of a forest. Between these two. Behind this one. The chains rattled as he nudged around their bodies. Nothing about him had changed in the twenty three years that had passed since I was a teenager. He had the same build. The same dark clothes. He was wearing that same mask. But he hadn't noticed me slip into the locker. He was hunting for me but had lost the scent.

I couldn't hold my breath, no way, but I breathed as quietly as I could so he wouldn't hear me, letting the short, fast inhales and exhales move through my open mouth. They echoed against the tin walls of the locker. Tears were flowing down my cheeks. My heart was doing everything it could to burst out of my chest. I felt the same way, like I was pressurized inside of that tiny locker, and I'd explode out of it any second.

I don't like enclosed places. I don't like not being able to run.

The killer stopped his pacing when he saw the lockers, like a bloodhound who'd picked up the scent again. He went straight to the first locker, flipped open the hasp, and swung open the door. The metal banged. He ransacked whatever was inside. All of this I heard but couldn't see. He was two lockers down from me. Then he went to the next locker. Same thing. First the little hasp and then the door. It banged against my locker, blocking what little vision I had through the vents. I went to dig the butcher knife from my hoodie's pocket, only there was so little room, I couldn't get my hand inside the pocket. It was so tight in there. It was so hot.

The door of the locker next to mine swung shut. I could see through the slits again, and there he was. I got a good look at him. Dark clothes. A face that refused to be seen. The robotic steady breathing as regular as a clock. His hand didn't need to undo the hasp on this locker. It was left open from when I'd pull the door shut after me. His body language told me he'd noticed. Glaring down at the unfastened hasp, he knew he'd found me.

Finally, like a bomb with a long fuse, I exploded out of the locker. A moment before he reached to open it, I shoved open the door, my hand found the handle of the knife, I crashed into him, and that knife went pumping, pumping, pumping like a boxer's lightening jabs into his torso. Each puncture was audible: wet and thick and hollow. If he made any noise, I didn't hear it. I was screaming so loud that it was all anyone could have heard. And I wasn't stopping. I plunged that blade from tip to handle all the way in and all the way out over and over again. We stumbled through the forest of my dead friends. His big machete clanged against the floor and when I'd backed him against the far wall, I switched grips with my knife and brought it down over my head, into his shoulder, into his neck, onto his scalp, and then catching the backside lip of that mask and dragging it down across his face.

The strap snapped. The mask fell away. Only then did I stop. He toppled to the floor. I stood over him, finally empty of tears and screams and hallucinations. The dream-like feel of that basement faded away. It shrunk down to a limited, reasonable size. Its red glow dimmed to gray. My friends were gone, but he was still there, coughing and hacking up blood, dying at my feet.

"And?"

And what?

"Who was under the mask?"

Tyler.

It wasn't the killer after all. Just my stupid ex-boyfriend who couldn't take a hint. He was the one who'd followed me in that black truck during my run, and rang my doorbell, and threw a rock through my glass door, and chased me across town and down into the basement of my old high school. And he'd brought a machete with him, to kill me. Because he wanted me to regret ever leaving him. Stupid, stupid Tyler.

"So, you confess to the murder of one, Tyler Haig?"

Oh, I killed him. But it wasn't murder. He harassed me. He stalked me. He invaded and vandalized my home. He followed me down into that basement. He went through those lockers. He brought the machete.

"The police never found a machete."

I took it. I didn't leave until I saw his chest stop moving, until after all his blood stopped pumping out onto the concrete floor, until he was dead, but there was no way I was going to leave it there with him. I don't know if you've been paying attention, but I've had bad luck with people I've made dead staying dead. I took the machete with me, went back out to Ruby, and left.

Chapter Fourteen

Back outside the school, Ruby and that big, ugly truck of his were still conspicuously parked near the back door. His keys were still in the ignition, so I threw the machete and the butcher knife in Ruby's backseat and hopped in the truck. I drove it out of the school and parked it in a strip mall just a half mile down the road, legally, between the lines, in the back row so no one would think anything of it. Then I ran back to Ruby.

Just a woman out for an evening jog. I wore all the right gear for it, and when I came to the "Don't Walk" light at the crosswalk, I stretched and jogged in place, just like I would have any other night. Yet the entire time I had my eyes peeled for that cop car that was supposed to be doing such a great job of keeping me safe. But I made it back to Ruby without being spotted by any cops. I pulled out of the parking lot and headed back home with no one the wiser.

Safe in the garage, I let Ruby nod off into a well-earned rest. The butcher knife and machete came inside with me. I rinsed the blood off in the kitchen sink and then ran them both through the dishwasher to cook away any DNA evidence. And then came the hardest part: I pretended like nothing happened.

"Why didn't you report what happened to the police? If it was self-defense–"

Stephen, despite all of his best traits, didn't trust me yet. I could tell that afternoon. And I suppose I shouldn't blame him. After all, when we first met I was charging at him with that same knife. Relationships take time! So I figured, maybe I would report it, but I had to find a way to do it so he'd believe me. I wasn't going to prison. Not for Tyler. Not for anybody.

So, I did the dishes. I did the laundry. I showered. I checked Ruby's carpet for drops of blood. I destroyed any evidence that might link me to Tyler's death. If there was no proof, there was no way they could arrest me for his death. It could have been anyone who knifed him like a Voodoo doll in the high school's boiler room. I was at home, enjoying a bottle of Merlot, scrolling through Pinterest. You can eat my ass if you think I'd admit to anything else.

I would have really liked to know whether or not that beat cop waiting to hand out speeding tickets saw me or not. He had to have, right? A lone woman driving a bright red Camaro? Even if he wasn't looking for me in particular, Ruby is a cop-magnet all by herself. Did that officer know I drove a red Camaro? Had Stephen even seen Ruby so he could pass along a description? I mean, the car's registered in my name and the cops have access to all of that information, so they at least had the ability to know what I drove. Did they look it up? Was that squad car hiding behind the trees even there because of me, or was it just part of their normal routine? Was he even awake?

If I knew that, then I'd know which lie to go with. If they'd seen me, then I'd say that I'd just gone out to stock up on some wine. A quick little necessary errand. If they hadn't seen me, then no, I never left the house that whole night.

I'd seen enough Law and Order. I read Alex Cross. Whichever lie I went with, I needed someone to corroborate my story of being here, at home, minding my own business. I needed an alibi. But who could I trust with that? Certainly not Barbara. Violetta hardly knew me, aside from the times when her head lived inside of my refrigerator. I think I'd rather strangle myself than voluntarily speak with either Robert or Roman. No way Jason would work. Doctor Hagari was fired. Tyler was dead. That left…

Bitch.

Bitch could corroborate my story. A digital story. One with time stamps. One that would without a doubt put me right here, at home, far away from the high school, precisely when Tyler was killed. All I had to do was change the time on my phone, set it back a couple of hours, and then build my own cover story. It took me a little while to find the place in the settings app to change the time. Not the time zone, but the actual time. It wasn't like I could go on YouTube to watch a tutorial. That digital trail would make my intended trail useless. Worse than useless. It would be evidence against me. But I found it, without any help from the internet.

I dialed Bitch back two hours and then started shopping. Mister Amazon and Miss Etsy made some money off me that night, let me tell you. I ordered books, clothes, and some cute little bits of home decor with witty little sayings like, "I'm great in bed. I can sleep for DAYS!" "It's okay if you don't like me. Not everyone is blessed with great taste," "I'm a Sass-a-holic!" and "Sometimes you win and sometimes you booze!" Kitsch and tawdry, I know, but what you don't understand is that I could pull it off. I drank wine. I ordered movies on the TV, sappy, Hallmark movies with actresses from the 90s making their comebacks. I even sent a work email. Nothing complicated. Just something like, "Sorry I didn't get to this earlier. I'll check in on it first thing in the morning and be sure to get back to you."

As I did these things, I checked the time stamps. They all happened, according to Bitch, during the time Tyler followed me through town, into the high school, and down into that hellscape of a basement where he met his untimely demise. I drank more wine. Because if I was drunk at home, then surely I couldn't have been across town murdering my ex-boyfriend.

When the dishwasher was done, I put the butcher knife back in its slot in the block with all the other knives. As for the machete, I have to admit, I played with it for a little bit, got a good feel for its black plastic handle, felt its heft as I swung it, admired its shine in the reflections of my recessed lighting, tested its razor-sharp edge with my thumb. It was sharp. One good swing would have taken me out. Me, or anyone else. It was dangerous possessing it. Even more dangerous to hold it in my hand and swing it around my living room like a five year old with a plastic lightsaber. If the neighbors saw me with it through my windows, well, that would undo a lot of the work I'd done to cover my tracks. As soon as that dawned on me, the feel of the machete changed from fun toy to poisonous snake. I tucked it away and out of sight.

Was there a cop out there in the night? Watching my place like Stephen promised? I doubted it, after everything that had gone on that night. See, trust is a two-way street, and we had a long way to go before we met in the middle.

And maybe you're thinking, you should have just gotten rid of it. You should have thrown it in a lake and let it sink to the bottom. After all, there are only, like, ten thousand lakes in this state. Pick any one at random and chuck that murder weapon into the water and no one would ever find it. But I didn't want to let it go. It was so much more lethal than the kitchen knife. So much more agile than the ax that had gone missing. I wanted to keep it. It was mine now.

I thought about putting it in my garage with the leaf rake and snow shovel, where it might make sense to keep a machete, as if there were any legitimate reason for a person to own a machete here in Twin Cities suburbia. But I wanted it close by, and I didn't want anyone to ever find it. So instead of putting it with the tools in my garage, I went to the air register near the floor in my living room. Two screws held the vent in place, but they came out easily enough and once the grill was off, I set the machete there in the duct, handle toward the opening. I twisted the screws back into place but didn't torque them tight. If… *when* the time came for me to need that machete, I could unscrew the grill with my fingers and reach the weapon in no time.

Then I went back to my couch and my Hallmark movies and my wine. As I sipped and thumbed through Pinterest, my eyes spent more time on the air register than they did on the movie or my phone.

I'd killed him, that son of a bitch. And I didn't feel bad about it! He'd been the last in a long string of terrible boyfriends and had become the worst of all exes. How many times had some jaded, neanderthal ex-boyfriend or ex-husband or run-of-the-mill stalker tracked down some woman and left her raped or beaten or dead? But that wasn't me. I got the jump on him. I got the best of him. I got him before he got me. Finally! Some fucking justice!

And you want to know why I didn't go running to the cops to file a report? Why I didn't retreat to all the men who would call me a menstruating, psycho bitch? Why I didn't go and surrender to them the power I'd finally found? No. Fuck no. Not on this Earth. I'd won. Don't you get it? I finally came out on top, and I was not capitulating my position to a bunch of cops who'd love nothing more than to make another arrest and another conviction and get another "killer" off the streets. That wasn't going to be me. I'd done it, and I was going to get away with it.

I woke up sometime between midnight and dawn, my wine glass of merlot tipped out of my hand and the dregs spilled on the couch. The TV was still on. The movie about that girl who goes to prom covered in pig's blood. I didn't know the plot. But the look in the eyes of that poor girl in her pretty, white, homemade dress, bathed from head to toe in red gloss was instantly recognizable and innately, barbarically relatable. The rage in her eyes when she slammed the doors shut to the school gymnasium. The focused intention when everything and everyone caught flame. The determination as she strolled through it all and out into the wider world. Carrie White was all of us.

Still, I told Bitch to turn off the TV and kill the lights. Then I shuffled over to my phone, reset the time to resync with the rest of the world around me, and left the wine stain for the morning.

I woke up with the sun to the snorts and slurps and wheezing of Chuck the Pug licking my face. I don't know where he'd gone to or why he decided to come out of hiding, but as soon as I heard those struggling respiratory gasps, even before I could peel open my eyes, I knew it was him.

"Chuck! Baby!" I wrapped him up in a big tight hug. He moaned and groaned, uncomfortably out of control and in my grasp, but I still didn't let go. "I thought I'd lost you, baby!"

We ate breakfast together at the kitchen counter. He scarfed down the chopped up hotdogs and lapped up tap water from the Tupperware. I enjoyed a cream cheese bagel and a glass of cabernet sauvignon. My stock was running low, which meant we'd have to make a trip to the store today.

But first I had to tend to my responsibilities. After all, I was a professional working woman climbing the corporate ladder in a bold new technology company, and I had an eight o'clock call-in. I showered and dressed, brushed my teeth, and put up my hair, and I even got around to following through with the email I'd sent last night while I was absolutely, positively, demonstratively NOT killing my ex-boyfriend in a high school boiler room. And the whole time I hardly even glanced at the air register grill and thought about what waited in the dark behind it.

Much.

And the day rolled on. No cops knocked on my door to arrest me. No "Breaking News: Brutal Homicide Discovered in Anoka High School" banners splashed across my feed. No calls or texts from Tyler. No ominous ringing of my doorbell. No more rocks through my glass.

During my lunch break, Chuck and I took Ruby to the liquor store for more wine. Reds of course. Nothing too sweet. Something strong and dry with a little bite. Something that could kill softly. On the way back, I called my home insurance company, filed a claim for my broken deck door, and made it back to my home office with enough time left in the workday to catch up on some reports. I was the queen of work-life balance and professional self-realization. All while sipping a bold and savory, but not overpowering, California Pinot Noir from a coffee mug. Take that, Mary Tyler Moore.

It wasn't until after work hours, after I'd drained the bottle of pinot and dropped it responsibly into the recycling bin, that anyone called me. I let Bitch pick it up.

"Taylor, it's Barb," she said over the speaker.

"Yeah, I know. Caller ID," I said and suppressed a hiccup.

"Have you heard from Doctor Cal?" she said, getting right to the point. No patience. No sense of humor.

"Why would I have heard from Doctor Hagari? I'm not seeing–"

She cut me off. "I haven't either. No calls. No texts. No one can tell me where he's gone to," Barb said.

"Well, you said he was put on administrative leave. Why would he be contacting his patients?" I asked as I rummaged through my utensil drawer for a corkscrew. I usually don't have to bother. Most of the brands I buy are screw-offs. And don't think that makes me basic. Did you know they did a study, and metal screw-off caps actually do a better job of preserving the flavors of the wine than an old school cork? It's true. You can Google it.

"I'm not just– It's not as if– Look. Just listen," Barb false started. "I know something isn't right. This isn't like him to go off the grid. I think this investigation, or whatever it is, has really messed with him. He's a distinguished professional, and to have people question his work and his ethics… I just don't think I could deal with it if I were him. Do you…?"

She hung on to that question, hesitant to ask it, or maybe restructuring it mid-deliver.

"Do you know what may have led to all of this?" she finally got out.

"I don't know, Barb. Maybe he fondled one of his patients," I said, shutting out the harsh memories of his spidery hands traipsing over my body as I lay in that chair. There was the damn corkscrew! You'd think a connoisseur such as myself ought to have an integral tool of the trade more available.

"Did someone say that?" Barb said. "Did you hear something about him being accused by one of our clients?"

"What? No. I'm just… Look. You asked, so I threw out one possible answer," I said.

"Do you know something I don't?" she asked, her voice sharp and curt.

Oh girl, me, the Library of Congress, and Wikipedia could play a tight game of Jeopardy! with categories like, "Things I know that Barb Doesn't."

"Do you have something to do with all of this?" Barb asked before I could respond.

"Barb, why would you even ask that? I'm out of his program. He's on administrative leave. I haven't had any contact with him. None. So leave me out of whatever weird, little obsession you have with him," I said.

"Weird? Little? Taylor, this is serious. This is a man's career!"

"I gotta go," I droned, fighting with the corkscrew and the bottle. It was one of those with the metal arms that rose up as you screwed it in as if it were a little man raising his hands to the sky while stretching his mouth agape, screaming. When the hands were all the way up over his head, I pulled them down and sucked the cork out of the bottle. A rich, aromatic Zinf. "I'm gonna put on a movie. We'll talk tomorrow."

"Don't hang up on me!" Barb said, but Bitch was right in front of me and all I had to do was give her a tap on the head and the call ended.

The TV already had a menu of movies up on display. Chuck waited for me eagerly on the couch. Shuffling through the selections, I settled on a trashy 70s exploitation flick. *Last House on the Left*. Not the two thousand nine remake. The original version that came out alongside other grind house B movies like *The Hills Have Eyes* and *Sleepover Massacre*. Not much polish or production value, but plenty of sex and violence to make up for it.

Chapter Fifteen

When I logged in for work the next morning, that's when the news of Tyler's death hit my feed. I wasn't even looking for it. I don't watch the morning news or the evening news or any of the local TV channels for that matter. But you know how when you open a new window it defaults to the browser's news feed? And you know how it customizes it based on whatever you've clicked on, and whether or not it thinks you're male or female, and where your IP address originates from? Well, the algorithm had me figured out, because right there, front and center, in big, bold, clickbaity text was "Slain Man Found in Basement of Local High School. Authorities suspect…"

Before giving up any more details, the browser flipped to the next headline. Some political scandal in DC. As if that was anything new. But I could hit the little arrow button to bring me back to the last headline, and I could click to read all about what exactly the "Authorities suspected." But I didn't. That would leave a digital trail and unwind the alibis I'd spun around myself. It would leave evidence that perhaps I had something to do with whatever happened at the "Local High School."

So they found the body. So what? I knew that would happen. Eventually. I was counting on it. Sure. It was summertime and the only people who ever went into that building between May and September were the janitors, but I knew they were going to find it. Thinking about it now, I probably would have been better off if I'd killed Tyler in the tenth grade biology lab. Maybe stuck him in the freezer with all those undisturbed, baby pig fetuses waiting to be dissected come second semester. But this changed nothing. As a matter of fact, it was more important now than ever that I maintained my cool.

As chill as a pig fetus, I logged in. I answered emails. I attended meetings. I nodded my head and concurred at all the smart quippy things Jason said. I sipped my wine. Always from a coffee mug so it raised no one's hackles. At noon, I laced up my running shoes, stretched out so I was nice and limber, and trotted down my driveway and out into the maze of the neighborhood's sidewalks. When I got back from my run, a good three miles today, with no suburban horror flashbacks or big black trucks to be spoken of, or attentive cop cars for that matter, I showered and logged back in just in time for our one o'clock meeting. I fed Chuck. I scheduled a time with the glass repair people to come out and fix my door. This was my normal routine. I was doing nothing I wouldn't have done had this been any other day.

No one said anything.

And neither did I.

I went to bed.

The next morning, Stephen called. I was in a chat with Robert and Roman about finances for the work retreat. They wanted to see invoices and estimates from the venue and caterers, which I didn't have, but whatever. I, very politely, excused myself so I could answer Stephen.

"Good morning, Stephen," I said, as chipper as a cheerleader.

"Taylor," he said, not so tickled. "Have you seen the news lately?"

"You know, I don't really watch it," I up-spoke. "Mostly just politics and derision. So-and-so did this. This bill is going to strip us of all our rights. This person is having sex with his person. Just a bunch of noise to pit us against each other if you ask me."

"The local news," he said.

Of course, I knew what he was talking about. But he didn't know that I knew what he was talking about, so the game played on.

"Hmm. No. Can't say that I…"

"Tyler Haig, your ex-boyfriend, was found dead yesterday," Stephen informed me.

"Oh my god. Like, in his sleep? Was it a heart attack? He was so young!"

"Nope. No, it wasn't a heart attack," Stephen said. "You really haven't seen anything on the news since, say, yesterday morning?"

"Like I said, I don't watch it. Nobody told me he died. We're not really a thing anymore. It's not like–"

"His body was found in the basement of Anoka High School. Someone stabbed him a total of forty eight times with what, our forensics department says, was an ordinary kitchen blade," Stephen said.

"Oh my god," I said, earnestly taken aback. Had it really been forty eight times?

"Care to make a statement about that?" Stephen said.

What I wanted to say, what I wanted to ask, was if they'd found the mask down there with him. And what they had made out of that. Instead, I played ignorant. "No. I mean, that's terrible. Who would do such a thing? I mean, we were through, he and I. I don't really know what he had going on in his life after we broke up. Did he have any gambling debts or owed any money or…?"

"Hmph," Stephen said. And then he asked what I was waiting for him to ask since I left Tyler dead in that basement. "Where were you between the hours of eight and ten PM on the night of August Sixth?"

"I was at home. I watched a movie. I think I bought a bunch of stuff off Amazon," I said, and I'd be ready with the evidence as soon as anyone asked.

"It might be a good idea if we meet in person," Stephen said.

"Oh. Okay, Stephen. Are you asking me out?" No! Stupid stupid stupid! What the hell was I thinking coming on to him now, when he just told me they found my ex murdered in a school basement?

"No," he said slow. "I'm asking you to come to the station to make an official statement."

"Oh. Well. I don't know…"

"You're not a suspect," he said, the first soothing tone he'd taken during the whole conversation. "It's more of a formality. If you were home all night that night, we just want to get it on record. We have a lot more investigating to do, and you're in no way, shape, or form our number one suspect."

"Oh. Okay."

"Can you come to the station? The sooner the better," He stated plainly.

"Well. Um… I've sort of been drinking," I told him and took another sip from my coffee mug.

"It's nine AM."

"I might have a problem," I admitted.

"Okay. Well. It doesn't have to be right now, but we should get your statement," Stephen said in that cool, understanding way of his. "Soon."

"Oh, of course. That will be no problem at all. I just didn't want to when, you know, I'm not in full control of my faculties," I said.

"Yes. No. That is true. Taylor?" he said my name. "Are you seeking help? Normal people don't drink at nine AM on a Thursday morning."

"No. I know. This isn't like a usual thing I do," I lied. "This is just, well, my way of getting through some stuff this morning. This isn't like a part of my normal routine."

"Are you sure?"

"Yeah. Totally. It's my demon. Let me fight it."

He sighed, concerned for me. "Well, call me when you're ready to make that statement. And take care of yourself, Taylor."

"Oh, I will. It was nice to hear from you. We should meet up sometime, like for lunch maybe. You know, to catch up. So much has happened since high school," I said.

"Yeah. We'll see about that. I'll be in touch," he said and hung up.

That could have gone better. Although, it could have gone worse. He said I wasn't a suspect. And now we were through that whole awkward phase of our relationship where he had to tell me they found my murdered ex-boyfriend. Now we could move on. It wasn't like he said "No," when I asked him out to lunch. I reminded myself, this was a process.

Although, I have to admit, it was difficult to refocus on my job with everything else going on around me. For instance, during my lunch, I went to the fridge to make a sandwich, and guess who's head was back? That's right. Violetta's! And it was even worse than before. It was as if her head had been in my fridge the whole time since the first time I'd seen it in there and had continued to decompose. The eyes were rotted, and a massive swarm of houseflies launched from her scalp. Maggots, like actual, white, squirmy, little worms were crawling in and out of her nose. The blood from the stump of her neck had dried up and turned black. And the smell! Oh my god, did it reek! The whole thing scared the shit out of me.

But after I fell on my ass and slammed the fridge shut, I picked myself back up and opened it just an inch.

Stink and flies poured out between the gap in the magnetic seal. I smacked the door back shut and tried again. The third time, there were no flies. No stink. Growing some courage, I opened the door further and there were no maggots, no rotten eyes, no pool of dried blood, no disembodied head. Good. Good for Violetta. Good for me. Good *for* me.

Bringing my lunch back to my desk, I almost hit my head on the ax handle jutting out of the wall. That gave me another good start, and I just about spilled my food and drink all over myself. And I had my camera on! How embarrassing would have that been? But I kept my composure and after a few deep cleansing breaths, the ax disappeared, and I could enjoy my lunch and listen in as Jason briefed us on this past quarter's sales.

"Taylor?" he stopped his speech.

I unmuted my mic and said, "I'm here. I'm listening."

"Is that wine?" Jason asked.

I had to look at the glass in my hand before I realized that when I'd poured my lunchtime refreshment, I had not used a coffee mug. In one hand I held my half-eaten turkey and cheese sandwich, and in the other I held a full glass of merlot by the stem. "Shit," I said before I could stop myself. Before I could put my mic on mute.

"I'm sorry! How did that happen? Let me dump this out," I said and carried the glass off-camera but absolutely did not dump it down the drain. What I did was find my coffee mug and pour the wine out of the glass and into that. Then, back on camera, my best smile shined. "It was in the fridge. I must have grabbed it by accident. Sorry for the interruption, everybody. Go on, Jason. You were talking about gaining traction amongst older demographics?" I said and sipped from my coffee mug.

Smiling, even while the blood seeped down the frames of my dual computer monitors and down the screens, was tough, but I did it. Even when the wine in my mug turned to blood as if Jesus fucking Christ had poured me my drink, I grinned and bore it. Even while Robert whistled. Even while Roman bitched about the empty cup of coffee. Even while Barb let her stupid, dough-faced husband and their little redhead interrupt the call. Even while Jason used those ridiculous made-up sayings like "core competencies," "low-hanging fruit," and "synergy!" I smiled.

"You know what, gang?" Jason said after slapping his thighs. "I think we need to rally the troops on this one. Tomorrow. At the office. Everybody bring your A Game, and let's drill down and generate some action points."

If our team had developed any core competencies since coming under Jason's wing, it was the ability to suppress groans. They all acknowledged and concurred and made notes in their calendars. I smiled because that's what sweet, innocent, sober Taylor does. I hoped they didn't notice when I smeared the streaks of blood off the monitors. It only helped a little. The blood was just thinner now as if I attended the meeting from the other side of a red lens.

"Nine o'clock around the big conference table. Violetta, can you have the slide deck ready?" Of course, she could. "Outstanding. Good job, today everybody. We moved the needle, but I think tomorrow we're really going to make some hay."

Toward the end of the call, just before I hit that "Leave Meeting" button, I swear all of them were gargling on that blood, but I ignored it. This was the product of years of corporate training. I could keep that smile while standing on my head on a bed of coals.

That night, the sun sank early. As the blood ran down the frames of my windows, it changed the hue of my home. Chuck barked, unsettled by it. But he was just a dog. As for me, I unscrewed the register and pulled that machete out of the air vent and poured myself another glass of merlot. I didn't get weirded out. I didn't scream. Even as the TV flipped onto static and unstable, gray light splashed over my living room. Nope. I stayed cool and kept a tight grip on that machete.

But I saw him.

"Wait. What do you mean, you saw him?"

When I ran my palm over the front window and cut a clean swath through the blood, I saw him out there in the street, watching my house, holding that ax across his chest like a soldier on guard duty. He still had that mask. The one with only eyes and a narrow gulch of a mouth, deep and black. No nose. No features. That same mask I'd cut off Tyler's face just before I watched him bleed to death from forty eight of my stab wounds.

Because it wasn't Tyler who murdered my friends in that boiler room. Of course, it wasn't. He was two years younger than I was. Three years younger than the others. He would have been a freshman shrimp back then. Maybe he had followed me on my run in that black truck. Maybe he tailed me and Ruby the other night. And yes, it was definitely him who followed me down into the old high school basement. I absolutely killed him down there in that boiler room. But he wasn't the killer.

All of these memories were so fresh in my mind it was as if I could smell them. You know how you can really put yourself in a point in your past when you remember the smells? It was like that. The dank, stall mildew of the boy's locker room. The polish of the waxed hallway floors. The slow rot of moldy textbooks. That steamed bleach smell of the school kitchen. The hormones pumping through all the pores of our skin that we couldn't hide no matter how much deodorant and body sprays and perfumes we layered on. All of those smells and sounds and images and memories were as fresh and pungent as wet paint. I recounted every detail, but the only person I wanted to share them with was Stephen. And he was the one person in the world I couldn't tell. He was one call away. All I had to do was ask Bitch to dial him up, and I knew he'd answer. But I couldn't tell him a word. The less connection he had with me and the basement underneath Anoka High School the better.

Meanwhile, my entire house bled all around me. Chuck snorted and sniffed and yapped at the oozing windows. The TV flickered static, then a shot from *Friday the 13th*, then *Hellraiser, Creepshow, Children of the Corn, The Thing, They Live, Critters, Alien, The Exorcist, Poltergeist…* endlessly.

Outside, a killer waited for me in the dark.

I clutched that machete and sat on my couch and watched, trapped. I don't like not being able to run. I don't like enclosed places. I don't like horror movies.

Chapter Sixteen

Morning's clarity came the same way alcoholics brag in dingy, church basements about finding Jesus: inevitably and unsolicited. I didn't sleep that night. At least, I don't think I did, but everything got strange after midnight. Too much wine and blood and flashing nightmare images on the TV. Morning brought an end to all that, but it also brought the heartache-inducing shine of the sun and all the tasks of another weekday spent in corporate hell. All of that waited for me outside of my bed, begging me to step out into the sun. Surely, even you can relate to that?

"Yeah. As a matter of fact, I can."

Jason had called us in for another one of his round-ups today. So, I showered my dog and fed my body and did my teeth and brushed my hair and gargled shampoo and put on a work-appropriate outfit under my armpits and wore Costco-brand deodorant that smelled like memories and diamonds and rust.

Getting into Ruby was the best part of my day. Nothing could go wrong when I was behind her wheel. With me inside of her, we controlled the world. Let the stalkers and murderers linger behind the bushes and chase us with their slow, ungainly trucks. When we were together, none of them could touch us. What a shame that we reached our destination in such a short time. In the parking garage, I procrastinated killing her engine. But I did, and all the demons crept out of the dark and gathered in concentric circles around us.

In the daylight, Minneapolis hummed with its mid-workweek bustle, a thing that had also come back from the dead, more and more each week. Still, the city had her scars, a lot of healing left to do, and some hard lessons left to learn. But the tourists and joggers were back on the Stone Arch Bridge. Indie music bands were playing at 1st Ave. Bigger bands were going on stage at The Armory, and the real big names were filling up US Bank Stadium. The food trucks had returned to The Commons on Fourth Street. The skyways were as populated by the suit-bedecked, business folks as they were by the drug-addicted, hopeless homeless. In other words, things appeared copasetic. But the demons were still there, just beyond the periphery.

I parked in the City Center parking ramp because my plastic tag hanging from Ruby's rearview mirror was good for it, and a walk would delay my inevitable arrival at the office. And because, I admit, the warmth of the day was dragging me out of my mental dungeon. Along the way, I sipped wine out of my protein-mix shaker bottle and blended right in with all the other office drones going about their business on the busy streets.

At the corner of Nicollet and 7th, I came upon that statue of the old TV sitcom star joyfully throwing her cap into the air. A ghost held in perpetuity, whose only chance for resurrection came from hard-working women such as myself. And then I met a real ghost.

"Taylor?" someone called from behind me. "Taylor Mosley, is that you?"

I turned back toward the corner, and there coming across 7th with a leather laptop bag, a cup of Starbucks, and that huge, unforgettable, devilish smile, was Cheryl. I knew it was Cheryl instantly because there are things about people that never change. A twist in their eyes. A turn in their smile. A lift in their nose. A glint in their eye. Except now there were more wrinkles between all of those energetic and enigmatic traits. Her cheeks sagged. Her posture drooped. That fire hidden in her pupils hadn't gone out but had dimmed ever so sadly. But it was her. Unequivocally, unmistakably, undeniably, her.

"Cheryl?" I said with a quiver in my voice because it couldn't be true. Maybe my eyes and ears could have deceived me, but when she wrapped me up in a hug that only a best friend from twenty plus years ago could deliver, the smell of her hair and the touch of her skin told the truth with utter certainty. It was her.

"Oh my god! Girl, I haven't seen you in so long!" she beamed as she held me at arm's length underneath the Mary Tyler Moore statue, examining me more thoroughly than if I'd stripped naked next to a campfire. "Why have we not connected? Aren't you on Facebook?"

"I– I– Cheryl?" I stammered.

"I can't believe it. Do you work downtown? You know, I've been going to work just three blocks from here for, oh jeez, it's gotta be ten years now. I can't believe we haven't run into each other! What are you doing for lunch? We have to meet up," she went on. "I have so much to catch you up on. My god, has it really been since high school?"

"I– I–," I what? I moved away? I went into treatment? I never went on the internet? Yes, I have been working downtown, and no, I absolutely can't believe we wouldn't have run into each other after all these years, and no, I can't believe that we've run into each other now because maybe I didn't move away, maybe I never signed up for a Facebook account, maybe I hadn't reached out to you, but that was only because "You're dead."

She pinched her face shut and did this little shake that told me she didn't think she heard me right. "What?"

"You died," I told the real ghost standing at the corner of Nicollet and 7th. "You, and Scotty, and Ash, and Linda, and… and…and Shelton. You all died."

"Who? Taylor. Are you okay?" Cheryl said, concern filling her unforgotten features. "Have you really been out of touch with everyone from high school since graduation?" And then, painting a smile on her suddenly pale face, she said, "We have a class reunion coming up!"

"No," I said. "You can't be real. I know some things I'm seeing are real, and I know some things are not. And you–" I pointed at her now as I backstepped off the curb and into Nicollet. Damn the screeching tires and barking horns. "You aren't real. You're dead! I saw you die! I watched you get murdered!"

I turned and ran the rest of the way across the street, down the block, and to the entrance of the IDS Center. I couldn't afford the hallucinations. Not today. Today, I had to go into work, pretend like everything was just hunky-dory, and do my job.

In the atrium of the IDS Center is this big, huge, US flag, hung down like a banner with the stars and stripes in the upper right hand corner, big enough to blanket everyone who walked underneath it. The perfect display of post-9/11 patriotism. Have you seen it?

"I've been there many times."

A spectacle at first, but nothing after the first hundred times you walk underneath it. All the towering glass and steel and the proudly hung red, white, and blue. It doesn't mean anything after a while. Like when you say a word so many times in a row until it loses all meaning. Because really, how many other tragedies and world-changing events have we lived through between 2001 and now? But it's still there, reminding us of when the IDS and the Wells Fargo and the Capella were on the list right alongside the Hancock and the Sears Tower as the next potential terrorist target.

"They call it the Willis Tower now."

Ghosts from the past. They're everywhere if you stop to look for them.

I took the elevator up to my floor. Coming into the big conference room, composed and with the appropriate amount of "a little late to work" fluster, I apologized to the gang. "Sorry guys, but I ran into an old friend out on the street that I haven't seen in like, twenty years. I guess she works just like, three blocks from here, and we've never bumped into each other until today. What are the odds of that, huh?"

"Oh, that's so cool, Taylor," Jason said in his ever-polite way of saying everything. "It's no problem. We were just about to get started."

"Give me just a minute to get settled in," I told them as I set my shaker bottle on the table, sloughed off my shoulder bag, and played my best Mary Tyler Moore.

Robert whistled the theme song to Friends.

Roman set a big box of doughnuts in the middle of the table. "Eat up, everybody."

"No gluten for me, thanks," Violetta said.

"Oh my god. Wes just loves this bakery," Barb said. "We're supposed to be on this keto diet, but really, it's more for him than me. That spare tire around his waist isn't getting any smaller."

"How far along is he now? I'm in my third trimester myself," Robert said and slapped at his belly bulge.

The whole team got a good guffaw out of them. I chuckled right along and finished with, "You guys," mocking exasperation.

Workplace banter. Give me thumbscrews or bamboo under the fingernails or the iron maiden or sandburs ground into my eyeballs. Just please, for the love of God, no more workplace banter. I took a good long pull from my shaker bottle like it was this poison's antidote.

The meeting persisted. Violetta clicked through slides. We all took dutiful notes. We tallied up figures on a spreadsheet Violetta brought up on the big screen. We were going to stay "solutions-orientated," and "crack this nut," and "make some hay." Give me a polygraph test, put a gun to my head, and honest to God, I couldn't tell you if we actually made any decisions.

After the torture session, another hell awaited me. Jason called me into his office for what I assumed was an update on the retreat. I had nothing to tell him, but I could bullshit with the best of them. After all, if a cutting edge, on-the-rise, tech-firm like Team Next Paradigms, (ranked Number Thirty Seven on Forbes' list of America's Most Promising Companies,) couldn't decide on a course of action, why should I be expected to make any real progress on something as trivial as Jason's ridiculous retreat?

Predictably, right on cue as if this was a sitcom and he played "the boss," as soon as I sat down in front of his desk, he asked, "So, where are we at with the work retreat?"

"We have a venue," I said. "I'm at a ninety percent solution on a cater and guest speakers, so really, it's just putting the bow on a few last items and–"

"Taylor," Jason stopped me. "It's tomorrow. The work retreat is tomorrow and you're telling me we don't have a caterer or a keynote speaker?"

"I do. We do. I have a list of action items that I can–" I went digging into my shoulder bag to produce some documents that I figured had at least a fifty-fifty shot of passing inspection and caught my shaker bottle with my elbow. It clunked over sideways and glug glug glugged a quite savory Sangiovese all over Jason's desk.

He didn't pick it up to stop the spillage, not even when the puddle spread over the BS papers from my shoulder bag to his desk calendar with all the ink and highlighter circles around the different days of the week. Not even when it crept under his monitor and keyboard. He just stared at it.

"Oh. Oops. I... must have grabbed the wrong shaker bottle?" I tried.

"You brought alcohol to the workplace? You've been drinking on the job? Again?" Jason asked, appalled by the very notion of needing a little help from a bottle to get through the day. "Have you done anything to prepare for this retreat?"

"What? Yes, but. No. Yeah, I have everything laid out for the retreat. It's fine. Everything is going to be fine," I said.

"Show me. Show me who you have booked for a keynote speaker. Show me the menu from the caterer. Show me something, anything, to give me the slightest reason to keep you on the team," Jason said, not at all like his usual, passive-aggressive self.

"I… I don't have a menu *with* me," I smiled.

"You're fired," he said. "I've never had to fire someone before, never gave up on a team member before, but Taylor, we gave you a company-provided counselor. I gave you a second chance when no one else said I should. I went to bat for you after word of what you did got to corporate. I stuck my neck out for you, and this is how you return the favor?"

"What? No. You can't fire me. I completed the sessions. I have some things done for the retreat. You can't just…" I said. All the while the aroma of the Sangiovese wafted up from his desk. "I… It's just that… I've been dealing with some things."

"Taylor—"

"Jason, I need this job," I said, my skin turning cold and a ringing filling my ears. Did he not understand that my nice house and my dream car came with monthly bills that needed to be paid?

"I'm sorry, but you've left me no other options. Hand off whatever you've done with the retreat to Barbara, collect up anything you have in the building, and go," he said. And there it was. Naked and exposed. Free of euphemisms and jargon and catchphrases. I had to give him credit. For once, he'd said something as plainly and clearly as could be said: You're fired. Pack up your shit and get out.

On my way to the door, not having to pack up a thing out of my little cubicle I was never supposed to even have at this remote position anyway, I stopped by Barb's.

"Here's what I have for the retreat," I said and slapped some completely unrelated wine-soaked papers on her already cluttered workspace. "Jason canned me. It's all yours now. Knock yourself out."

"I'm sorry, what the shit?" she called after me.

I strolled past Robert as he whistled the opening to the Andy Griffith show and Roman begged someone to take the last donut. On my way to the elevator, I reached into the box and snatched up a raspberry-filled Bismark with vanilla frosting.

"I'll be seeing you, Violetta," I told her on my way to the elevator. "You were the only one I never dreamed of running through with a goddamn rusty pitchfork."

"Excuse me?" she said, not taking it at all for the compliment that it was.

"Fuck you, Team Next Paradigms! It's been a living hell!" I called across the cubicle farm.

And just as the elevator doors were about to close on another nightmare chapter of my life, a hand reached through and caught the closing edge. I hammered on the > < button, but the door's safety sensors kicked in and the elevator opened back up. And who of all people followed me in? Of course, it was Barb.

"What the fuck is this?" she waved the sopping-wet pages in front of my face.

"I don't know. Probably my taxes from last year. Keep 'em. I got 'em on digits," I said.

"This? This is what you have for the retreat?"

The doors closed but neither of us hit a floor button, so we just sat there, two idiots sharing a motionless elevator. I chewed on the donut and washed it down with what was left in my shaker bottle.

"I got a venue," I said.

"*I* got a venue!" she said.

"Fair," I said. She had found the place. All I did was click on the link she sent me. "Listen, Barb. Do you really think I give a shit about this fucking dog and pony show of a work retreat? Do you really think I give a fuck where you guys decide to hang out and get drunk and pretend to be edgy and play at pushing boundaries when you're really just jostling in line to see who gets to be next to suck corporate's dick?"

"You–" she jabbed the finger of a fist still clutching the red-stained papers, "do not get to get off that easy."

"What do you want from me?" I asked her, as earnestly as I could between chomps of donut and gulps of Sangiovese.

"Taylor, you don't get to… to… to just take our donuts and leave like this!"

"Jason fired me!" I explained to her. "I don't work here anymore. So take a hint like I did and fuck off."

"Where's Doctor Cal?" she demanded.

"This again? Jesus, Barb, how the fuck should I know?" Running out of patience, I hit the 1st floor button and finally, the elevator started moving.

"He's missing, and you should care. But you don't, which tells me you have something to do with it. You have something to do with the investigation too, don't you? I know you're the reason he was put on administrative leave, so tell me, God damn it! Tell me what you did to him?"

"What *I* did?" I snapped back. "You want to know what *I* did? To *him*? How about what he did to me? How about what he probably did to you too and probably did to a hundred other broken and fucked up women who went to him for help? How about that, you doting Stockholm-syndrome-brainwashed bitch?"

"I don't know what you're talking about," she said.

With a pleasant little chime, the elevator door opened to that beautiful, sun-bathed atrium of IDS Center. I stepped out. The big red, white, and blue blanket caught the daylight like stained glass.

"Of course, you don't," I said and threw the half-eaten donut in her face. The raspberry jelly smacked against her cheek. "Keep your donuts. I'll keep my wine."

Chapter Seventeen

I had the start of a decent buzz by the time I got back behind the wheel of Ruby. Breaking my own rule, I know. But to be fair, most of my wine was all over Jason's desk or absorbed into whatever papers I'd left with Barb. We got home just fine. No dinged fenders. No DUIs. No runover children. Hardly any visions of massacred bodies or black trucks or suspicious, mountainous, pedestrians wearing dark clothes and faceless masks. Call me Miss Responsible.

Or don't. See if I care.

As soon as I had Ruby in the garage, I went inside and got to work building on that buzz, because if there's one thing you don't want to be after getting fired, it's sober. You get me?

"I can sympathize with you, but I can't empathize."

Yeah. Sure. Anyway, it was life as usual back in Casa De La Mosley. Bitch taking my Amazon orders. Wine going into glasses and then going out of glasses. Bottles clunking heavy into the recycle bin. Screaming, half-dressed teenagers getting murdered on the TV. Blood running up the walls. It might sound humble, but you know the saying about no other place being like home.

Only, I learned something in the passing days. Something had shifted in my mind after getting fired. Yes, I was a victim of all these things, but by losing my job, losing my ex-boyfriend, and losing my mind, I had gained some control. I couldn't stop the TV from switching from horror movie to horror movie. I couldn't keep the walls free from those long, thin, red tears running from the carpet to the ceiling. I couldn't find Chucky. I couldn't tell if the ax was lodged into my wall or not. I couldn't open my refrigerator without first checking for flies and the smell of rotting Violetta head cheese. Sometimes things were as they should be. Other times I was in a Satanic funhouse mirror version of real life complete with long, leaning angular shadows, upside-down crosses, a pale full moon, and an unsettling violin soundtrack. But you know what made the difference?

"What was that, Taylor?"

I did.

I let it swallow me. Let it digest me. Let it become a part of me. I groveled in the madness of it all. And when I saw the killer standing in my backyard, half-hidden behind laundry hung out to dry, I didn't cower. When he looked at me through that mask with those burning-ember eyes, that mask that I had knifed off Tyler's face the last time I saw it, I stared right back.

Then I found the ax buried half-blade deep in my sheetrock, ripped it loose, and threw open my still-broken, sliding glass door. I charged into the bright afternoon light, clutching the ax like a soldier charging out of a World War I trench with rifle in hand. I sprinted down the steps after him, screaming bloody murder. He didn't run. Of course, he'd never run. The image of him leapt from one spot to another, but I didn't let him go that easily. I chased him down past every sheet of laundry, every bush, every corner of the house. I wouldn't be afraid of him anymore. He wasn't Tyler. He had never been Tyler. He'd always been something more. Something darker, and stranger, and stronger than my stupid, pathetic, dead ex. And I had him cornered.

When I came around the corner of the house, to the box canyon dead end of my house and the privacy fence on the side with no gate, I had the ax held with both hands at the very end of the handle, blade behind my back, ready to swing it over my head and into him so I could kill him again, just like I'd done up by the lake and in Cheryl's front lawn and down deep inside of the boiler room.

But there was no one there. The dead end of my backyard was empty. No mysterious masked killer. No ax in my hands. Just me, panting and sweating and my throat hoarse from screaming. And maybe you think that's just another example of my hallucinating, fevered, troubled mind. But that's where you'd be wrong. I was just starting to see things clearly.

I couldn't forget my horrors, even if I couldn't remember them, and I couldn't escape them. So I assimilated with them. I surrendered to them. I bathed in them. I became them. There was a sort of homeostasis to be found in that balance between abject terror and conventional suburban boredom.

So, having chased away the killer, however temporary, I went back inside and poured another glass of wine and browsed the internet for succulent holders. Chuck jumped up on my lap and didn't seem to mind the screaming heads pushing through my living room walls, stretching the egg-shell white paint around their tortured faces, but never breaking through.

When the doorbell rang, it was like someone had taken a needle to my little surrounding balloon, but rather than shreds of latex rubber exploding out across the neighborhood, a million crystalline shards of glass fell down around me.

Ask me how long it took me to get that machete out of the air duct. Come on. I put it back before I left for work that morning, turned the register's screws in finger-tight and everything. But from the time my doorbell rang to the time I had it in my hand and down to the front door, ask me how long it took.

"Okay. How long?"

Well, I don't know, but he didn't have to ring twice.

And after all the terrible luck I had that day, that week, that life, just when I was expecting more shit piled on top of an already tall mound, finally something good had come my way. Someone good had come to my door, and that someone was Stephen. I opened the door and tucked that insanely wide and long blade behind my back, holding the handle low by my buttocks so the point wouldn't reach over my head. He was wearing his, I'm-a-cop-but-not-a-beat-cop black polo with embroidered name and badge and those khaki trousers. His gun and gear hung tight around his waist, never jostling, as if it were glued there. A corner of his lips turned up when he saw me.

"Stephen! So good to see you! I was just thinking about Mister DiMaggio's classroom down in the English department wing. It was always so dark and quiet down that hallway," I blathered. Embarrassing, I know. Also careless. I shouldn't have said anything about Anoka High School. All those details that were so fresh in my mind belonged inside my mind and only inside my mind. But what can I say? He caught me off guard. "Tell you what? Wait out here just one second while I tidy up and then you can come right in."

He started with a "Miss Mosley–" but I shut the door before he could go on. Cops are a little like vampires: you have to invite them before they can come inside. Not that I didn't want Stephen in my house.

I ran upstairs, looked for a good, quick place to ditch the machete, and threw it in the dishwasher. "Bitch, turn off the TV," I said, and she obeyed. Then I lowered a finger to Chuck's flat, wet, snorty nose. "And you behave!"

He sneezed back at me. I'd have better luck with Bitch.

On my way to the front door, I checked the windows for blood: none. I checked the walls for axes: none. I checked the fridge for heads: one half of a lettuce. Everything just as it should be. I went down and let Stephen in.

"Sorry about that," I said. "But a lady is allowed her secrets. Come on in."

He stepped across the threshold with those big rubber-soled boots, and what was done was done. Once you let the right ones in, you don't get to kick them back out.

"Do you want to sit upstairs on the couch? I can get you something to drink," I offered.

"Actually, Miss Mosely," he said. "I'm going to need you to come with me."

"Oh, are we going out? Well, you'll have to give me a minute to powder my nose," I said. "Where are you taking me for our first date? I don't mean to ruin the surprise, but I need to know what to wear."

"To the police station," Stephen said. "The situation regarding your ex-boyfriend has continued to develop, and I'm afraid I need to take your statement."

"Oh," I said, stopping halfway up the steps, meaning to preen myself for going out to dinner. "Well, I have been drinking. I probably shouldn't–"

"We can't put this off any longer, Taylor," he said. "I'll drive you there and back, but we need you at the station to make a statement."

I smirked. "Well, that's not a very romantic first date, but I guess I'll take what I can get," I said, and when his hard demeanor didn't break, I eased the tension. "I'm just messing with you, Stephen! Of course, I'll come to the station and make a statement. Whatever I can do to help resolve the case."

You need to understand, I'm not just some dingy broad who trips over herself every time a cute guy shows up at my door. I knew where we stood. I knew he wasn't taking me out on a date, but I was manipulating him as much as he wanted to use me. Guys can't help but like it when a pretty girl shows some interest in them. It disarms them. It gets them off their script. It killed any antagonism between us. Sure, Stephen was a gorgeous man with those eternal eyes and that firm but smooth skin. Yes, I would have loved it if he'd actually been there for a date instead of taking me into some grimy police station to answer a bunch of stupid questions. And of course, the last thing I wanted to discuss with him was my ex-boyfriend who I just so happened to stab forty eight times with a kitchen knife in the basement of our old alma mater. But he was playing his game, and I was playing mine.

Want proof that I knew what I was doing? When we rode to the station, I sat next to him in the passenger seat. Not in the molded, plastic, puke-proof seats behind the plexiglass and wire-mesh cage in the back. No handcuffs. No reading of rights.

"Remember when that was like, *thee* mall to hang out at?" I asked, pointing out the window.

"Oh yeah, I remember. Spent way too much time inside of that place. Didn't have the money for it, but I sure got good at pretending," he said.

"Ugh, same! I pretended to try to work there. Took some applications, back when you had to go in and actually ask for a paper application, before the internet. I filled out some. Maybe even turned in one or two," I reminisced. "Probably wasn't too bummed when nobody hired me."

"That place has really gone downhill over the years," he said.

"Yeah, well, it's like the line from that one movie, 'Sometimes, dead is better,'" I quoted.

What movie was that anyway?

"Are you asking me?"

No. It doesn't matter. He didn't know the movie either, but that didn't matter either. We chatted and joked the whole way to the station. Both of us laughed. Not just me. It was almost as if we were going out to the newest restaurant in town, each of us trying to impress the other.

"I was pretty straight-laced. Graduated high school, went right to work on my Criminal Justice Degree, worked some security jobs, then as a sheriff's deputy, and now here," Stephen said.

"A detective," I said, still impressed by the fancy title. "So, do you still watch all the cops shows? NCIS? Law and Order? Which one is *actually* the most realistic?"

He hummed it over for a bit. "It's a tough call, but I'd say either Reno 911 or Brooklyn 99. If there was a Midwest suburban blend of those two shows, that'd be my life."

I laughed good and hard at that because it was funny. Here I was thinking of all the dark and gritty police procedurals, and his mind went straight to Officer Dangle. It made me like him all the more, that humble deflection of what had to be an extremely difficult job. An extremely difficult lifestyle. It was a fun ride. I was disappointed when we finally reached the station and it ended.

Chapter Eighteen

Once we got inside and around other officers, the mood changed. The banter died. The smiles retreated. He still never cuffed me. I wasn't under arrest, but the vibe changed. And the atmosphere. Why are police stations always dimly lit? Why are the tiles always chipped? Why was the carpet so thin and ugly and stained?

He brought me to a room, showed me a chair where I was to sit, and followed me in with just his head and a single shoulder.

"It will be just a minute. Can I get you anything? Coffee? Bottle of water?" he asked.

"A nice merlot?" I half-joked.

"Coffee it is," he said with a wink. Then the door closed.

If you've never been in a police interrogation room, good for you, I guess. But the old Hollywood-style rooms with big, wall-sized, one-way mirrors are a thing of the past. They have cameras now, and microphones. I bet you've even seen footage from those cameras. Grainy. A dull washed-out hue one notch above black and white. A lone suspect sitting on a chair in a small room. An officer in a shirt and tie slowly working the criminal into a corner with his own words.

This room had a camera too, hidden behind a black, quarter-dome in the corner of the ceiling. I tried not to look at it. I reminded myself I wasn't under arrest. I reminded myself that, if all else failed, I could still claim self-defense. Because that's what it had been. Self-defense. I didn't set out to kill Tyler. Well, maybe I set out *prepared* to kill Tyler, but that was only if he did exactly what he did, which was try to kill me first. I just couldn't trust the cops to see the difference. If I got by with killing him, if I walked, got away scot-free, then there would be no trial and no possibility of being thrown in prison with a life sentence. But once I confessed, once I resorted to self-defense, it was all out of my hands. It was left up to lawyers, and judges, and well-meaning, civically-responsible jurors.

When Stephen came back, he brought with him two cups of coffee. Black. Steaming. Sobering. They were the paper cups with the little wings that unfolded to make a handle. We didn't sit across from each other but around the corner of the little table. I think they set up the room that way so that we weren't directly opposed to each other, just by our seating arrangement. The message was, "Cooperate. We're not against you. We're your friends. And never mind that little black ball in the corner of the ceiling. This is just between you and me." It was manipulation if you weren't smart enough to notice it. If you came in expecting to sit on opposite sides of a table, handcuffed to it, lying while you threw sideways glances at the wall-length mirror you knew wasn't a mirror, this sort of thing might throw you off.

"So, let's start with the basics," Stephen said. And he took down the basics. My name. My date of birth. Where I lived. Where I worked. The boring stuff. Although, I was already lying when I didn't mention my recent breakup with Team Next Paradigms, but I figured he would be more interested in my breakup with Tyler. He scribbled it all down on a long, frayed, yellow legal pad.

"Now tell me about your relationship with Tyler Haig," he said.

"We were nothing," I said. "We broke up like, over a month ago."

And then he asked me all kinds of details about the breakup, about our relationship, who broke up with whom, how Tyler took it, what contact we had afterward, and for the most part, I was honest. Because if they really pinned me to the wall with some undeniable evidence, then I wanted them to know exactly how crazy, and abusive, and obsessed Tyler had really been. This wasn't a motive such much as it was justification. Besides, they didn't have any undeniable evidence. I'd left nothing at the scene. I had the murder weapon neatly tucked in my knife block. I had my alibi. I had everything. They had nothing.

"Where were you on the night of August Sixth?" He asked, not for the first time.

"Well, you guys should know," I said. "You had the extra patrol watching my house."

Only they didn't. I read it as plain as words printed on his face. The nearest cop was doing his best to either catch some speeders or some Zs. He wasn't even paying enough attention to follow the hot girl in the red hot Camaro he was supposed to be watching. If he had, he would have pulled us both over, given Tyler and me speeding tickets, and probably would have inadvertently stopped what had happened. But I played it up as a way to reinforce my alibi. If they wanted to manipulate me, I could manipulate them right back.

"So you were at home?" Stephen said.

"All night. I watched a movie, bought some stuff off Amazon, enjoyed some wine... Another boring night at the Mosley residence," I told him.

"When was the last time you were inside the Anoka High School?"

"I mean, can you at least tell me what you found there?" The mask! The mask! I had to know if they had found my killer's mask. And when they did find it, what had they done with it? Who had access to it?

"Before I can answer any of your questions, Taylor, you're going to have to answer mine," he said. "So, when were you last at Anoka High School?"

"Well, you should know that too," I said, polishing off my patented, tension-breaking smile. "You were there!"

"And when was that?" he asked, not returning my smile even a little.

"I don't know. Graduation? The last day of school? Whenever it was that they last herded us unruly eighteen year olds inside of that building. Whenever it was, it was probably the last time you were in there too," I said.

"So not recently," he said.

"Not since we partied like that Prince song," I said.

He raised an eyebrow.

"You know, 'Two thousand zero zero party's over, oops, we're out of time. So tonight let's party like it's nineteen ninety nine,'" I sang and did a little shuffle in my chair. "Oh my god! You know what I just remembered? Y two K!"

"Taylor," he said, but didn't stop me.

"Remember? We hardly even knew what the internet was, but everybody was so convinced all the computers were going to just stop working at the stroke of midnight. Stop lights were going to quit working. Planes were going to fall out of the sky. Lawnmowers were going to turn around and gobble up all those suburban dads tending their lawns. Vending machines were going to fire cans of pop at unsuspecting baseball coaches like bullets from a gun. ATMs calling people assholes! Man versus the machines! Utter chaos! Anarchy in the streets! Human sacrifice! Dogs and cats living together! Mass hysteria!"

"Ah!" Stephen said. "I caught that one. Ghostbusters. I love Bill Murray."

"Huh?" I said.

"But…" he dragged out, tapping the point of his pen on the legal pad. "If we can stick with the questions we'll get through this much quicker, and we can get you back home to all your movies. So, the last time you were inside Anoka High School was when you were a student there?"

"When we were students there, yeah," I said, taking a page out of Jason's book. Always use collective pronouns. Never I or you. Always we and us. The eternal persistent message being: We're a team. We're in this together.

"Was Tyler ever violent with you?" he asked next.

I paused at that. Why hadn't he lingered on the high school longer? After all, he knew what had happened to me there. To *us* there. He had to. He was in my same grade. It happened at our school. He must have attended the candlelight memorials for Cheryl, Scotty, Ash, Linda, and Shelton just like the rest of the student body. After all, that's why he acted so aloof when I first described what happened to me happening at a cabin up north. Because he knew the truth! Even though I couldn't see it through my own fog, he knew. And now he wasn't going to ask me about how I dealt with all that? If I had therapy? If I had any intrusive memories of it? If I'd become prone to high-risk behaviors? If I just maybe, perhaps, had developed a chemical dependency?

"Were your fights ever physical?" he asked the same question in a different way. He was good at this, I have to admit. Of course, he'd be good.

And how should I answer that? When we were together, no. Really, not until he came after me with the machete currently secreted away inside my dishwasher. But how did I want to spin this? "Yes, he was violent," reinforcing my self-defense story? or "No, he wasn't," distancing myself from any motivation I might have had to end him?

"Taylor?" he asked.

I split the difference and feigned distress. "Do I have to answer that? Can't we keep talking about the good old days instead?"

His eyes softened. He reached across the corner of that table and put a hand on top of mine. And oh my god. That touch sent a giant crack right through my emotional dam. I couldn't remember the last time someone touched me in that comforting way. So many things were stirring and boiling inside of me and not once in all that time had someone shown genuine sympathy for me. When I came to that police station, I wasn't expecting it. Certainly hadn't asked for it. Didn't even know I needed it. But his look and his touch, that was all it took. He broke me.

I cried. I scooted closer to him and draped my arms over his wide shoulders. He hugged me back. I got tears on his sexy, black, police detective, polo shirt. He didn't seem to mind. I answered his unasked questions.

"It's just that, I'm overwhelmed. I'm alone. I don't have any resources or anyone I can confide in. I have these memories I can't get rid of, but nobody understands that, and they just keep on expecting me to be normal, and I'm not normal. I want to be like everybody else, happy, and social, and likable, and comfortable, but I'm just not. I'm not normal. If normal is New York, I'm in Kalamazoo, nowhere near normal! I try to be, but my whole life is just fucked, you know? Ever since that night–"

"Which night is that?" he asked.

"What do you mean, which night? You know which night. That night!" I allowed myself but refused to go any closer to anything related to Anoka High School.

"Taylor, if you want me to help you, you have to tell me everything," he said.

"I am, but you're still not understanding me. *I'm* the victim here."

"But you're not," Stephen had the gall to say. "Maybe at some point in the past, a long time ago, you were the victim, but we're here to talk about Tyler. He's the victim. He was killed, and we need to find out who did it."

"So what? You think I did it? You think I had anything to do with that? I suppose you think I'm guilty because I'm not wearing black and weeping over his death? Tyler was a royal asshole, and no, I don't miss him, and no, his mother didn't call me and tell me, and no, we didn't share a good cry together, and no, I don't care that he's gone, and no, that doesn't mean I had anything to do with it. Is that what you need me to say? Is that good enough for you and your little notepad?"

If he tried to write down everything I said, he hadn't kept up. His pen sat dead at the top of the page, just below my name, age, and place of birth.

The ride home was quiet. I was still uncuffed and still riding shotgun. We sat next to each other, saying nothing, and not making eye contact. Sort of like when a date ends with embarrassingly bad sex. Before I left the station, they took my fingerprints and swabbed my cheek for DNA. After all my cleaning and tidying up, I didn't once think about DNA evidence. And now they had mine. And Stephen didn't seem to mind that they were treating me like a suspect. Like a perpetrator. And the whole ride back he said nothing to alleviate my fears. I felt exposed and violated and stupid. *Just* like after a date that ends with bad sex.

I should have refused to talk. I should have clammed up. I should have asked for a lawyer, but in my mind, I just repeated to myself, "It was self-defense, it was self-defense, it was self-defense."

When we pulled into my driveway, he walked me to my door. Because after everything, Stephen couldn't help but be a gentleman. On the stoop, I turned to him.

"Sorry for freaking out back there," I said.

"You've been under a lot of stress," he admitted.

"Remember when we first met?"

"How could I forget?" That was the closest thing to a joke he'd said in hours.

"Well, I know I won't," I said, playing bashful. Maybe this night didn't have to end like he'd prematurely ejaculated while dry-humping my unwashed granny panties after all. "I still can't believe you didn't shoot me."

"Gotta admit, you caught me off guard when you came screaming around the garage like that," Stephen said. "But I've also gotten to know you quite a bit since then. I'm glad I didn't shoot you, Taylor."

"So you don't think I'm a criminal?"

"If so, you're one smooth criminal," he said, and as if recognizing my blushing and seeking a way to keep things cool, "That's Michael Jackson. Smooth criminal."

I reached out and held his hand. He didn't pull it away.

"That stalker, whoever rang my doorbell and broke my deck door, I think he's still out there," I said.

"You don't think Tyler did those things?" he asked.

I shook my head. "It's just that I've seen things since… since when you said he was killed. I think the person who did those things is still watching me. I don't think I'm out of danger yet."

"We can keep the extra patrol in your area," he said. Convenient. For the cops. They'll probably keep a closer watch now that they had me pinned for murder. "You need to tell me right away if you see anything suspicious, okay Taylor? I'm still on your side."

"Thank you," I said and meant it, and we shared another hug.

No kiss. Not on our first date. But that hug was worth all the hassle.

Chapter Nineteen

I woke up the next morning on my couch with a headache and hazy eyes. The house was quiet. Empty wine bottles lay on the floor like dead soldiers at Antietam. Dried Ramon noodles had glued themselves to the table. The fuzzy belt of my bathrobe hung over the back of the couch. The robe itself hung open around my naked body. My small, smooth, pretty, pink vibrator which I always thought of as chic, discreet, and not one of those big, gross, veiny, rubbery monstrosities, was stuck between two cushions. It poked into my hip. The last of the juice in the batteries ground away the mechanics inside, too slow to excite anybody. Black little smudges from my inked fingertips dotted all the white and pink things like leopard spots. My phone wasn't on the coffee table, or hidden in the cracks of the couch, or tucked away in the big pockets of my robe. And of course, it wasn't on the charger.

But the walls were clean of blood. No tortured faces pushed through the paint. No axes hung from the sheetrock. Rather than beating like the interior of a human heart, the walls stood straight and stiff, just like any other boring, cookie-cutter, suburban home. The menu of my streaming service was silently cycling through movie teasers. For the first time in a long time, the house seemed still.

My memories of what happened after Stephen dropped me off were foggy, but clearly, I was in a celebratory mood, and honestly? That mood lingered into the morning. I'd been set free from the prison of my previous life. I'd chased down my worst fear. I'd met the man of my dreams. So what if it was in a police interrogation room and ended with inked fingerprints?

Looking around at the debris of my debauchery, it was clear I should have felt guilt, shame, embarrassment, and admonishment. What did you do last night, Taylor? Get a hold of yourself, Taylor. Clean up your act, Taylor. Get your shit together, *Taylor!* Right?

Wrong.

All those people out there, you, them, everybody, they all want me to feel like shit for being me. They want to harass me. Follow me. Stalk me. Haunt me. Belittle me. Fire me. Shame me. Control me. Keep me under their thumb. That was supposed to be my place. And how dare I spend a night rejecting the nice, little box society squeezed down around my shoulders?

I didn't feel guilty. I didn't feel ashamed. I was never going to apologize. As I wandered through the wreckage of my house, I felt justified. After all the nonsense and insanity life had thrown at me, was this anything but an appropriate response? The only truly insane reaction to this insane world was trying to pretend it made sense.

The kitchen was in no better shape than the living room. The machete I'd taken out of the air vent when Stephen rang my doorbell never made it back inside its hiding place. Rather, I'd taken the opportunity sometime during the night last night to practice swinging it into my wooden dinette stool. There were dozens of hack marks, and the blade was still buried into the seat. There was another empty wine bottle in the sink and a few of those tiny 99 Bananas shooter bottles along with it. My cell phone was in a tub of melted ice cream, power and auxiliary port up, so at least the melted dairy didn't have much to seep into and fry the electronics. It came back to life, and a long series of notifications blanketed the lock screen.

17 Missed Messages from Barb From Work
6 Missed Calls from Barb From Work
3 Voicemails from Barb From Work
5 Emails from barbaracarpenter@teamnextparadigms.com

I found the vague memories of receiving these messages in the fog of last night. They explained why I ditched my phone in the tub of Cherry Garcia. I wasn't about to call her back. Why should I? We weren't coworkers anymore, and I was more than satisfied with our goodbye, but naked curiosity forced me to open the text app and scroll through what she thought was so goddamn important.

Taylor I need your help.
Call me please as soon as you get this.
Seriously I need a hand. Its something only you can do or I wouldn't ask.

And on and on they went. Seventeen messages, and not once during any of them did she allude to what she actually wanted. And sure, I was curious, but not so curious to open the emails or listen to a god damn voicemail. Who leaves voicemails anymore? What kind of monster was she? After wiping down my phone with a kitchen towel and getting most of the ice cream off, I left it on the kitchen counter and continued my survey of last night's indiscretions.

No blood on the walls. No heads in the fridge. No broken glass on the floor. That was good. It was late in the morning according to the clock on the stove. That was fine. It wasn't like I had a job to make it to. Besides, it was Saturday. Would have been the first day of the work retreat.

And then it hit me. That's why Barb was being so damn persistent. Something to do with the work retreat. The work retreat I was supposed to have put together. The work retreat I dropped on her plate at the eleventh hour. I was back in the living room when my cell rang. My shoulders shot up in surprise at the sound and then slouched low when I admitted to myself I already knew who was calling.

"Incoming call from: Barb From Work," Bitch confirmed my suspicions.

"Fine," I said. "Let's get this over with. Bitch, answer the phone."

"Taylor?" Barb's voice came through the speaker immediately. "Are you there? Please God, tell me you're there."

"Yeah, Barb, I'm here," I said.

"Oh, thank God. Thank God, you picked up," she said. "Are you okay? I've been calling and messaging you and trying to get a hold of you any way I could. Are you not on Facebook?"

"No, I'm not on– What is it? What's so important?" I cut to the chase.

"The venue for the work retreat. They're not letting me check in," she said. "Because you're the one who booked it, they need you to be here. They need to see your ID and the credit card you used to book it."

"I used the corporate account," I said. "Why would I ever use a personal card?"

"Well, they're saying it's on your personal card, and they need you to come here and get it sorted out," she said.

I collapsed back down on my couch. The nearest wine bottle had a few dregs in the bottom. The rim dangled above my tongue but wouldn't give up the last drop. This was going to be a rough morning.

"Can you put them on the phone? Maybe if I talk to them—"

"No, that won't work. I already asked," Barb said. "Listen, I know you don't like me. I don't know why you don't like me. I always thought I was nice to you, and I guess I thought we could've been something of a team, you and me, while you were here at Team Next Paradigms. And I know that's not how things turned out. Which is fine."

Was she getting emotional now? Oh, my god, she was.

"But I really need your help on this one. Jason is here. Everybody is here, and they're all looking at me to get this thing rolling. But I can't do *shit* without them seeing you first." She whispered the word shit, I guess in case her mother was listening in. "So please, from one woman to another. Help me out. Us ladies have to stick together."

I tossed the stubborn bottle across the carpet and sighed long and deep. This problem wasn't going to go away by ignoring it. If I didn't help Barb, Jason would be calling next. And if I somehow used my personal card to book the venue instead of the corporate account… Well, my future income stream was already looking bleak. I didn't need that debt hanging over my head.

And maybe Barb had a point. Maybe us ladies should have stuck together from the start.

"Text me the address," I exhaled the words as if I didn't want to speak them, but they escaped from me against my will.

"Thank you thank you thank you," Barb blathered. "I'm going to owe you big time. Come to the address, as soon as you can, and come right inside. I'll be waiting for you."

"Yeah. Yeah. Fine," I said. "But I'm only doing this so I don't get a charge on my…"

I was going to go on, but she'd already hung up. Busy was the life of a working woman. No doubt, she had a million more fires to put out under the direction of Jason and the rest of the team. But Violetta would give her a hand. If Jason had been smart, he would have dumped the retreat on Violetta's lap to begin with. What was he thinking of giving that responsibility to me in the first place?

Barb's text came in and jostled my cell phone on the sticky countertop. The resort was less than two hours west of the Cities, which was funny because I was sure we were planning on a location more remote. More "up north." But the shorter this trip, the better, so I didn't question it. Looking around the kitchen and living room, it was clear that there was some work to be done before I left anyway. Most notably, that machete needed to be washed of fingerprints and tucked away back into the air duct. The stool with all the bits of wood chopped out of the seat would have to be burned, but that was too time-consuming for that morning. Maybe after I got back I could have a little backyard campfire. As for all the empty bottles, dried-up food, and the errand sex toy? Nothing a little germ-killing dish soap couldn't handle.

By the time Ruby and I were together in the garage, ready to go, I was showered and dressed, the murder weapon was hidden, the toy was put away, and the house was clean. Mostly. I made a note to pick up more wine on the way back home.

The garage door opened, and sunlight poured into my vaguely sober eyes. I had to take care of this one little thing, this loose-end leftover from my days at Team Next Paradigms, and then I could get back to enjoying the rest of my crapulent life and deciding where to go from there. Ruby and I slipped into 1st gear and rolled down the driveway.

Chapter Twenty

An hour and a half later, Ruby and I sat in the parking lot. Where and of what, I wasn't sure. All around us, for miles and endless miles, were slow yellow stalks of corn. A construction site stood beyond the front of the hotel but nothing else. The asphalt underneath us was crumbled to rocks by weeds and time. The venue where Team Next Paradigms should have been hosting a rousing and motivating retreat stood in front of us, but this place didn't look like the sort of corporate-friendly, luxury, conference center by the lake Barb had pitched me. This looked like a dingy, out-of-date, foreclosed hotel in the middle of nowhere. Maybe at some point in the past, the wealthy and those who treaded on their coattails met here to swap industry secrets and build networks between power players. If so, that had been a long time ago. The building had that old log cabin exterior to it, but the stain was long bled from the timbers. The plastic front of the highway sign was missing, and the unlit bulbs underneath were exposed, leaving the entire venue unnamed. A rusted yellow bulldozer sat abandoned in the far corner of the lot. Nothing moved inside.

I'd checked and double-checked the address that Barb sent me the whole way up. My phone wouldn't charge during the drive, not with all the solidified ice cream in the power port, but I followed Bitch's directions turn-by-turn. When Ruby and I pulled into that decrepit parking lot, with just twelve percent battery life left, she confirmed that I had arrived at my destination. Maybe it was nicer inside. Maybe the lake was behind the building. Maybe everyone else was still on the way. But it didn't feel that way. It felt forgotten. Haunted. Cursed.

Was this the location I'd blindly booked at Barb's suggestion? If so, she'd fucked up, big time. And since I was no longer around to be thrown under the bus, Jason would have her ass over this.

Her Honda CRV was parked underneath the drive-up canopy.

"Barb, what the fuck are you up to?" I said as I got out of Ruby.

I strolled up to the entrance with my phone pressed to my ear, listening to it ring and ring. She wasn't answering. Bitch gave me a buzz letting me know she was down to ten percent. The glass door only gave a view of shadows. I didn't go inside. Turning back to the CRV, I looked inside to confirm it was hers. The Team Next Paradigms parking pass hung from the rearview mirror. Pictures of her dark haired husband and her redheaded little kid were clipped to the visor. It was hers, no doubt about it. And today was the day of the retreat. So why was she here? Her and no one else?

I replied to one of her seventeen text messages.

Okay I'm here. Where are you?

No response.

This didn't make sense. This couldn't be the resort, and this wasn't like Barb. The way I saw it, there were only two possibilities. Either Barbara, the domestic suburbanite wife and mother, diligent and loyal corporate drone, who'd developed an unhealthy relationship with her therapist, had lured me out to the sticks, far away from where a work trip she was supposed to have planned, to do what? Scare me? Or she'd gone to the wrong place by mistake, and something inside of here was keeping her from responding to my calls and texts.

I'd left the machete in the air duct. I'd left the butcher knife in the cutting block. The ax had disappeared from my wall. I had no weapons.

"If you're fucking with me, Barb, so help me…" I said and went up to the glass doors of the old hotel.

When I pushed, the unlocked door swung inwards and bade me to enter. Like an invited vampire, I crossed the threshold.

There were no lights on inside. Dust covered the elaborately woven Indian rug that led deeper into the lobby. The concierge was absent from his spot behind the front desk. As if the hotel had a need to prove its age, it displayed a rack of keys on plastic fobs. The brass was tarnished. The plastic tags with the stamped-on room numbers were faded. A pair of keys were missing for two rooms on the second floor. The hotel sat as if someone wanted to open it tomorrow, all they'd have to do is vacuum, dust, and turn on the lights. As if this place had been open and doing business not that long ago. Another tourist-dependent victim of a pandemic hungry to devour any business on the brink of failure. Ghosts are everywhere if you look for them. The little brass bell on the oak counter sat silent. I wasn't going to ring it and call up the haunts from the backroom to help me with my bags. You think I'm crazy?

"Well, I wouldn't use that word, but–"

Never mind. Don't answer that.

You know what else I wasn't going to do? I wasn't going to call out anything stupid like, "Hello? Is anyone here?" Instead, I texted Barb, again. Now I was the one building up a long string of unanswered messages on her lock screen. Wherever she was. Wherever her phone was if she was no longer by it. But I kept quiet, and I moved further inside.

There was a huge fireplace at the end of the lobby. Chairs with thick cushions embroidered with ducks and moose and bears and canoes and trout sat on either side of a coffee table. An out-of-date and dead tube television sat off to the side, so if anyone lounging here got bored of the fire, they could watch movies on VHS. On either side of the stone-worked chimney, were two grandiose staircases made out of more rough-hewn timbers. I could see tracks in the dust going up the stairs on the right. The treads of Barb's Skechers were as defined as Neil Armstrong's boots on the moon. Still, I didn't call out her name.

When I was four steps up, something cracked behind me. My eyes shot to the large voluminous lobby, and just like that, this place felt very familiar. From a dream? From a memory? It was as if I'd already been here. As if an encroaching threat had backed me up these stairs before. But no one was behind me, so what had made that noise?

My own mind was as likely a suspect as anything or anyone else. More likely, even. But I thought I was over all of that. I was certain that by killing Tyler, leaving my job, and winning over Stephen, I'd taken all my bad memories and trauma and demons and crammed them into a little box and sealed it shut with a heavy padlock. Just last night, hadn't I enjoyed a quiet evening to myself without speaking in tongues or spinning my head three hundred sixty degrees? I'd beaten my past. I'd silenced my paranoia.

Or so I thought.

Something was very wrong here. Something had made a noise down there. I should have left, right then and there. I should have leapt down the stairs, sprinted through the front door, jumped back into Ruby, and gone home. But coming here by herself, when she should have been with Jason and the rest of the team, was not like Barb. Not one bit. Yes, I could abandon her, surrender to my fears, run, and never look back. It'd be easy. Instead, I remembered her pleas and ignored the noise and continued upstairs.

As soon as I was on the balcony overlooking the lobby below, I realized why this place was so familiar to me. Like turning the pages of a book to uncover the mystery at the end, my mind cycled through all those locations where I thought the killer had attacked us back when we were teens. The cabin by the lake. The quiet suburban neighborhood. The basement of our old high school. The deaths of my friends replayed in my mind's eyes. Shelton strung up, spread eagle, blocking a narrow subterranean passage, his entrails at his feet. Linda thrown onto an elk head, impaled by all its antlers. Scotty and Cheryl pummeled to a pulp by a spiked Louisville Slugger. Ash with a kitchen knife buried in his face. Shelton, dangling from a ceiling fan with a barbeque fork stabbed through his sternum. Ash and Linda cut up like lumber, the buzz saw spitting red, rooster tail arcs across the lawn. Scotty hanging from a meat hook amongst a forest of the rest of them, ready for butchering. Shelton's naked corpse hanging out of my bedroom window like a flag on a beautiful, sunny Fourth of July. Cheryl, my best friend, wearing only her pretty, lacy, red underwear, getting hacked to pieces by a monster on a cool summer night. I paged through all of my memories, and when I got through them all, I arrived here. On this big wooden staircase. In this hotel.

This was where it happened. Not in any of those other places. Here. In a big empty hotel, tucked away in the woods in the middle of an impoverished Indian reservation, closed for the summer. It was Nineteen Ninety Nine. It was Year Zero. Everything was just beginning. Everything was ending. I was an innocent, inexperienced, unscarred, unjaded seventeen year old. And I came here on a dare with my best friend Cheryl and a few other kids from our cross country team, and I was about to watch as all of them got murdered before my very eyes.

All over again.

Just inside the glass doors of the hotel, the form of a mountainous man cut an all-black silhouette out of the sunlight. The cliffs of his shoulders raised and lowered in a rhythm set by a clock. His ice-white, blank face was fixed at his summit. His featureless face, which could be filled by anyone or anything glared up the stairs at me. It was a void of humanity, eager to be replaced by the worst of us. But I recognized him immediately. He was massive, thick, and holding a metal stake as if pulled free from an ornate wrought iron fence, its sharp tip protruding from arabesque petals. That old, fat, tube TV, the one set up for guests to watch movies, flickered to life. It splashed gray light over the killer as if lightning had landed inside the hotel. In that dull light, I saw Ash's severed head hanging halfway down the wrought iron spear, eyes turned up, agape mouth drooping down, the stump of his neck painting the shaft on which he was impaled red.

The sound of static played from the TV's speakers, but it wasn't itself static. Only the sound of static as part of a wider soundtrack. Unsettling music played from its old speakers, and when I looked at the TV, I saw inside the screen the image of a second TV, this one buzzing with whitewash. A little girl in a nightgown knelt in front of it. She reached her hands out and set them against the screen within a screen, then turned her eyes over her shoulder, met my gaze, and sang, "They're heeeere."

The killer's all-black shape sprung into motion as if he were a corpse jolted back to life by the electric glory of the television. He moved quick, faster than I'd ever seen him before. Fast enough to catch me if I didn't go, immediately and without thinking, deeper into the hotel. So I went. My foot only slipped once on the smooth dusty finish of the steps. My shin cracked against the lip of a wooden riser. I ignored the pain and put my running shoes to work.

As soon as I was up the steps, I was sprinting through an endless hallway flanked by door after door after door. To my right, I saw inside of a series of those doors, each open and showing an identical image in each room, advanced only by a frame as if animated in stop-motion. The flicker-show was of Linda and the killer. She stood at the foot of the bed as he brought a roaring chainsaw into her head. Her body writhed as the teeth tore through bone. Always still through each frame but moving like a dancer under a strobe light as I ran and watched through door after door.

I slammed into the end of the hallway and the jolting images stopped. The buzz of the saw and the screams of my dying friend continued. My body clung to the shape of a red metal box with a fire extinguisher locked inside. Why couldn't it have been an ax? Why just a big, stupid, unwieldy cylinder instead of a fucking ax? My life-long tormentor was still marching down the hallway behind me, his form blocking out the vanishing point leading back to the brighter entrance. To my right was another hallway, branching off to more rooms. To my left was a metal door marked "Stairs - Emergency Exit."

The metal door exploded inward as I shoved it. In the dim red light of the EXIT sign, I could see concrete stairs flowing down to my left and up to my right. I was about to go down because, of course, I should go down because I needed to get the fuck out of there. But then Shelton's body fell down the center of the stairwell. A noose snapped tight into his neck as the rope reached its end. His body bounced, then swung between me and the way downstairs. Fear of going any closer to him overwhelmed my logic, and I fell backward, into the hallway.

The killer stood over me, his feet planted wide next to my hip and shoulder. The starch-white, featureless face smiled down at me. I can't explain how he smiled. The mouth never moved. Those squared-off teeth were chiseled in stone, but I swear to God that mask smiled at me as if it knew exactly what it was putting me through and enjoyed every moment. He held a pickax now, like a miner would use, one end pointed and sharp, the other heavy and wide. The wrought iron spear and chainsaw both used up, he required something unique for me. And I had nothing. Not even a fire extinguisher. All he had to do to finish me off was swing.

Fuck that. I was the one who survived. Always. Each time, I lasted until the end, if for no other reason so that I could relive all these horrors again and again and again. As he hefted that pickax over his shoulder, I reached the latch of the fire extinguisher box and flung open the door. On the pickax's downward arc, it caught the metal door and stopped before the rusted tip could bury itself into my face. With all my strength, I drove the heel of my shoe into the side of his knee. It buckled sideways, in a direction knees aren't supposed to bend.

The pickax tumbled to the carpet beside my head. I twisted, put my feet underneath me, and bolted down the hallway, deeper into the hotel. As I ran, the left side of the building, the walls, the doors, the rooms beyond those doors, fell away. The carpeted hallway followed along a cliff edge. The hotel was in mid-demolition, and from that cliff edge, I looked out of the building and onto a star-sugared night sky looming over a dark forest. Below the cliff, there was no floor, but mounds of rubble, and rebar spikes, and splintered and broken two-by-fours. A bolt of lightning flashed overhead. Electric blue light reflected off rain-soaked cranes and bulldozers. All the while, I never stopped running. If I'd mapped it out right, if this hotel still obeyed the rules of geography, I was heading back toward the front. That big wide staircase would bring me back to the main entry, out to a bright and mild summer day, back to Ruby, and away from here.

When the killer exploded out of a hotel room door to my right, he carried Scotty by the collar with him. Scotty's feet didn't touch the ground. He was pawing at the mask and craning his neck around his shoulder, trying to see down into the pit below. It was useless. The killer heaved him out and over the abyss just as I sprinted by, determined to get back to the exit. Scotty cried as he fell. I couldn't help but turn and watch him land into a nest of steel rods and busted, sharp, wood studs. His cries stopped.

I didn't.

That cliff's edge of a hallway fed back into the middle of the hotel as if my path were a tunnel cut through rock. The hotel's wound sealed itself back shut. As I sprinted for the front, doors reappeared on both sides of me. That brought no comfort, only more terrible, terrible possibilities. He was still behind me, but that meant nothing. If he wanted to be in front of me or to either side of me or above me, all he had to do was wish it. This place was his home. He was the hotel's sole caretaker. It was as much a part of him as his mask. Still, I ran.

Until I heard my best friend scream my name. My feet stopped underneath me. Not because I wanted them to. They just did.

Both hotel room doors were open to either side of me. From which one came her cry, I couldn't tell. To my left, Room 237 was dark and empty. To my right, mist clouded the ceiling of Room 217. An orangish light shined from somewhere around a corner.

"Cheryl?" I called to her and stepped into Room 217.

A shower was running, making that TV static sound of no sound. I moved through the short entryway to the main area of the room. There was one bed, made and undisturbed. A familiar red, lacy bra and panty set waited there. The same set she'd been wearing each time. Because all of this had happened before. And all of this would happen again. The bathroom door was open. I took a wide path around the door to see inside but not get too close. Behind me, the hallway was empty. The killer hadn't followed me. Maybe he didn't see me slip inside. Maybe this was all a part of his game.

Steam filled the bathroom. The water ran. Nothing moved. My right foot stepped onto the tile.

The plastic shower curtain burst open. Cheryl fell through it, grasping and ripping the thin metal rings from the curtain rod. She crawled over the lip of the tub, her nails like animal claws did their best to grip and dig into the tile and pull her wet, sheening body out of the shower's spray. One of her nails popped free from her nail bed. Blood mixed with hot water. When she lifted her eyes up toward mine, her wet, blonde hair parted like stage curtains. Her face was painted in confusion and anguish. I backed away, because, of course, there was nothing I could do to help her.

"Cheryl, what's wrong?" I said. "What's happening here? What's happening to me?"

Her smooth, young skin bubbled and blistered. She stretched a palm toward me, almost reaching the fabric of my hoodie. "Help me. Taylor… Help. Please."

I staggered backward, out of the bathroom and toward the hotel room door, as if my body wasn't my own. I wanted to help my friend. I wanted to end whatever misery she suffered, but it was as if everything around me moved while I stayed still. Meanwhile, Cheryl lifted herself up on the frame of the bathroom door like a boxer climbing up the ropes while a ref counted to ten. Her skin flaked away and exposed black rotting flesh underneath. When her hand slipped on the doorframe, she left a bloody filet of her palm on the wood. Her other hand stretched toward me.

"The water… It was too hot… I'm… I'm falling apart," she said through her failing throat, tongue, and lips. From that splayed hand reaching for me, a finger came loose and fell to the carpet.

But she managed to stay on her feet, even as a thick slab of skin and muscle peeled away from her thigh and flopped dead on the floor. Her exposed breasts, when I'd seen them before, were icons of sexual beauty and maturity, everything I envied for myself. But this sight was nothing anyone would want. Her chest melted like wax. Her belly button and vagina bled an inhomogeneous black tar. Her skin fell away and exposed bare ribs and clavicles. Weak lungs under a thin layer of flesh moved the bones. Her ankle cracked with the sound of a base hit and her fibula and tibia stabbed into the carpet and kept her upright. She still came for me, both of her rotting hands groping for me.

"Help me, Taylor," she groaned. "Help me!"

Then we were out of Room 217, and she was following me across the hallway. Just as I crossed into Room 237, the membrane of her left eyeball ruptured and white ooze like school glue leaked down her decomposing cheek. Then the door slammed shut, closing her off away from me.

And in her place, previously hidden behind the open door but blocking my way out, was Barb. She was dressed plainly, casually, in clothes she might wear golfing or to an outdoor work function. Daylight came through the back of the hotel room and shined on her face. Nothing about her suggested rot or decay. Nothing about her hinted at maliciousness besides a nasty smirk stretched across her lips and a squint in her eyes.

"I knew you'd come here, Taylor," she said and backed me further away from the closed door. "I just knew it."

She shoved me as hard as she could, and with me already backing away, it wasn't hard for her to tip me over my heels. I fell, not just to the floor, but through where the floor should have been. I whirled my arms as I plummeted through the partially demolished second floor and down into what waited for me below.

Chapter Twenty One

I descended through the daylight into a pit of loose debris. Rather than being impaled on the rebar and two-by-fours, I landed on a pile of broken sheetrock and tumbled downhill into the bottom of a maw. Dislodged trash poured down over me. I sank through chunks of broken sheetrock, lumber reduced to splitters, bricks and concrete rendered back into mortar, and nails and screws and a million shards of glass. There was no bottom. As I grabbed and clawed at the rubble, the mass shifted over my head, and I slipped further from sunlight. I came to rest, deep below the surface. The weight of the material pressed down around me.

I must have gone through the second floor, through the ground floor, and down to the very basement of the hotel where all its broken remains gathered. But I could still see blue sky through the loose pieces of boards and steel beams above me. My hand still touched the open air. I could wave for help. There was hardly any room for my chest to expand and my lungs to fill with air, but I could still call out. My toe found the corner of a partially intact cinder block, and I could push off. I could get free. I could escape.

And then I was going to murder that bitch that put me here.

My foot pressed up off the cinder block. My shoulders wiggled around a two-by-four that was pressing down against it. My ribs found a little more room to expand. My right hand that was stretched toward the sky couldn't touch anything other than air, but my left found a chunk of busted-up concrete I could pull on for leverage.

The garbage pile shifted. My toe slid off the cinder block. My body slipped further down into the wreckage. But my one hand was still above the mound, and I could still breathe. I worked my feet and hands for more purchases, anything I could use to press against and worm my way back to the surface. A chunk of twisted steel. A sheet of particle board I managed to get my knee on top of. A vein of crumbling bricks I could shovel below me with my left hand. I worked my way up, slowly, patiently, methodically, never panicking, never letting reality free from my tenuous gasp.

Barb had lured me here, intentionally, for the sole purpose of burying me in this pit. She planned this. She took advantage of my past trauma. She followed through with it. She shoved me. As for the rest of it, the visions of the killer from my youth, the midnight rainstorm, the murdered corpses of my high school friends, the image of my best friend actively decomposing and reaching out to me for help I couldn't provide… Those things were just bad memories from my youth, from the first time I'd come to this hotel. Flashbacks from a time I'd already escaped. Hallucinations. They had no place here. I had to focus on shifting my way through the garbage, and then on what I'd do to Barbara once I was free.

And then she was above me.

"Ugh," she groaned through that hole that led up to the sky. "Are you seriously not dead?"

My hand, the only part of me above the trash, flailed and stretched out to her. All she had to do was grab it. "Help," I pleaded.

"What's that? You want me to help you?" Barb said, her hands firmly planted on her hips as she lorded over me. "Let me tell you exactly why that isn't going to happen."

"Grab my hand," I said as gravel and dust spilled down the hole and into my eyes. Beyond all rationale, I believed there was no way this mousey, polite woman from work would ever have the heart of ice to abandon me there.

"No. I'm not going to grab your hand, and here's why," she said, but had to gather herself, blink away some tears, and sum up her courage before going on, too prideful to allow herself to get emotional in front of me. "You took everything from me. Doctor Cal told me what you did. He told me all about how you lied and said he assaulted you, and how you reported it, and how, because of you, he's accused and under investigation and on administrative leave, and how you did it all to ruin his career.

"You took him away from me! Well, you tried anyway, didn't you?" she taunted me. "Don't you get it, you lonely, psycho bitch?"

From down by my hip, muffled by all of the old, broken, construction material, Bitch answered, "Yes?"

My cell phone! It was voice-activated and still had five percent or so left in it. I could call for help, and Stephen would come. All I had to do was say his name. But not yet. Not while Barb still waited above me.

"I love him!" she wailed from the surface. "Maybe you can't understand that, but Doctor Cal and I have something so much more special than anything you could possibly understand. He is the only one who knows who I should be and what I can become. He is my master! After Jason finally fired you, I figured it out. I went to Doctor Cal's home and found him there, alone, too ashamed to come out because of your lies. But he opened the door for me, and I'm bringing him back. He's coming to the retreat. He's going to be our keynote speaker. And I'm going to make sure Jason finds out exactly who you are, and what lies you told, and how you tried to ruin him. Then everyone will know just how great of a therapist Doctor Cal is. And down there, in that hole, you can't do a thing to stop me."

She stepped away to where I could no longer see her through the narrow tunnel of the garbage, and not seeing her was worse. The last words she said, spoken with such certainty, left no doubt it wasn't just a threat, but a promise for more. It didn't take me long to figure out why.

The thunk and whirl of hydraulics came from above, followed by the groan of strained steel. A shadow blocked out the sun. The open tailgate of a dump truck drew over the opening above my head. To the soundtrack of steel on steel screeching, tons of demolition waste poured out. A thousand bits of rubble, broken boards, and detritus dumped out of the steel bed and down into the pit. I sucked my hand back down below the surface and slipped my knee off the lip of the sheetrock. My toe let go of that cinder block and I slipped further down. I had to. My only shelter from the crushing debris was the farther depths of the pit. Bricks and steel beams and gravel and paper all rained down on me. The already present two-by-fours filtered out the worst of it, the largest most dangerous pieces, but the sand… There was so much sand and dust and mortar and gravel, I couldn't keep my eyes open. I looked away and the grit poured into my hair, my ear, and down my shirt. It blotted out the sun. There came a point where I didn't know if I was voluntarily digging myself deeper into the pit or if I was being pushed down by the new weight above my head. The trash compressed around me. Two pieces of garbage bore down on my right arm, clamping it in place like a vise. I couldn't see what those pieces were, if they were something forgiving like sheetrock that might break before my radius and ulna, or things that would snap my bones without ever giving an inch. Before my descent was complete, my knees were bent up by my chest, and I was rolled up in a tight ball.

The mound of debris settled. A few more nails and bits of glass tinkered down through the larger pieces like quarters from a spent slot machine. Everything was dark. There were no sounds from above. My lungs, crammed as they were, pumped in and out feverishly. When they sucked in, dirt and dust flew into my mouth. I coughed and sputtered, but that only forced me to inhale again and take in more dry particulates. Then came another bout of hacking and wheezing. The air around my head turned warm and rich in carbon dioxide.

I couldn't panic. I had to calm myself. I had to preserve oxygen. Until what? Until I could call Stephen to come and get me. It had to be him. If it was any other cop, they'd arrest me. They wouldn't believe me when I told them it was my coworker, that kind, chipper, Minnesota-nice gal from work who shoved me into a garbage heap and buried me alive.

Oh my god, I was buried alive.

I couldn't run. I couldn't move. Any attempt at repositioning a limb was met with firm resistance. Even if I turned my head, more dirt and gravel poured down to fill the void. If I kept at it, I'd only hasten my own suffocation. And Stephen was an hour and a half away. I'd be dead by the time he reached me.

"Bitch?" I called through what little gaps of air existed around me.

"Yes?" her upbeat voice, so eager to please, responded.

"I need help," I said.

"Shall I call 911?" she asked, her never-anything-other-than-pleasant voice was muffled through the rubble, but still audible.

"I don't want them near me," I said, the control in my voice beginning to unravel. I didn't know what I wanted, but I didn't want some beat cop from the sticks, some sheriff's deputy, coming only to throw me in handcuffs and in the back of his car.

The wet, sticky, warmth of blood crawled down my cheek. Was it from a cut in my scalp? Or was the blood from the hotel flooding into the garbage pit, soon to drown me in its cordial embrace?

"Is Ruby still out there?" I asked.

"Yes," Bitch answered.

"Is she okay?" I asked.

"She's okay," Bitch soothed me. "That cunt Barbara didn't even look at her when she drove that piece of shit Honda out of the lot. She doesn't appreciate things the way you do."

"I know," I said. "What about Chucky? Is my dog okay?"

"Chucky's at home. Safe and sound," Bitch reassured me. "He misses you."

"I know," I moaned.

"If you don't get out of this hole, you'll die down here Taylor," Bitch told me. The cheeriness drained out of her voice until only cold honesty remained.

"I know," and I did know it. But hearing it from someone else, someone outside of my own head made it so much more real. Fear soaked my every word. The tears were really flowing now, mixing with the syrupy trails of blood. The flow continued down from above me, onto my head, my shoulders, my limps. I tugged at my right arm to get it free, but it wouldn't budge. My thighs strained to straighten and push up, but the weight above me didn't shift.

"What are you going to do?" Bitch asked.

"I don't know," I sobbed.

"What are you going to do, Taylor?" Bitch asked again, stern now.

"Call the cops," I caved. "Call Nine One One. Whoever's closets. They need to rescue me."

"You never needed to be rescued," Bitch said, mean now, as if reprimanding me. No dish soap saleswoman or teen cheerleader sugar sweetness in her anymore. This voice was different than her default voice. More real.

I heard that other voice of hers too, beyond a veil and muffled by trash. The old boring, generic, corporate aren't-we-all-so-happy-with-the-product voice. It said, "Calling: Nine One One."

And following that, after just a few rings cut up by the intermittent connection, came another voice. "Nine One One. What is the— of— emergency?"

"I'm stuck," I cried. "I'm buried alive! I need help! I need to be rescued!"

"I'm sorry ma'am. I think we— connect— is this address?" the staccato voice came back.

"No one ever rescued you before," Bitch chided me. "You rescued you. You don't need them."

"I don't know the address," I said to the Nine One One operator. "Bitch told me how to get here. Barb sent me here. She's the one who pushed me down into this pit. She's the one who dumped more trash down on top of me. She's responsible for all of this."

"— explain to me— I can have EMS come to—" the dispatcher said.

"They can't hear you, Taylor," Bitch said, much louder, as if her lips were right next to my ear now. "If they do come, they won't help you. They have nothing to do with what you're dealing with anyway. Barb is responsible. Tyler and Jason and Doctor Hagari and all of the rest of them too. They put you down here. Each day of your life they dug this hole for you and set you up for the fall. And then when you were at your weakest, they had Barb push in. So. What are you going to do, Taylor?"

"I'm going to kill her," I said, some resolve coming back into my voice. "I'm going to kill them all."

"Get me out of your pocket," Bitch said. "Use my flashlight. I still have three percent of my battery left. There's a way out of here."

"I can't move my arm," I said.

"Stop whining," Bitch snapped back.

"Ma'am, help is on the way," the dispatcher's voice came in pure and unbroken for that one short sentence.

"I don't need help!" I yelled, even though it brought more dirt into my mouth when I did. I chewed the dry, salty granules. They couldn't choke me if I swallowed them.

"Use your other arm," Bitch coached me. "Your free arm. You can reach."

My left hand was free. My phone was in my hoodie's kangaroo pouch, I could feel it against my stomach. But the material was twisted and pulled to my right hip. There wasn't much room. In order to move my left arm, I had to create space by shifting my torso away. I twisted my hip. My fingers crawled across my belly, fighting to find the opening of the big middle pocket and work their way through. I sucked in my stomach and held my breath to create space. The tip of my middle finger brushed the phone case. It was coated in dirt now; the dried-up ice cream had acted like glue. My hand crept through the fabric, closer. Another two inches. Another inch. I pinched the corner with my thumb and forefinger.

"Don't you fucking drop me," Bitch said.

"I got you. I got you, you bitch," I said and pulled the phone free from my pocket. And then, with growing resolve, I addressed her other voice. Her pleasant product voice. "Bitch, hang up the phone."

"Call to Nine One One: Ended."

To get to the flashlight app, I just needed to press my thumbprint on the home button, swipe up, and tap at the lower left corner. I didn't need to see the screen to do that. Even as the lock screen and then the home screen lit up, I could see more of my prison. When I tapped on the flashlight, it was like a constant bolt of lightning illuminating the pit. I squinted my eyes shut until they had time to adjust.

There was more room inside of that garbage heap than I'd previously thought. All kinds of space between layers of particle board and sheetrock and lumber. There was no tunnel upwards. No way out that way. But there was room to move horizontally.

Now that I could see, I maneuvered my elbow into gaps and worked my left arm around to aim the flashlight at the things pinning my right arm in place. My head scrunched down, and a little more of the debris above me settled lower, compressing me further. My eyes got level with my trapped arm, and I saw right away what was holding it in place. Below my forearm was a solid cinder block. No wiggle room there. Above it, clamping my flesh in place, was a long length of rebar held down by the garbage above. My arm was a fulcrum between the cinderblock and the rebar. The rebar was a lever, and I had all the mechanical advantage right above my shoulder. All it would take was a little strength applied in the right place.

Slipping my phone into the waistband of my yoga pants, I kept the bulb up and outward. My hand squirmed up and found the end of the rebar. I pressed up with all my strength and ignored the dust filtering through my grinding teeth. Things shifted. The pressure alleviated from my right forearm. My own blood lubricated my skin and let me slip a few inches until my wrist caught against the cinderblock. My strength gave out. The weight came back down.

"Stuck. Still fucking stuck," I said.

"Stop whining," Bitch said. "Another push. Do it again. Again!"

I inhaled and swallowed more dirt. I flexed my thighs. I regripped the rebar and, all at once, pushed with my left arm and pulled with my right. A gap opened up between the metal bar and the cinderblock. My wrist came free. It hurt like hell. I must have ripped open a good amount of skin on that last pull because my whole arm was wet now. But as unsanitary as it may have been, the dirt and mortar dust staunched the bleeding quickly. I wasn't going to suffocate, and I wasn't going to bleed out.

"I still can't go up," I said.

"You don't need to go up," Bitch said, growing tired of my stupidity now. "The closer to the bottom, the bigger the pieces are, and the more room you'll have. Don't climb up. Crawl out through the gaps."

Nursing my right arm, I relied on my left to do most of the work. I jostled the bits of wood and rubble I could out of the way, then dug my phone out of my waistband to scan each empty space with the beam of the flashlight.

"There," Bitch said. "That gap right there, between the big sheet of plywood and the broken bricks."

I saw the same thing she did. "There's not much room," I said.

"You don't need much room. You just need enough room," she said.

"I don't like tight places," I said, the very sight of that slim space in the debris brought up bad memories of laundry chutes and metal lockers. "I want to run. I just want to get out of here and run!"

"Then crawl!" Bitch demanded.

I could do it. I didn't want to. I *really* didn't want to. I'd have to contort my body, going sideways so my shoulders wouldn't catch, but I could at least get into the gap. That wasn't saying I could go any further than that, but it was a start. As I twisted, more rumbled sifted down in the empty space I abandoned. No going back. My head ducked into the space. My toes pushed me further inside. My arms were forced to my side. I couldn't aim the light from my phone ahead of me.

"I can't tell where I'm going. How do I know if this goes anywhere?" I said.

"Do you want to stay down here? Do you want to die a victim? Or are you going to do what you said you're going to do?" Bitch asked, her voice snarls now.

"I'm getting out of here," I growled as I pushed further and further through the space.

"And then?" Bitch asked.

"And then I'm going to get into Ruby, and I'm going to track them all down, and I'm going to murder every single one of them," I promised.

Bitch made a digital noise like a swoon. Then her battery gave up its ghost and the flashlight blinked out. Dead.

The collective weight of the debris pushed down on me. The darkness closed in around me. As I pushed forward with my toes, I wedged myself into the tightest space yet. For a moment, the terror of being trapped down there flooded in to fill a void left by Bitch's flashlight.

But I wasn't left in total darkness. There was a dim shine ahead. A trapezoid shape of soft, filtered daylight. That mound of rubble had been dumped into the hotel's basement, but it didn't cover all of the basement. There was a way out sideways, and I was inching toward it with every push and pull. The gap narrowed closer, so close my ribs didn't have the room to expand. But there was no going back. Not after everything I'd been through. Another shift of my hips, another creep of my toes, and I came closer to the edge. The weight of the trash lightened, and I could push it off my shoulders. I made myself more room. I wiggled. I pushed. I dug my right hand out ahead of me and slapped it against a cold, hard, concrete floor. Pushing, pulling, squirming, straining, grinding my teeth, I slipped free and tumbled down onto the basement floor.

Gasping for breath, covered in dust and mortar and dirt and blood, dusty eyes still burning and adjusting to the dim basement light, my ears detected the faint wail of police sirens in the distance.

"Now," Bitch said into my ear. "Now, you can run."

Chapter Twenty Two

I hobbled up the basement staircase, dragging along a right ankle that felt like a bag of broken glass. By the time I reached the hotel's first floor, coming into an industrial laundry room, the pain dulled, and my strides grew longer and stronger. I pushed through the doors into the main hallway and daylight met me. Police sirens were loud and coming closer as I trotted through the lobby. That TV was dead again, just an ashen screen with no sound. I shoved through the front doors and broke into a healthy jog. Barb's Honda CRV was gone; no surprise there. She'd played her cards. Now it was time for me to play mine. I ran full speed toward Ruby, all those aches and pains and cuts forgotten. I slipped into the cradle behind her wheel and pressed the ignition button. She awoke singing that finely tuned song from deep under her hood. All the needles on her dash launched over to the far right side of the gauges and then settled back to the left. We found first gear together, just as two police cars poured into the parking lot.

With the wheel cranked all the way to the left, my right foot all the way down on the accelerator, and my left feathering the brake, Ruby's rear tires smoked, and her back end rotated around her nose until we were both pointed toward the entrance of the lot. We shifted into second gear as a fire truck followed the cop cars. When I eased off the brakes and straightened the wheel, we catapulted away from the flashing lights and onto the highway. We cut off traffic and swerved between curbs, found overdrive, and barreled down the center white stripe. We were well over sixty miles per hour when I spotted those cop cars with their sirens and cherries in the rearview mirror.

I was supposed to be the victim, but they didn't understand that. Run from the source of a 911 call, and they'll only see you as a perpetrator.

They didn't understand what we had humming under the hood either. Just by starting the pursuit, they'd underestimated who we were and what we were capable of. Ruby's tachometer and speedometer climbed to the right in sync. Her engine found its chorus. We weaved around slower, weekend travelers like trout swimming around river rocks. One hundred miles per hour. One twenty. One thirty. One forty. The cry of the sirens faded to inaudibility. The lights were distant flickers in the daylight. Soon, they'd call off the pursuit. It was too dangerous for them. Too risky. Besides, they had some poor woman to dig out of a hole back there. She was the one who called them and needed their help. Because she was clearly the victim in all of this. Clearly whoever was driving the Camaro was the perpetrator. Right?

"Well…"

Right.

If I was lucky, I'd come across Barbara's CRV on the highway. I checked each blue SUV crossover we passed just in case. She had to be heading for wherever they were actually holding the retreat, but the problem was I had no idea where that might be. I paid no attention when I'd booked the place, if the place I booked was even the place where they were holding the conference. Most likely, Barb sent me some bullshit to throw me off and then canceled that transaction and booked it somewhere else. For all I knew, she had me book the abandoned and half-demolition hotel we'd just come from. But I had a better, more certain plan. I had to go to the office. She'd have records on her desk. Printed out receipts and contracts. Barb loved hard copies. Always had mounds of random papers scattered over her desk. It'd be her downfall.

The cops were gone from the rearview mirror, but I kept Ruby running hot the whole way back to the cities. Barb's CRV was nowhere to be found.

Minneapolis on a Saturday morning is either a ghost town or packed with all the drunk sports fans of whichever team is playing in town that day. It must have been an away game that Saturday. Ruby and I rolled in, unabated by traffic congestion and herd migration of beer bellies crammed into replica jerseys. I found street parking on Eighth Street and set Ruby next to the curb. She slept there, ready to fly again as soon as I needed her. All fifty seven towering stories of the IDS Center loomed over us.

A quick flip of the sun visor showed me my reflection. It wasn't good. My hair was caked and matted. The blood and mortar had hardened to my scalp. My eyes were dried up and bloodshot. Dust covered my face everywhere except where tears and snot and drool had cut clean riverbeds through the grim. My clothes were filthy, soiled, and peppered with tears and holes like a World War II bomber that had barely made it back from the last run. Not exactly appropriate work attire, but if I had a paper cup and a seat on the sidewalk, I bet I would have had a source of income. I snapped the visor closed and stepped out.

The doors to the big glass atrium with the big patriotic flag were unlocked. Plenty of natural light shined through the glass, but no one was behind the security desk. Violetta must not have prioritized my separation because my Team Next Paradigms ID card still opened the elevator doors. I hit our floor number and rode up. When the doors binged open, I stepped into a darkened version of the offices that was all too familiar. Nothing changed since I'd last left, sans my job. The automatic lights popped on, silently, one after another, following me into the interior of our cubicle farm. My workspace had the same scant bits of office supplies it had before I was fired. But two cubicles over was Barb's, and that workspace looked like an industrial-sized recycling center. Papers. Everywhere.

The address of the venue. That was all I needed. A receipt. An itinerary. An invitation. All of which, you would think, would be digital and locked away securely inside of her dual-authenticated work computer. But that wasn't Barb. If a series of ones and zeroes entered her computer, they inevitably transferred to the printer where they became toner and paper. Each sheet was another addition to her chaotic collection, like eight and a half by eleven leaves fallen from an oak tree in October. I had no doubt I'd find what I needed in one of the stacks on her desk, but why did she have so much bullshit? Seriously, who prints out a spreadsheet? What good was it as soon as it was printed and stripped of all its functionality? A good amount of it wasn't even work-related. She has the results from an online Genealogy and Me test. She had articles on dealing with a toddler's "terrible twos." And under that, was a print-out of a Wikipedia page on

Neolithic death masks. I was about to give up until I glanced up, paranoid of security investigating an off-hours entry of the building, when I spotted the sticky note glued to the side of her computer monitor.

In her own hand-written scrawl was the reminder, "Deposit for Bayview Lodge."

Bayview Lodge was one of those classic, Minnesota, up-north resorts with a PGA-rated golf course, on-site catering, conference rooms, hotel rooms, cabins, and of course, a big, beautiful view of a lakeside. Just the kind of place Barb wanted for the work retreat. Bayview Lodge, just north of Brainerd. That's where the work retreat was. That's where they all were. I snatched the sticky note off the edge of the screen and confirmed what the words spelled out in her loopy, semi-cursive handwriting. It said what it said, and I knew what it meant. And I was about to take the sticky note with me and go until I looked down at the papers I'd scattered across the desk.

Underneath the Wikipedia article on the Neolithic death masks was a printed-out email. It was dated July 24th, in the middle of my treatment. It was from Doctor Hagari to Barb. Like one leaf from the pile, I slipped the paper out of the stack.

> Everything you warned me about her has come to fruition. You're a very insightful woman. But I believe I have an apt solution you might find fitting. I can't pass along all the details, but the attachment will give you a hint of what I have in store for our little office problem.

I didn't understand what that meant. Not yet. But there were more emails lying below this one. Fast forwarding in time, the next Barb sent just yesterday. The whole team was in the To: line. The whole team except me. The Subject was "Doctor Cal needs Us."

> I'm sure by now, you've all heard what has happened to our most senior and most respected provider. Doctor Cal Hagari has been put on temporary administrative leave due to false and baseless accusations of sexual harassment. And you can probably tell who made those accusations

based on who's not included in this email. That's right, our little office problem has branched out!

I can tell you from my own personal and professional relationship with him that Doctor Cal is a good man. He needs our support now more than ever. If each of us reaches out to corporate's HR department and vouches for his constant professionalism, dedication, kindness, compassion, skill

… and on and on and on.

After her gushing was over Hagari, Jason replied. All. It was brief.

Doctor Hagari is a valued resource. Team Next in the Twin Cities wouldn't be where it is without him. We'll be sure to support him through these difficult times.

And what was this about "our little office problem?" Is that what they called me behind my back? In their cute little private chats and calls? That bitch! Barb had told them all about my confidential, mental health sessions and now she had them gathering up pitchforks and torches to hunt me down. All for that smiling, touchy-feely pervert of an old man, the Good Doctor Cal Hagari. She wasn't even supposed to know. None of them were supposed to know that I'd attended sessions with Doctor Hagari, or that I filed a confidential, sexual assault report with corporate. Besides Jason. And only him because he assigned me to the counseling session. But they all knew, and they were all just fine turning on me after I'd filed my claim. That's what I got for trying to hold Hagari accountable. For saying anything. I was mocked, shunned, fired, and buried alive.

When I thought I'd found the end of it, I found more. From just below the printed-off email, there was a list of prescriptions that looked strikingly familiar. It should have. My name was at the top. Names, doses, frequencies, and instructions followed. Percocet, Ambien, Lunesta, Sonata, Mirapex, Cortisone, Adderall. The funny thing was, I don't remember taking these drugs. Or any drugs! There was a place for my signature at the bottom of the sheet, and some looping blue-ink swirls were above the line, and it sort of looked like my signature, only bigger and sloppier. The cute underscore of the Y of the last letter of the last name didn't end in the flourish the way I did it but dragged across the page as if I'd fallen asleep while writing it. But I had written it. I could tell it was mine. Just… drugged.

All these prescriptions I read with the paper still sitting on the stack, undisturbed, as if touching it would burn my fingers. As if I'd break through this false mirror world into reality and cut my hand on all the broken glass. But I had to look beyond it.

I slid the list of prescriptions off the stack for a closer inspection, and from below, two hollow eyes, a blank white face, and an eerily, toothy smile looked up at me. The face of the killer. The man who'd haunted me since the night by the lakeside, through my quiet suburban neighborhood, in the basement of our school, through the old, abandoned hotel. The man who killed all my friends and left me a mentally broken, alcoholic mess of an adult. As if the image of his mask was a snake coiled up to strike, I dropped all the papers in my hands and stumbled backward until I collided against the thin wall of Barb's cubicle. Sticky notes and birthday cards and photos of her and her dark haired husband and her stupid little redheaded kid flitted down to the carpet. My eyes fixed on the printed-out picture of my killer's mask.

How in the fuck did Barb have a picture of my killer's mask?

And that's when I noticed the picture was stapled to the list of my prescriptions. And if I flipped past the mask? What would I find stapled under that? Treatment notes? Diagnosis? I had to see.

Pushing off the cubicle wall, I approached the stack of papers on Barb's desk as if they could lash out with venomous stingers and teeth. Not wanting to touch it at all, I pinched the corner of the sheet of paper of my killer's mask and flipped it over. The next page was another email, this one from Doctor Hagari's personal, non-business, Yahoo account sent to Barb.

> Barb. You're the only one I can trust. Remember all the things we worked on together? I need you to handle our little problem. Permanently.

Nothing more than that. Just a single line of instructions from Hagari to Barb. He'd started all of this.

His office was just two floors up.

Chapter Twenty Three

"What did you think you'd find in Doctor Hagari's office?"

I don't know. I don't know specifically what drove me there. But I knew if I was going to find answers, I needed to get back inside of that office. Back where it all began.

"Is that where everything began? What about when you were seventeen? Back in '99?"

I wish my memories were clearer. More tangible. I wish I could grab them in a stranglehold, wrestle them to the ground, and force them to confess. My memories of "that night" back in high school. Of those places. Of my murdered friends. But also of my sessions with Doctor Hagari. They were as much of a blur as my distant past, and after seeing that list of prescriptions, I was beginning to understand why.

There were other offices on the fourteenth floor, so there were no security precautions getting off the elevator. As I marched down the hallway toward Doctor Hagari's office, I had my Team Next Paradigms ID card ready in my hand. When I first started my sessions, building security had added the credentials for his office onto my card. If they hadn't revoked them for Team Next Paradigms, there was a good chance my card would still get me into his office space as well.

And oh god, did I need to see what he had inside his office.

The frosted glass door of his lobby read "Hagari and Associates Mental Health Services." Below those words, printed in plain black Helvetica font on a sheet of printer paper was, "Due to Unforeseen

Circumstances, Dr. Hagari is no longer accepting any new clients." I swiped my card over the little magnetic reader embedded below the handle. It beeped cheerfully, flashed a green light, and a heavy piece of metal inside the lock withdrew. I eased the door open and slipped inside. All the lights stayed dark. The receptionist's desk was empty, as were the rest of the offices. Doctor Hagari's was straight ahead.

His door was similar to the outside door in most ways: frosted glass, copper letters spelling out "Doctor Calvin Hagari, Pys. D," but it had no electronic sensor for me to wave my card at. I tried the handle, and it rattled in place, refusing to rotate.

Locked. Okay. So this was going to take a little more gumption. Taking a step back, planting my front foot, and conjuring up my best Detective Stephen Hansen, I wound up and put my heel into the door, right below the locked handle.

The noise echoed through the solemn offices. The wood cracked but didn't break. I reset my feet and tried to ignore the pain radiating from my heel. There was just a small metal mechanism inside of that handle holding me back from what I needed. That was all. Another kick started with my knee in my chest and finished with all of my weight slamming against the door. That frosted glass pane rattled in its sill. If it came down to it, I could always break the glass and unlock it from the inside, but something about busting into this office, not breaking but busting in and shattering that metal mechanism, felt good. One more big, SWAT Team kick sent wood splinters airborne, metal bits chiming off the floor, and the door flying inward until it bounced off the back wall.

I was in.

And then it was like an FBI raid. I wasn't trying to be sneaky. This wasn't Watergate. I wasn't out to prove anything to the police or some journalist or to anyone other than me. I needed to know what he'd done to me. I needed to know why he'd prescribed all those meds that I never remembered taking, and why he had emailed an image of my killer's mask to, of all people, Barbara. I knew I told him all about what had happened to me back in high school. So sure, he could have done some research and found an image of it after I'd described it to him. Only that wasn't the case.

The date on the email he sent to Barbara was July 24th. Before I'd left the program. Before my last few sessions when I recounted to him the memories of my youth. But just after I'd reported his ass to HR. He sent her the image of my killer before I ever told him about my killer.

I ransacked his desk and found only the standard items you'd expect in an office desk during this modern age of emails and online calendars. Pens. Blank notepads. Paperclips. Trinkets. Unlike Barb's heap of a workstation rich in personal identifiable information, Hagari at least seemed to understand the surface-level legalities of sharing people's private health data. But I found a pair of keys on a ring. And there was another door behind me.

As best as my extremely faulty memory could recall, my initial sessions with the good doctor started in this very room. Beyond the desk with the computer and phone was a comfortable set of plush chairs and a chaise lounge. Just the setup you'd expect from any psychoanalyst worth his cigar since Sigmund Freud. We sat across from each other, in the chairs, me not feeling comfortable enough to lay down with the top of my head toward him, leaving him out of sight and me vulnerable. It turned out, I had good reason for that. But later on, when the sessions became hazier and harder to see clearly through the mirk of time, we were in a different room. One with a very different sort of chair. A chair with washable vinyl cushions and restraining straps. A chair you'd find in a dentist's office, or a dominatrix's dungeon, or maybe an insane asylum.

I eyed the door between the desk and the Freud-inspired furniture.

But there was another lock to open before I tried that one.

A locked filing cabinet drawer sat on the bottom right side of the desk. The smaller of the two keys slipped right in. As soon as I twisted it, the lock popped open, and the drawer rolled out on its casters. There were file folders, one after another, like the kind you'd put your tax returns in. Each folder had a plastic flap with a label, but rather than years going back a decade like your tax advisor recommends, these tabs had the names of patients. Sorted alphabetically by last name. Each hanging folder had a classy leather-bound notebook inside. It took me no time at all to find, "Mosely, Taylor." When I pulled out my notebook, it jarred loose memories of him holding it in his lap as his pen whirled away and took down notes.

The small leather book fell open to the front page as soon as it was in my palm. Handwritten notes in that old school cursive the elderly are so proud of scrawled across each lined page from top to bottom. The first few sheets were of little interest. I remembered these things. Most of it was rehashing "the incident" at Team Next which landed me in the doctor's care in the first place. "Shit happens," could have summarized it, but of course, he had to bloviate and pontificate in order to justify all those degrees he had hanging in frames on the wall.

After our first few sessions, he dared to jot down a bit of analysis: "Patient displays as a physically healthy forty year old female. Not married. No children. No strong relationships with parents, siblings, or family. Mother suffered from years of untreated alcoholism. Absent father. Patient has a history of alcohol dependence manifesting in binge drinking when feeling lonely or threatened. Aside from the incident—"

The "instance" being, of course, me coming to work blasted and putting each of my coworkers and my boss on blast in turn. My words; not his.

"—patient is high functioning. Denies use of illegal street drugs. Denies driving or partaking in high-risk behaviors while intoxicated. Denies multiple sex partners but is still dealing with a recent breakup with a possibly abusive boyfriend."

Possibly? This motherfucker…

"Patient remains defiant with typical antiauthoritarian and nonconformist traits even when not under the influence. But remains amiable with peers and socially aware. Perhaps due to her high-functioning alcoholic tendencies, patient is resistant to change."

Yeah. Pretty much. That was me. But he'd failed to mention a big part of what had shaped my entire adult life. Clear bouts of post-traumatic stress disorder manifested from the time a brutal fucking manic murdered my friends when I was seventeen. Never mind that. I'm sure that has nothing to do with why I'm a "high-functioning" mess of a middle-aged drunken woman-child. But what do I know?

The following pages were a lot of the same. Memories of the early sessions came back to me. Him trying to earn my trust. Me giving him the cold shoulder. Him coming on to me. Me doing everything I could to keep him at arm's distance. Him giving me his best smile as he stroked that "salt and cayenne pepper" beard of his. Me growing more distant and trying to use my suburbanite, passive-aggressive personality to paint him a picture that all I wanted from him was a god damn signature so my boss would let me come back to work. Not all of that was written down on those pages.

It didn't need to be. I remembered it. Every hellacious, insufferable, miserable visit.

Enough of what I did remember. It was time to sink my head under the filmy surface of the swamp and see what the murky waters hid down below.

I ripped the keys from the drawer and walked them over to the door. The bigger of the two keys slid in nicely. Each tooth and tumbler clicked into place. With a twist, the door eased open into a windowless chamber. My empty hand found the light switch, and with a flick, everything was laid out before me.

The dentist's chair stood in the center of the room. Thick leather and Velcro straps waited at the arms and ankles. A computer monitor on a multi-jointed armature hung over the chair's head. On a very clean and sanitized counter, next to a wash sink, were stacks of DVDs. And not any kind of psychiatric reference DVDs, or rewritable data DVDs to be put into a computer. These were movies. Horror movies with glossy black and blood-red cases.

I've never liked horror movies. Have never gone out of my way to watch any of them. But I knew their names by heart. Their names. Their characters. Their plots. Their quotes and quips. Their tropes. Their sequels. Their spoofs. I had an encyclopedic knowledge of everything stacked there on the counter. *The Exorcist* with the scariest little girl to ever appear in a horror flick, despite all the black-haired, soaking-wet mimics that came around in the late nineties and early two thousands that followed the path that Regan blazed. *Texas Chainsaw Massacre* and its "true story" that brought 70s exploitation films into the mainstream. *Halloween* that solidified "Slasher Flick" as an enduring genre. *Friday the 13th*, with Jason in his famous hockey mask not appearing until Part III that perfected the art. *A Nightmare on Elm Street* and its inferior, more surreal, but campier sequels. There were more. Plenty more.

My feet propelled me forward. The doctor's notes dangled from my fingers, almost forgotten. I'd been here before. I'd been in that chair. Tied down and vomiting obscenities, not all that dissimilar from Regan herself. Not only had I seen those cases sitting on the counter, but I'd watched those movies. *A Clockwork Orange. Re-animator. Scream. Child's Play. Rosemary's Baby. It Follows. Hellraiser. Jennifer's Body. Alien. House of a Thousand Corpses. I Spit on Your Grave. Paranormal Activity. Get Out.*

Silence of the Lambs. Hereditary. Nosferatu. From Dusk Till Dawn. The Blair Witch Project. The Cabin in the Woods. The Hills Have Eyes. The Conjuring. The Shining. The Thing. The Omen. The Fly. Saw. Us. X. It. Old. New. Big budget. Grindhouse. Oscar winners. Cult classics. All of them.

My shaking arm went to pick up one of the cases and knocked a half dozen orange prescription pill bottles into the sink. Percocet, Ambien, Lunesta, Sonata, Mirapex, Cortisone, Adderall. Each had my name, last then first, printed on the label. None of them were full. Most of them had only a few pills rattling around as the bottles skateboarded up and down the basin of the sink. Meanwhile, my hand landed on one of the DVDs. I turned it over and looked at the cover.

The Evil Dead. A woman was climbing out of a grave, only for a bloody arm to grab her by the throat and pull her back down. I remembered this one as well as the rest. Ash, the hero, was forced to kill off all of his friends as they each turned into zombies, one by one. There was his best friend Scotty, his girlfriend Linda, Cheryl, and…

Oh my god.

The characters. Ash and Linda. Scotty and Cheryl. Shelly instead of Shelton. And no Taylor.

But those people. They weren't my friends. They were Ash's.

I threw the DVD across the room. The case exploded against the wall and the disc went bouncing and rolling across the tile floor. It circled round and round until it spun like a dropped nickel, never coming to a stop but spinning faster and faster. My hip bumped against the chair. I hadn't realized I was backing up until it stopped me. Turning to see what it was, I saw the last surprise in that office waiting for me in the seat.

An oval white mask, featureless but two round hollow eyes and an open teethy grin, looked up at me.

Picking the thing up made me lose sensation in every part of my body except my fingertips. It was heavy, thick, and made of coarse unpolished clay. There were no straps to hang it over your head. Not like Jason's hockey mask. Small holes were carved where the ears should have been, and someone could tie string through those holes, but no one had. The only way to wear the mask was to hold it up in front of your face. That idea dislodged a memory from the cavern ceiling of my mind. An image dripped down my cranial stalactites and cleared away the moss from the pond. In it, Doctor Hagari with his curly red and white beard lifted the mask to his face as I lay in the chair looking up. His boring, pedestrian eyes peered through those dark circles. His lips moved behind those clay teeth.

"Take your medicine, Taylor. Take your medicine and enjoy the show." Then the monitor swung into place and the opening credits of another horror movie filled my vision.

Here in the present day, I collapsed into that chair while still holding the mask and the doctor's notebook. My thumb held the notes open to a page dated July 25th. Just after I'd reported him. Just after he sent that first email to Barb, hinting at his solution to their little problem.

"Barb was right. The patient is a vindictive, disaffectionate, unreachable, nonconformist. All my previous patients, Barb especially, were much more malleable and accepting of my influences. Never before in my professional career have I met a woman so unaccepting of my guidance and affection. And now she has created more than just 'little' problems.

"I've decided to attempt a different sort of treatment for this patient. While she is highly resistant to my counseling without intoxicants, she has shown a remarkable level of susceptibility to suggestion while influenced by certain prescriptions. I have done some research and have decided on a blend specifically selected to induce anxiety, confusion, and hallucinations. A cocktail of narcotics and nonbenzodiazepine sedative-hypnotics. She has so many things I can still teach her. I have such sights to show her!"

And all those things he showed me still clung to the gray matter of my brain, integrated into my memories so seamlessly there was no way to tell reality from fiction. The killer had never come to the cabin by the lake. Had never stalked through our childhood neighborhood. Hadn't lured us down into the basement of Anoka High School. Never murdered us in turn inside an abandoned hotel. Those killers had been Jason Vorhees, Michael Meyers, Freddy Krueger, and Jack Torrence. My only real villain, I understood now, was Doctor Cal Hagari.

He molested me. He drugged me. He built a past for me out of Blockbuster leftovers. He brainwashed me and turned me into what I had become. And I hated everything about him for it.

Chapter Twenty Four

I took the Neolithic death mask with me. I stole it, I suppose, but I felt like I had more of a right to it than anyone else on the planet since it was first carved from clay. It was my past, my personality, and my compulsion. Where Doctor Hagari got it, I had no idea, but it belonged to me now. Bringing the mask out of Hagari's office, down the elevator, and through the IDS atrium felt like repatriation. I was bringing it back to someone who knew death well. And to others who would learn death very quickly.

"So the police never had it."

No. I understand now that Tyler never brought it down into the Anoka High School boiler room. That was as much a figment of my brainwashing as the bodies of the friends I found hanging from meat hooks.

There in the Minneapolis, midday shine, I was the soulless, lumbering undead, clawed up from the grave to meander the mostly abandoned financial district and torment the living, and I had the creepy clay mask to prove it. Even the homeless dared not harass me.

I was coming around the corner of Nicollet and 7th Street, ready to fall back inside Ruby and hit the road when I heard the sirens. My first thought was that they'd caught up with me from the old hotel out west. But when the unmarked, blacked-out, Dodge Charger came screeching around the corner, I knew this wasn't some country bumpkin sheriff from the sticks. It was Stephen, and maybe it was only the silent alarm set in the frame of Doctor Hagari's private office that had called him here, but he was coming for me.

The black Charger with its flashing red and blue LEDs hidden behind the grill and windshield skidded to a stop perpendicularly across 7th Street. It washed me with a tide of aerosolized tire rubber and brake pads. No other police cars followed. MPD had more important things to worry about than a tripped alarm in some corporate office, but Stephen no doubt knew what it meant, connected it with me, and raced out of his own suburban jurisdiction to stop me. As if his one, lone, cop car could block off all of 7th Street. As if any boring, old, standard-issue, squad car was any match for Ruby.

As soon as the smoke rolled past me, he was standing outside of the Charger's door. His sidearm was leveled directly at my haggard face.

"Taylor!" he bellowed into the city, so loud, it stopped me three steps from Ruby's door. "I don't know what you think you're doing, but I know what you've done."

If he wanted to, he could have pulled the trigger then and there and made me dead all over again. The blocky end of that gun quivered between his eyes and mine, but it didn't fire. He was close enough to kill me but not close enough to catch me. His jaw muscles clenched and eased, clenched and eased, clenched and eased. His non-firing eye hung lazy, half shut. The pupil behind the sites bored into me deeper than any bullet could. But he wasn't going to shoot.

"Come catch me and find out," I said, then took the last three steps to Ruby, fast.

I fell in her seat as if she were custom-molded for me. The steering wheel, the pedals, the shifter, the mirrors all reached out to me as I reached out to her. With the push of her button, she awoke. Lights and vibrations and songs surrounded me. I've said before that Ruby sings. She doesn't growl or roar or rumble, and while she certainly had that deep guttural range, none of those words were accurate. Ruby was a choir. The basses and baritones of her engine harmonized with the tenors of her fans and the altos and sopranos of her supercharger. When I shifted into gear, she took a breath. When I put my foot down into her accelerator, she wailed.

The Neolithic death mask fell to the passenger seat next to me, eyes and smile up.

We could have just gone past Stephen. Around the front or rear bumper of his black Charger. There was plenty of space on either side. But he'd shown up with a flourish, skidding in sideways like a kid on his BMX bike thinking he was cool for kicking up a fan of rocks. I couldn't let Ruby be upstaged like that, so I shifted her into 1st and then stood on the gas and brakes till her fat tires burned. I cranked the wheel and eased up on the brake pedal until the rear end began to swing around like a screen door. Then it was Stephen bathed in a blue-gray cloud, and Ruby and I were pointed in the opposite direction. A quick shift into 2nd and a release of the brake pedal sent us catapulting down the glass and steel canals of downtown.

7th Street was a one-way, and I was going the wrong way. Thankfully, the streets were relatively clear on that Saturday, so I only had to weave once or twice around oncoming traffic before coming to 5th Avenue. A glance into the rearview showed me that Stephen was in hot pursuit. I expected nothing less. We hung a sharp left, Ruby's ass end kicking to the outside of the turn, me counter-steering into the skid to bring her back straight with the road. Stephen followed.

I had to get off the surface streets. Cross-traffic or a slow bus or the goddamn light rail train could bring me to a stop at any moment. And I couldn't really let Ruby off the leash until she had room to stretch her legs. In the meantime, we slipped under skyways and through intersections. The Armory, that big Art Deco concert venue the length of a whole city block, flashed by in a blink. 3rd Street was just ahead, and back toward the northwest, it funneled directly onto I-94. Then we'd be off to the races. With no turn signal or hint of my intentions, I whipped Ruby into another hard left, taking the turn as fast and as wide as I could, going from the outside edge of Fifth Avenue, nipping the curb of the inside corner, and skidding to the outside bike lane of Third Street. There were no cyclists, but I did have to swerve around a parked garbage truck. The momentum sent us swinging over the opposite curb and it took us a good three swoops before we were barreling straight down the center lane again.

Stephen was keeping pace, only a hundred yards behind me, following me turn for turn and weave for weave. I loved and hated his abilities and his car in equal measure. If I had lost him after the second turn, it would have left me unsatisfied and disappointed. I needed him to follow me just like he needed to chase me. But I wasn't going to take it easy on him. After all, I had other business to attend to, and he knew it, and he intended on stopping me, even if he didn't know all of my plans just yet.

Two blocks ahead, Hennepin Avenue crossed 3rd Street, and so did a whole lot of traffic. My light turned red just as their light turned green and released a sortie of slow-rolling civilians. There was no space to weave between them, and my only turn-off, Nicollet again, zipped by me before I could catch it. I had no choice but to stand on the brakes. All four of Ruby's thick tires seized up and left four long trails behind us. The Charger was braking too, and for a moment, I thought Stephen was going to rear-end us and push us into the crossing traffic, but at the last moment, he veered to my right. We came to a stop, side by side. He had his window down.

"Taylor?!" he yelled, half a demand and half a question in a way that told me if he had a few more seconds, he had all kinds of things to ask.

I hit the button on Ruby's touchscreen. Bitch played Miley Cyrus' cover of Blonde's "Heart of Glass," with the chaotic drum fill and cymbals buildup. Before Miley hit the first lyric, a gap in the traffic appeared before me. I racked Ruby into first gear and floored it. Stephen had a split-second delay waiting for traffic to clear. Then he plunged across Hennepin and was back on my tail.

Second and Third gear followed in quick succession. There was a red light across 1st Avenue, but not as much traffic. We plowed right through. 2nd Avenue was also red but with little traffic. I jacked the shifter back into fourth, and then forward into fifth, giving Ruby a breath between each of her lines as she and Miley sang their duet. As we crossed 2nd, a city bus rushed through the intersection to T-bone us. With only a split second to react, I cut to the right and pressed down harder on the accelerator. The bus's front bike rack slipped past Ruby's rear bumper by inches.

Stephen braked, the mist of his brake pads catching up with him for a breath. He cut left and then reappeared around the back end of the bus just as I charged up the ramp leading to I-94 and the open interstate. Finally, I slipped Ruby into overdrive. She was off the leash.

We crested the rise of the on-ramp, and when the roadway sloped downward there was one single moment where Ruby and I were removed from terra. All of it disconnected. All of it gone. All the noise of life momentarily and blissfully silenced. I would have been happy if it were possible to stay suspended there in that place and time where we were fluid and pure kinetic energy, riding the wave of chaos both behind me and ahead. It was zen. Not surrender. Not peace. Those things never interested me. But that sense of sustainable euphoria teased me as her four tires lifted off the pavement and we flew, still accelerating, still driving for what we needed, never satisfied but cumming in the middle of the effort… I could have been happy there, forever. But bliss is fleeting. Her four tires squawked when they touched down to Earth, and then it was back to business.

Warehouses and new hipster apartment complexes rolled by underneath us. Target Field, where the Twins did their best to play baseball, fell away to our back left. A check in the rearview mirror showed me that Stephen was still after us. Those red and blues still flashing from their hidden places in the all-black Dodge. The sound of the sirens still cried, but I couldn't hear it. The on ramp swooned down and to the right. We followed it and slipped into the furthest right lane of I-94's six northbound lanes.

The sky was himmel blue. Only a spattering of clouds. A perfect summer afternoon for a car chase. On I-94 proper now and in the highest gear, my right hand moved from shifter to the wheel. My eyes focused forward. Glances measured the black Charger behind us. I didn't want to lose him yet. I knew I needed to. But I didn't want to beat him so easily, not when Ruby and I were only now finding our top speed.

Stephen didn't disappoint, again.

Before I bought Ruby, back when she was just another car in the dealer's lot, I shopped around. I checked out the latest Chargers, Challengers, Mustangs… even a Porsche. Dodge had a wide spread between stock and insane models. Stephen's Charger was certainly an SRT with the supercharged V8 Hemi, but was it the Hellcat Redeye model with an additional two hundred and twenty five horsepower? I was confident that between Ruby and I, we could outmatch Stephen and a basic Charger, but if he was hiding something more under the hood?

We were redlining it, all needles on all the gauges buried to the right, when Bitch rang. "Incoming call from: Stephen The Hot Cop." This should be interesting. My finger mashed against the touchscreen.

"Well, I didn't think I'd hear from you so soon," I said.

"Taylor, what the fuck are you doing?" Stephen said back, no humor in his voice. Was he really pretending like this was all just part of his job?

"Giving you something to chase. What do you got under that hood? Did the local cop shop really spring for the Hellcat package, or are you actually managing to keep up with just the Scat Pack?"

The interstate flowed in calm, shallow curves alongside the Mississippi. We slipped around slower traffic like ribbon tails navigating the wind. Smoothly, naturally, never slowing down but instead propelled forward by the medium around us.

"I can make one call and have helicopters and half a dozen different departments all coming down around you. You can't out-run a radio, Taylor," he said.

"Speaking of, you're interrupting Miley Cyrus, so you better make this good," I said, slightly but honestly annoyed over it.

"Pull over and we can sort this out," Stephen said. "Whatever you think you're doing, won't work."

"You have no idea what I'm about to do," I told him.

"But I know what you've done," Stephen said. "The lab came back. We matched your fingerprints. We found hair samples that match yours. We know you were down in that basement where Tyler died. And I caught you red-handed breaking into offices in the IDS. If you ever want to stand a chase in court, pull over now and let me help you."

"And what if I don't? What if I don't want to go to court? Are you going to make me?"

He hesitated, not telling me "Yes." He didn't want to haul me into his boring and tedious legal system just to see me dressed in baggy oranges for some old judge and pedestrian jurors to tell me what I'd done and what should be. We were better than that. We were that perpetual orgasm of running and chasing, of breaking laws and straightening them back out again, of order and chaos. He belonged in this dance with me. He enjoyed it as much as I did. This was our zenith.

"Where are you going, Taylor?" he asked instead.

"If you're good enough, if you're smart enough, you'll get there shortly after I do," I said and pushed the "End Call" button on the touchscreen. That was the thing about men. Always leave them wanting more.

There were several exits coming up. I-694 drew to the east and west, but also Highway 252 to the north. I feinted toward the left exit, toward I-694 West, luring Stephen out of position. I waited as long as I could until

I wasn't sure if even Ruby could make the turn. A moment came when a slow delivery van was to Stephen's right, and we made our move: the tried and true pick-and-roll. I cut the wheel hard. Rubber tires melted to mist as they dragged along all four lanes of the concrete freeway from the far left to the far right and then across the yellow lines cutting a wedge between the 252 and 694 East exit ramps. Careening around the curve, Ruby's right tires found grass and churned up rooster tails of mulch and black dirt behind us. Eastbound and down, we poured onto 694.

Stephen hadn't reacted quickly enough. He was northbound on 252 and would be stuck that way until he could find a turnaround. It wouldn't take him long, but it was all the time Ruby would need. Multiple exits lay ahead. Highway 47. 65. I-35W. I could take any one of them, and he would be none the wiser. I stayed on until I-35W veered north toward Duluth.

And I never let off the gas.

Chapter Twenty Five

By the time I reached Bayview Lodge, the last light of the summer evening was bleeding down into the horizon. Darkness drew over the sky like a pall, as if hiding the horrible things that were about to happen from the innocent blue above. The resort was on the shores of a remote up-north lake, surrounded by swaths of pines. The main lodge was a modern and massive hotel with a pool, a bar and restaurant, conference rooms, and a convention center. Bitch was dead, and without a working charging port, there was no bringing her back to life. That meant I had to navigate by highway signs and billboards as if I was traveling with Louis and fucking Clark. But Ruby and I found our way. If Bitch had survived the combination of ice cream and gravel that kept her in the grave I'd escaped, I would have called the front desk and politely asked the receptionist where Team Next Paradigms had their accommodations. By now, this late in the evening, they'd be done with the "conference" portion and would have moved on to the "no-host social" which really just meant they'd be drinking back in their rooms.

I hoped they were staying in the isolated cabins along the shore and not inside the main lodge. After all, I wasn't trying to spoil any family's idealistic summer vacation. I just really needed to murder a few people.

With Ruby humming her quiet idle, I turned off the main road and onto a winding gravel driveway leading through the forest and down to the cabins. I turned off the music and Taylor Swift cut out. With the windows rolled down, I listened to a million crickets and leopard frogs and whippoorwills and other creatures of the night.

Despite everything I'd found in Doctor Hagari's office, despite knowing what he'd done to me, even as I built myself up to admit that the very night of my youth upon which I believed to be the foundation of my whole personality was a lie, my memories came back. This place… It was too similar to my initial recollection of "that night" at Scotty's uncle's cabin. All those night sounds, the gin-like smell of the pines, the blackness of the shadows, the bruise-colored evening sky, the diamond stars and opal moon shining through the boughs, the faint thumps of music and murmurs of laughter up ahead. No matter how often I glanced down to my passenger seat and reminded myself that the mask was with me and therefore couldn't be out there in the dark waiting to kill me, the memories persisted.

And blended.

Part of me knew, just knew, that I'd find myself stuck between floors of one of these cabins, or trapped inside a narrow changing room locker, or buried alive under mounds of construction waste. I'd find Shelton and Linda and Ash and Scotty and my best friend Cheryl hanging out of broken windows and on meat hooks and impaled on steel stakes and elk's antlers and swaying at the ends of nooses. I knew it. Even though those things never happened, I knew they were about to happen all over again. You can tell me those people aren't real, but you can't remove them from my mind. And if they're not real, am I?

"Cheryl is real. And alive. She told me about how you met on the street outside the IDS."

And the others?

"I'm sorry, Taylor."

What about you? I still can't see your face.

"I can assure you, Taylor, I am very real."

But if those memories were false, which were true? I don't remember anything else. I don't remember a typical, peaceful, boring, uneventful summer between my junior and senior year. I don't have any recollection of my "true" experiences. I only have these visions of slaughter and torture and torment. What did Hagari do with my real memories if the only things I remember are lies? I didn't understand as I idled Ruby down that narrow drive through the woods, but I was determined to find out.

Her lights splashed across a gravel parking area in front of three rustic log cabins. I killed her lights and let her roll to a stop. Around the gravel lot were all my coworker's cars. Jason's Tesla. Barb's CRV. And there in front of the far left cabin, was Doctor Hagari's BMW. How did I know it was his BMW? Well, first off, because of course that's what that pompous prick would drive, and secondly, because the license plate said, "DOC CAL."

"Bingo," I whispered to Ruby and let her motor purr her back to sleep.

The sounds of the woods amplified around me. A loon sang out on the lake. I took the mask from the passenger seat.

Even as the images of my friend's hung corpses filled in the gaps between the pine trunks, hatred boiled up inside me. Hagari was here, having a good old time with all of my former coworkers. Even though he was under suspension, under investigation, and even though they all knew why he was put on administrative leave. Barb made sure they all knew, and they had him here anyway. As their one and only keynote speaker.

I risked trying the driver's side door of his Beamer and found it unlocked. No alarm. Reaching under the dash, I popped the hood. The positive cable slipped off the battery terminal fairly easily. I tucked it down below the battery and eased the hood shut.

The music was coming from the cabin on the far left. But I wasn't going to just kick in the front door, screaming, waving my arms around like a maniac. I needed to know where everyone was before I did anything. And I needed a tool in my hands. Still holding the mask, I sulked around the outer side of the far-right cabin. There was still no way to wear it. It had no straps or strings to slip over my head, so, for the time being, I slipped the hood of my sweatshirt over my hair and stuck to the shadows.

Around the back, the conjoined lawns sloped down to the lakeside. Light from patio doors painted orange trapezoids across the wet grass. A cozy gazebo sat in the middle, empty and dark. A small dock jutted over the water. Tiny waves lapped against the thin strip of beach. Three unlit fire pits waited for packs of teenagers to pass around cinnamon-flavored whiskey and play naughty "adult" versions of Never Have I Ever and Truth or Dare. A tool shed stood over in a shadowed corner under the pine branches. Even as the dew soaked through my running shoes on the way to the shed, I could hear the muffled music from the far cabin. And laughter. They were all laughing at me. They were inside, together, partying and drinking and no doubt toasting their brilliant solution to their "little problem."

The wooden shed door opened and closed on rusted hinges. Once inside, the sound of the work retreat muted. A cricket silenced its violin as I took another step. A twine cord brushed my face. When I pulled on it, a dim light bulb burned a dirty orange. I didn't know what I needed out of that shed, but with one glance I knew I'd found it. To my left, Shelton hung crucified against the shed's wood frame. Screwdrivers pinned his hands out as wide as they could stretch. His throat was slit, and a curtain of blood hung down his bare chest. A few beads even made it across his pelvis, through his sparse patch of pubic hair, down his thighs, and to his feet which had been nailed in place with a metal tent stake. To my right was a wall covered with various groundskeeping tools hanging from hooks: rakes, shovels, hedge clippers, and a wood saw on an extendable pole for pruning tree branches. On the back wall was a workbench with a metal toolbox, a cast-iron vice, and a chainsaw. Outlines of wrenches, pliers, saws, hammers, and various tools had been drawn on a pegboard behind the bench. Two screwdrivers were missing from their places. A dark part of me that had survived on covetousness felt glee for the first time on seeing all those rusted sharp edges. But it was the roll of electrical tape that drew me in first.

I snatched the tape off the bench, and my fingernails went to work finding the start. A centimeter came up, and it was gummy and sticky and stretchy. Without fully understanding my own need to do so, without knowing my own motivations or even consciously deciding to do it, I pressed the rough clay bowl of that Neolithic death mask against my face. The ancient porous interior felt like cool, dried-up bones against my skin, as if I was putting a new skull over my own. The tail of the electrical tape stuck to the mask's forehead, and when I wound it around the back of my hoodie, it stayed in place. By the third wrap of tape around the mask and my head, I didn't need to hold it in place anymore. When it held firmly in place, not slipping down even a bit, I pulled the tape tight until it snapped off from the roll. I thought I heard him breathing behind me, that ultra-regulated, interminable cycle of inhales and exhales. Heat seemed to radiate through the mask's eye holes as if his bright red, burning pupils also sat behind the clay surface. But he wasn't there. It was only me. I breathed through my killer's smile. I looked through my killer's eyes.

Tools seemed to call out to me. The pitchfork. The hedge clippers. That jagged serrated saw at the end of the pole. I gathered them up like I was on a supermarket shopping spree.

"You won't be able to carry them all," Shelton mumbled through bloody lips.

"Shut up. You're just a character made up inside of my head," I told him.

"That doesn't mean I'm not real," he said and didn't lie.

Dragging implements behind me, I followed the lake shore across the three connected backyards. The porch lights cut long, triplet, gazebo shadows across the grass. As I stalked toward the far cabin, the one with all the music and laughter coming through the walls, I ducked behind the gazebo and watched the big glass patio doors through its spindles and lattice. The pruning saw slipped out of my grasp. A ball pein hammer followed it. I abandoned them in the wet grass and made my way to the edge of the forest. There, a shovel and a tire iron fell into the underbrush, and I was left holding the hedge clippers in one hand and a D-handled pitchfork in the other. That was fine. I was really only here to kill two people anyway. As for the others?

They were all inside the cabin in front of me. I watched them from behind the trunk of a thick and flaking Norwegian white pine. Jason sat at the kitchen table just on the other side of the patio door with a Four of Clubs stuck to his forehead, calling toward the kitchen. Barb's dull-eyed husband, Wes, sat next to Jason. An Ace of Spades was glued to his forehead. On the other side of the kitchen window, Robert and Roman cracked open two beers from the fridge and toasted them together. Roman's Joker slipped from his head as he tipped back his can. The next window over looked into a bedroom, and someone was moving around inside that orange square of light as well, pacing back and forth. When he paused in front of the window, my heart paused too.

It was Hagari. His red turning gray beard hid most of his face. A glare of his glasses shielded his eyes. He never looked my way, but the very sight of him sent me into a cold sweat. And he wasn't alone. Like an actress called from stage left, Barabara entered into frame. She was distressed. Alone in the bedroom together, and Doctor Hagari, being the steadfast therapist that he was, he comforted her. His hands lay on her shoulders. Her forehead sank into his chest. He petted her hair. When he lifted up her chin with the side of a finger, their lips met.

In the kitchen, good ol' black-haired Wes nudged and play-fought with Jason. Robert and Roman joined them at the table.

In the bedroom, "Doctor Cal" and Barb's lips reluctantly pulled apart. He brushed his patient's hair over her ear, leaned in, and whispered something just for her.

So Barb was having an affair with him. That explained quite a lot, but was I supposed to care? Did it matter to me one bit how her relationship with her husband was going? It didn't. I only cared that she knew everything that Hagari had done. That he tortured me and drove me insane and removed any possibilities of this run-of-the-mill, lonely, white, female alcoholic had for a healthy life. And if that wasn't enough, she had buried me alive and tried to kill me, all so she could maintain her naughty little affair. The others? In the kitchen? They were by no means innocent. They knew about it, and they allowed it to happen. They never spoke up. Never intervened. Refused to help. Sanctioned my abuse. Jason and Roman and Robert and yes, even that stupid, ignorant, husband Wes, were bathed in culpability.

"You'll be just like them," Linda said.

She hung from pine boughs like a baby at a mother's bosom, but instead of soft motherly hands, branches had punctured through her back and protruded out of her stomach and chest. She wore only underwear, the same as she had that night. Her head was lolled back. I must have looked upside down to her.

"If you kill them, you'll be just like the man who did this to us," she said, her hair dangling down toward the ground.

"I am him, and he is me," I told her.

The patio door opened. Barb had left the good doctor, collected her husband, and was now leading him outside. Theirs must have been the cabin nearest the tool shed, all the way back across the three shared lawns. She held him close as they walked in that way where she pulled his arm into her so he couldn't pull away. She was saying something to him. I couldn't hear what over all the crickets. Not that it mattered. They were going to their cabin, maybe to retrieve a sweatshirt, or more drinks, or maybe to have that first, honest, difficult conversation that would inevitably lead to divorce. Who was to say? No one, because Barb and Wes weren't going to be alive long enough for anyone to find out.

Carrying the pitchfork and hedge clippers with me, I shuffled, hunched over, out of the tree line, back to the gazebo. From there, I watched until they ducked into the patio door of the far cabin. That steady, mechanically-timed breathing followed me. No exhale faster or slower than the last. Every inhale like the slow pause between the ticks of a clock. But the two tools were one too many. I dropped the pitchfork so I could work the garden shears with both hands, then shuffled to the patio, up the steps, and to the side of the glass door. There, I waited.

"You seem to be in a good mood tonight," Wes said from the kitchen.

Where Barb went to, I didn't know. I couldn't see from my hiding place next to the patio door. Only hear. Their voices traded locations and volumes.

"It's just good to have everybody together in one place, you know?" Barb said.

"And without that bitch what's-her-name around to mess everything up," Wes added.

"Taylor," Barb grumbled. "And I hope to hell I never hear her name again."

Hope to hell was right. In her mind, I was still buried in demolition refuse at an abandoned hotel in the middle of nowhere. She was in the kitchen now. Had Wes gone into one of the back bedrooms?

"Well I'm glad you included me," he said, quieter now. "I know you've been planning this retreat for a long time."

She's cheating on you, you dumb fuck! That's why she's so happy. Her daddy doctor is free from his administrative leave, and she's happy because he's here. Not you! You stupid toilet clog!

"Oh, you're such a sweetheart," Barb crooned, and I swear she was right on the other side of the glass when she did.

So when the glass door slid open, I imagined her traitorous face peering out, and I didn't hesitate. Pivoting in front of the door, I opened the hedge clippers wide, stabbed them forward, and clamped them down as hard as I could on the neck standing there waiting for me. Wes never looked dumber than he did in the moment when those two giant scissor blades sliced into his flesh. Eyes as wide as lakes. Mouth open like a mine pit. Skull as empty as a jar. He'd managed to catch the right blade with his fingers, keeping that side of the shears away from his neck, but as I squeezed, blood splattered out from those fingers and the opposite side of his neck.

I plowed into the cabin, pushing his stunned mass over the dining room chairs, and knocking over the table as we went. When he tripped over one of the legs and fell over backward, I followed him, coming down on top. The tips of the clippers stabbed into the cabin's hardwood floor and kept me from snapping them further shut.

All the commotion brought Barb out from whatever backroom to find me on top of her moronic husband on the verge of cutting his head free from his torso. Like the typical victim she was, she stood at the end of the hall with a wine bottle and corkscrew in her hands and screamed. Wes uttered a series of monosyllabic objections and confused profanities. His flailing hand pawed at the mask and stretched out the electrical tape until it hung loose around my neck. That was fine. Let them know exactly how big their "little problem" had become.

With some effort, I pulled the tips of the garden shears out of the hardwood floor and turned them sideways so one handle rested on the floor. Then I heaved my weight up and back down on the higher of the two handles. Pumping the shears closer and closer shut, the blades sliced through Wes' fingers. They spilled to the floor like frozen pizza rolls on a microwavable plate. Then the blades met his carotid arteries with all the fanfare of red, liquid confetti poppers. He made a lot of weird guttural noises when they sliced through his trachea and esophagus, but shortly after that, with a few more pumps on the handle of the shears, the edges cinched through his spinal column. His head tumbled to the floor and rolled through the wet and bumped against his detached fingers.

Chapter Twenty Six

Barb hadn't stopped screaming.

But when her husband's head rolled toward her feet, she did come unglued from the floor. She dropped the wine bottle, added a liter and a half to the reddening floor, bolted around the displaced kitchen table, and tried to make it past me. I didn't have enough time to swing the garden shears at her, but I reached out and snatched one of her ankles. Faster than I was expecting, she stabbed the twisted pointed end of the corkscrew down into my hip. Her ankle slipped free, and she was out of the open patio door before I could come to my feet. Two steps and I was at the door myself, watching her run and slip and fall through the wet grass.

"I'm coming to get you, Baaaaaarrrbara!" I sang to her as she ran.

I let her go to the far cabin and tossed the bloodied hedge clippers aside. Of all the implements I could have gone with, they were probably the most unwieldy and the least effective, although still lethal enough for Wes. Back in the cabin, his stump was pouring a kiddy-pool worth of crimson onto the floor.

Ash's body, only clothed in a pair of plain white boxer shorts, was splayed out on the patio. His mutilated face lifted up to look at me. "No going back now."

"That's right," I told him. "I'm the devil, and I'm here to do the devil's work."

"That's not your line!" he called after me. But what did he know? He had a barbeque fork buried in his forehead. I wrenched the corkscrew from my hip and tossed it in his general direction.

The pitchfork was still lying in the grass by the gazebo. I swaggered over to it, limping from the wound in my hip. My fingers were inches from the pitchfork's handle when the sound of a sliding glass door and the poorly whistled melody of "Carry on my Wayward Son," reached my ears.

Robert stood on the patio of the middle cabin. His insufferable whistling finally clipped to an end. He held a six-pack of beer in each hand and the curious look of a yellow lab on his face. Roman bumped around him, also carrying more beer, a big ungainly case of Michelob Golden Draft Light, to resupply the party.

"Taylor?" Roman asked. "What are you doing here? What was all that screaming about?"

From inside the shadowed gazebo, the fibrous hemp rope that led down to Scotty's noose eked as it turned ever so slowly. When the lazy spin turned his purplish face my way, he said, "There's two of them. God knows you can't kill them both."

As I took up the pitchfork, I snarled at him, "I am God."

Before either of them spotted the pitchfork, I had it up like a spear and was charging like a bull. Roman squealed like a pig and bolted right. Robert stood still; the only thing moving in him was his bowels. Right before the prongs plunged into his guts, he swung one of the six packs and deflected the attack. The four points slid to his side as a shower of foam and beer splattered over us. We twisted and traded positions: My back to the cabin and his back to the lake.

"Taylor! What the fuck are you doing?" Robert stammered while stepping down the patio stairs.

"I'm finally putting a stop to that fucking whistling!"

As I charged again, he launched a bottle from the surviving six-pack at me. It missed and detonated against the cabin's logs. The next beer I caught with the wooden shaft of the pitchfork. The third bottle he still held by the long neck as I ran the tines between his ribs and into his chest. As the holes emptied the air from his lungs, he gasped, trying to refill the vacuum. The rest of the beer tumbled onto the lawn, and I swear to God, as he followed them down to the grass, the holes in his lungs whistled.

Eventually, thankfully, finally, they silenced, and he collapsed over sideways with the pitchfork irretrievably lodged in his body.

Roman was in the middle of the lawn, not running, but slowly backing up while clutching that case of cheap beer to his chest like he was a scared kid up after bedtime, hugging a stuffed animal tight to his heart. He was shaking his head no, over and over again, as if he couldn't fathom that one day, all of his brown-nosing and bitching about making coffee would never come back to haunt him. As if he hadn't left me to the wolves. As if he couldn't have prevented this. As if he could let them have their way with me and I'd have nothing to say about it. As if life had no consequences. As if I'd let all his slights slide.

"Don't kill me, Taylor. I wanted to say something. It wasn't right how they treated you. I wanted to help. I really did," he babbled.

"But you didn't, did you?"

"I don't want to die," he begged, still backing up, still hugging that beer like a teddy bear.

"I didn't want to be a serial killer, but here we are," I told him as I picked up the pruning saw from its place next to the gazebo.

He let out a yelp, then turned and ran. I don't know where he was going. Down to the dock? Was he going to jump in the water still clinging to that case of beer like it was a life preserver? Was he planning on swimming across the whole lake to one of the distance pin-prick-of-light cabins?

I hefted the prune saw like a javelin, hung it over my right shoulder, took two preparatory steps, and launched in through the air. The long handle wobbled in midflight. The serrated blade sunk deep between his shoulder blades. The case of beer crash-landed on the dock next to his face. The cardboard tore open and twenty four cans bounced and rolled and splashed into the water.

With no need to run, I nursed my bleeding hip and hobbled past the center fire pit, onto the dock, and over the lake. Roman wasn't dead yet. His fingers dug into the spaces between the deck boards and pulled himself further over the water. Where *did* he think he was going? There was no danger of him getting away. There was no salvation for him. I straddled his torso and got a good two-handed grip of the shaft of the pruning saw. When I went to pull it out, it caught resistance, so I shoved it further into him. He crowed like a bird. When I pulled it back up, I heard the saw teeth grind through some bone deep inside of him. So that was how he'd die: getting his internal organs sawed apart as he crawled on his belly for a lake that couldn't help him. After a short while, he stopped moving and the pruning saw came loose. I cast it aside and let it splash into the shallows.

Before I left the dock, Cheryl's drowned visage drifted beside me as beautiful and as dead as Ophelia. She was wearing her lacy, red underwear. Her once beautiful skin was molting and rotting. Her eyes were clouded over with decay. Her lips had decomposed to a point that they couldn't hide her teeth, even when they closed. Nevertheless, his eyes still blinked. Her lungs still filled as if she could take oxygen from lake water. Her lips still formed words.

"They did this to me, Taylor. The ones left inside of that cabin. The only ones that really matter," she said, her voice coming through the water unhampered. "Kill them, Taylor. Kill them! Don't let them get away! Don't let them live!"

My eyes fixed on the orange rectangle of light coming from the third cabin. Jason. Barb. Hagari. They were the only ones left. They'd lied about me. They sent me to be tortured. They never helped me. They fired me. Brainwashed me. Assaulted me. Tried to kill me. Left me for dead. But I was back from the grave now, and I could never die.

Next to the nearest fire pit was a familiar setup: a small pile of split logs and a chopping stump. The blade of a felling ax was half buried in the wood. I put one foot against the edge of the stump and pulled the ax free. As I marched with it toward the patio of the last cabin, Jason slid open the door, stepped outside, and posted in front of that patio door, the hero in his own biopic. He held both his hands up, one holding a phone. Had he watched me saw Roman's spine in two? Had he noticed Robert lying dead against the gazebo, gored by a pitchfork? Did he think he was somehow different than them, by merit of a corporate office knighting him as our "regional manager?"

Ax in hand, I didn't break my stride.

"Taylor, stop where you are right there," he ordered me. *Ordered* me. That officious little child in charge of his tea party. "I already called the police. They're on their way now."

When his weak threat didn't slow my steps, he appealed to my dearly departed sense of reason.

"Taylor, whatever you're going through, whatever you're dealing with, he can hash out some solutions, together. Let's break this down, get to the meat of it, and problem-solve."

My foot landed on the patio step.

"Listen. Taylor. I know I had to let you go from the team. But I never forget one of my players." He was pleading to what? To my sense of team spirit? "Just tell me what you need!"

A primal roar unbottled from deep inside of me and boiled up when I was two steps away. The ax head reared back as I closed the distance. He crossed his arms over his head as if to ward me off. The light of the phone glinted in my eyes. Then the swinging ax blade caught a shimmer of moonlight. It made a thick hollow thud as it cleaved through his clavicle. Then he was the one screaming.

I yanked the blade loose and a geyser of blood followed it. Cocking the ax back gave him a single insufficient moment to beg, and it gave me all the time I needed to explain.

"You knew."

The ax sent another wet and dense report through the night.

"You knew!"

The phone clattered to the patio. His arms couldn't stay up to fend off the next blow.

"YOU KNEW!" I screamed at Jason and buried the ax into his skull.

The bone cracked like split lumber. His body dropped sideways to the patio. His arms and legs convulsed as a million confused nerve endings fired randomly from his destructed mind.

I admit it. By the time Jason was just a corpse, I was panting for air. That machine-steady respiration of my teenage killer was a farce. My own breaths were ragged, harsh, dry, and short of oxygen. The truth was, I was nothing like the killer from my youth. I wasn't calm and methodical. I wasn't stoic or silent. I wasn't big or physically imposing. But I had gone mad.

Don't we all?

Sometimes?

Barbara waited for me on the other side of the glass door. She'd retrieved a butcher knife out of a kitchen drawer and brandished it at me as if there was anything in the world that could come between her and me. Beyond Barb, Doctor Hagari pinned himself against the dining room wall, that manipulative, cowardly, opportunist of an old man. Of course, he'd let Barb come after me with a kitchen knife while he watched. He was the chess master, in his mind, and we were the pieces, moved about and arranged on the board until we were both right where he wanted us, here, glaring at each other through glass like neighboring animals at a zoo.

Barb bared her teeth at me and took a swipe through the air with the knife as if testing if she could wield it. But she wasn't opening the door. No. She would wait until I did, and then lunge at my heart with that glistening blade. I wasn't stupid. I wasn't going to fall for her trap.

With the flick of my wrists, I turned the ax backward in my hands. The blunt end of the head whizzed through the cool air and into the glass door. It punched a hole in the double panes and spiderwebbed the glass from sill to sill. I swung again, and the sheets peeled away from the frame like dead skin. A third attack and the glass collapsed inward, shattering against the kitchen floor and sending Barb screeching and backing away. Her ass pushed back the kitchen table, clearing out the dining room and giving us a space to meet each other, but she was not my equal. Fear glazed her eyes. Fire glazed mine.

"Don't let her intimidate you, Barbara," Doctor Hagari coached from behind her shoulder. "Don't let her defy you. Remember, we created her. She is nothing but our child."

She regripped the kitchen knife and a shot of steel stiffened her spine.

"Oh, really?" I asked. "Now, you're going to grow a backbone? After being his pet this whole time? After betraying your husband and your stupid little family? After betraying me? Now, you're going to pretend like you have some conviction?"

"You can't scare me, Taylor," Barbara managed to speak through her quivering lips. "And you can't fool me anymore either. I know you meant what you said to me when you came into work drunk, you two-faced, backstabbing slut. Doctor Cal told me all about your bullshit complaint to HR, lying about him assaulting you. He told me all about you, and your substance abuse, and your absentee father, and your drunken whore of a mother. He was the best thing you ever had. I bet you were begging for it. You wanted him to assault you. You wanted the kind of relationship that we have. He and I, we share something beautiful, and you got jealous. So you lied. But you'll never be good enough for him."

"Barb, you silly twat. He came on to me, and when I pushed him away, he put his hands on me. And when I told him no, he drugged me so he could do it anyway. I remember now. I remember everything," I told Barb. And then to Hagari, hiding behind her, "I found your little library in your office, Doc. I know what you did to me after I reported your perverted, fondling ass."

"Don't you like who you've become, Taylor?" Hagari said with growing smarm and confidence. "Don't you like how you feel? The energy boiling inside of you excites you, does it not?"

"You can't be angry with us," Barb said as she kept the tip of the butcher knife aimed at my throat. "Not if you like who you are. We created you. Doctor Cal and I both. The Taylor you are right now? We did that. And if you don't appreciate our work, then you really don't remember anything. You should have seen yourself before your sessions. A lonely, shallow, vapid, stupid, dependent, subservient woman. I could have summarized your personality with a Facebook Minion Meme."

"I! Have never! Been on Facebook!" I lashed back at her.

"You were nothing until we made you into something." The quiver in Barb's lip was gone. It transformed into a smirk.

"Well, then you're really going to love your handy work when I bury this ax in your stupid, bitch face," I said.

"What will you do, Taylor?" Hagari asked me. "After you murder Barbara and I? You can't simply return to the life you previously lived. The changes I've made in you are irrevocable."

At that, Barb laughed. She laughed! "Do you really think you're just going to go on with your quippy t-shirts and throw pillows about drinking wine and being sassy? You would have never been who you are now without us stepping in and changing your banal, boring, borrowed bullshit," Barb said. "You're the frog we boiled and were too stupid to notice."

"So, what do you want me to do? You want me to go back to how I was? You want me to forgive you? You think just because you tell me you made me this way, I'm supposed to believe you and go on with my life as some copesetic forgettable, abusable, suburbanite slob? Do you really think you can unboil me now?"

"Or you can let us finish our work," Barb said.

"You are my masterpiece, Taylor," Doctor Hagari dared to speak.

"Barb, I'm really sorry you got mixed up in all of this, but you only have yourself to blame," I said because enough was enough. She and her good Doctor Fuckbuddy weren't going to talk their way out of this. "Besides, your work will only be complete when I'm finished with mine."

I stepped in. She struck out with the tip of the knife. It sliced through the sleeve of my hoodie as I slipped sideways, but it cut nothing else. Then I brought the slower but longer reaching ax head around horizontally like a baseball bat. It plowed into her shoulder, nearly separating her arm from her body. She cried out, more from frustration than from pain it seemed, even as spurts of red sprayed the walls. But I'd cut into her left shoulder, not hurting the arm that brandished the knife one bit. She lashed out again, the knife darting at me like the fangs of a cobra. It hissed past my throat as I swung the ax again, a little bit higher this time. The head plunged into her neck, bending it over as more and more blood gushed from her veins and redecorated the cabin interior. The knife clunked to the floor. I kicked her once in the hip to send her backward. She slammed against the doctor, pinning them against the wall. Her hands went to her spurting neck as if her fingers could plug the gash.

I thought of lumberjacks falling trees, taking notches out of both sides as she managed to mutter in wet gargled words, "No. No, you can't. We made you–"

I sent the ax into her neck from the opposite side. The blade made it all the way through this time, and her head toppled over like a watermelon falling off a fence post. Dual shots of bright, arterial blood shot up from the stump of her neck. Her shivering hands had enough nerves left in them to reach up for where her head should have been and feel about her served neck. But there was no brain left to report back to, or to keep her body balanced, or her legs standing up. She toppled down onto the hardwood.

Doctor Hagari, painted with her blood, reappeared from behind her.

"Take a good look, Doc," I said. "Look what you made me do."

Chapter Twenty Seven

With the ax still in my hands, and with Barb's headless body still twitching on the floor, I locked in. I got tunnel vision. I fixated. I couldn't help it. It was too easy to keep swinging the ax, over and over again into Barb's torso, finishing off the removal of her left arm, hacking through her ribs, scooping out the viscera and orange and bluish guts inside, dissecting her deeper and more thoroughly than Hagari ever could. I dismantled her. I ravaged her.

Doctor Hagari ran.

There was no will in him to stand and try his best to mind-fuck me into not killing him. Or to try to fight me off like Barb had. No. His fight-or-flight coin always landed on RUN. Too bad for him, he had nowhere to go.

I took my time taking apart Barb. Eventually, the ax blade lodged deep into a bone. Probably the spine. And with the rest of her body as loose and sloppy as it was, there was no place for me to post my foot to pull out the ax. It stayed there, the handle like a half-raised Iwo Jima flagpole on a hilltop of gore. The kitchen knife was just outside of the blood pool. I gathered that up and followed the doctor out of the front door of the cabin.

The small cluster of cars was still parked in front of the three cabins. Ruby was to the far left, untouched and waiting for me to come back to her. Jason's Tesla was right in front, and Barb's CRV and the rest of my coworker's rides were all neatly lined up after it. I walked past the all-blacked-out Dodge Charger to Doctor Hagari's BMW with those god-awful "DOC CAL" personalized license plates. He was at the driver's door, frantically fighting with the handle, dropping his keys, picking up his keys, dropping them again, and finally managing to work the latch and open the door. He fell behind the wheel as much as sat, a clumsy oaf devoid of courage, completely confused and kerfuffled the moment I ripped away whatever control he at one time had over me.

By the time I limped over to the side of his car, he'd managed to close and lock himself inside and had even inserted his keys in the ignition. But as much as he twisted and cranked the ignition and pumped the gas, there was no life in the BMW. Not with the battery under the hood disconnected. And he said I had poor impulse control and never thought ahead! With the tip of the knife, I tapped on the glass.

The Neolithic death mask, the symbol of my victimization, still hung around my neck by the stretched-out electrical tape. Before looming down to meet the good doctor's eyes, I brought it up and set it back in place.

"Remember me?" the voice inside the mask asked him.

He reeled back as if falling further into his car could keep him safe. I tilted my head back as well, getting a good glimpse of the black, night sky littered with diamonds, before sending my head forward again, face first, leading with that clay death mask, through the tempered glass of Hagari's BMW passenger window. It shattered. Tiny kernels of glass twinkled just like stars. I spit a piece out through the open grin of the mask. Another bit must have cut the skin around my eye. I blinked away blood. Hagari was still inside his car, but not for long.

I got a good fistful of his shirt and pulled him closer to me. Then, while he fought and tried to bat my hand away, I got an even better grip of his salt and cayenne pepper beard. He unfurled out of the broken window like an afterbirth, wet and sloppy, unwanted, and soon disposed of. Then he was on the gravel. I put a knee down on his chest, pinning him in place. I hoisted the kitchen dagger over his chest. He threw up splayed hands and begged me, "No no no no!"

"Remember, doc. You're the victim here!" I said, eager to send the knife point down into his heart.

"Taylor!" a bark froze the night.

The crickets stopped chirping. The breeze cooled to a hush. The knife hung above Hagari like a guillotine waiting for a neck. I looked up to see Stephen in his khaki pants and black polo with the embroidered badge, standing on the porch of the cabin I'd just exited. He held his pistol in his hand, steady this time, his previous reluctance washed away, I suppose, by what he'd found in the backyards and inside the cabin behind him. His focused eye beyond the sights was certain now.

The blacked-out Charger. I'd noticed it when I first came out here but hadn't registered what it meant. Stephen must have seen Ruby and followed my path through the backyard, around the Gazebo, down to the dock, and back through the cabin, seeing my handy work along the way.

"Drop the knife," Stephen said.

"Aww," I cooed. "This is how we first met."

"Drop the knife, Taylor!" he said louder.

"Or what?" I asked.

"Or I'll shoot," he said, without a drop of doubt in his voice.

"Nothing you can do or say is going to stop me from ending this man's life," I told Stephen.

"Taylor, please, no," Doctor Hagari was saying. "You're confused. You and Barbara both. You were both terribly confused!"

"Yeah, you did a real bang-up job on that, doc!" I said. The blade lifted a bit higher into the night.

"Taylor!" Stephen yelled and stilled the night again. He took a step down the porch steps. A board creaked under his boot. "I don't want to shoot you. I don't want to kill you. But if I have to, I will. Too many people have already died tonight."

"Please, daddy? Just one more?" I said with a pout. But I wasn't really asking. I'd stopped asking for permission a long time ago. That was Doctor Hagari's gift to me, and his demise.

"Don't make me–" Stephen began, but never got a chance to finish.

I sank the butcher knife through Hagari's protesting hands and into his throat. The metal plunged down until the hilt and my tight fist met his skin. As if the blade were a bomb, the night exploded when it hit flesh. A shockwave of air and sound perforated my eardrums. Blood jetted skyward from Hagari's neck. A spray of dirt shot up from the ground around me, coating the fresh wetness with grit, but I didn't understand why. Had Stephen tried to shoot me and missed?

But I didn't have time to hesitate. If Stephen missed once, I knew he wouldn't miss again, and if I died, my brain blown apart before my eyes saw Hagari dead, it would be the last injustice in a lifetime full of them.

He hacked and spat and sputtered on his own blood below me. I heaved the knife high above my head. The stars danced on its wet blade.

"Taylor!" a voice shouted.

A different voice. A new voice. A voice I'd heard before, but not Stephen's voice. A voice out of place. Was that you?

"Go on. Don't stop now. Tell me what you remember."

Violetta straddled Stephen's prone shape. She held the shovel I'd dropped outside of the tool shed in her hands like a choked-up softball bat. Her shoulders lifted and fell, lifted and fell as she panted over him. His right hand protruded from the pile, loosely holding the gun without any strength left in his fingers.

Nodding back down to Hagari, I told Violetta, "I have to kill him."

"You. Killed. All of them," she said, each breath its own sentence.

"They deserved it. Every single one of them," I said. Under my knee, Doctor Hagari still choked on his own blood. The first blow hadn't been enough. "Him more than all the rest."

She crept forward, almost crawling over Stephen's inanimate body. Her fingers spider-climbed for the gun. I had no idea what she was going to do.

"He was one of the good ones!" I shouted, gesturing with the knife blade toward Stephen. "We were supposed to be together! What have you done to him?"

The gun found Violetta's hands. You picked herself up to your knees and brought up the barrel.

"Do you have any idea what this man has done to me?" I asked.

"I know," she confessed. "I saw everything. I saw when Jason assigned you to his care. I saw your report to HR, of him sexually assaulting you. I saw the prescriptions billed to Team Next. When they seemed strange, I dug deeper. I saw Hagari's treatment plan for you. I went into his office after hours. I saw the DVDs. The chair. The mask. I reported it. When they did nothing, I reported it again. After seeing you leave his office one afternoon, seeing you drugged and dazed and staggering like a zombie, I went to Jason and demanded something be done. And I told him everything I'd found. And he threatened to fire me. So I went to corporate.

"I risked my job for you, Taylor. I could have ignored all of it. Maybe I should have ignored all of it and never showed up to this retreat. I know you'd do something like this. Something crazy. Something irrational.

Something way overboard. But I never imagined it would go this far. This was the best job I've ever had. I'm finally paying all my bills, and climbing out of debt, and I can buy my kids nice clothes so they don't have to get picked on every time they go to school. We were making it. Don't you get that Taylor? Do you realize what you've done?"

"They made me, Violetta," I said. "They made me do all of this."

"You're not the fucking victim here," you said. "Stop being so fucking selfish."

That is you, isn't it? Underneath my mask. You came looking for me, didn't you, Violetta?

"Finish your story, Taylor."

"What about him?" I asked, gesturing with the knife to the man underneath me. Doctor Hagari still breathed. Poorly. Struggling and coughing up blood that kept draining into his open windpipe, but I hadn't severed his carotid arteries. Not yet. "He doesn't deserve to live."

Violetta rested the tip of the gun against Stephen's head. "What about him?"

"Don't you take him away from me," I growled.

"He's going to wake up soon," she said. "A blow to the head never lasts long. And when he wakes up, he'll want to save that piece of shit under your knee and throw us both behind bars."

"So let me finish," I said.

Doctor Hagari pawed at the side of the knife as if he had enough strength to knock it from my hands. He didn't.

"Let him go," you said. "He's going to die anyway."

"Not good enough. He stole my previous life from me, rewrote it into a tragedy, wound me up, and then set me loose on everyone and everything around us," I said. "After everything he's done, he deserves to reap what he sowed, and I have to see him die."

"And what then?" she asked.

"We both go," I said. "You were never here. Stephen wakes up, and finally, he'll know what it was like for me all those years ago, scared, confused, wandering through a field of bodies, only to stumble upon a horde of police cars and reporters and lights and cameras. They'll haul him away, the last survivor of a brutal mass murder, and he'll finally know how I felt."

She paused. Violetta's body waited as her mind churned through the possibilities. Like a one-armed bandit, spinning Cherries and Bars and Lemons until her mind came to rest.

"Make it quick," you said. "Then, I go my way and you'll go yours and we'll never see each other again."

All Cherries it was. I dropped the knife down into the good doctor's chest. You turned away. And then I was entirely consumed by animal rage. I was all murder. I couldn't stop myself. I didn't want to stop myself. I pumped the blade in and out, in and out, each time blood gushed upwards into the night sky, painting me and the off-white, Neolithic mask with tiny red polka dots. The chromatic opposite of a robin's egg. That knife raised and lowered, raised and lowered, machine-like, like a press stamping out license plates over and over again without the assistance of any human mind. I punctured him. I sucked the blood out of his wounds and sent it vaulting into the night. I drained him of life. Before the light burned out of Hagari's eyes, all I saw in them was confusion. The doctor's protest grew weaker with each plunge until finally, he was an inert mass, a water blivet growing more and more useless with each leak until he was a sloppy, deflated bag.

I'm sure I must have looked completely insane when I looked up to you. You didn't hold the gun against Stephen's head any longer. You held it toward me as if I was a rabid dog capable of any irrational act. But I wasn't going to hurt you.

We said nothing else. I don't think that you thought I was capable of speech after watching me give the doctor what he had coming. He died a warm, wet mess, as whole as a spilled bowl of chili. All that blood must have loosened the glue of that electrical tape. The mask fell to the ground next to him, and I left it there. I assumed I was done with it. I had finally killed my monster. I ran to Ruby, fell inside, and tore off like a beast hunted. But I'm not a monster.

Chapter Twenty Eight

That is you, isn't it, Violetta? Isn't it? Why can't I tell who you are?

"You're a very confused woman, Taylor. It's okay to be scared. It's okay to make mistakes. You nearly killed me, you know. If the ambulances hadn't arrived so quickly, I surely wouldn't be here today. But I won't give up on you. Barbara, she was too wrapped up in her own life. I couldn't mold her into her full potential. But you, Taylor. You have so much possibility. I have so much to show you, but for now, let me wear the mask, and I'll tell you where we can go from here."

I know you're not him. I murdered him that night. Of all the things that happened up there by the lake, I know I left Doctor Hagari dead in the dirt. You can't be him.

Take off that mask.

"I will. In good time."

In good time? Since that night, I've been on the run. I couldn't go back home. No one has fed or taken Chucky for a walk since I left. Bitch is broken, and I couldn't use her even if she wasn't. As for Ruby, she's too recognizable. I can't drive her anywhere. I haven't eaten or slept in days. I've been hiding in this old abandoned, half-demolished hotel for too long now. I need help. I need to see who you are.

How did you track me down? Stephen, is that you behind that mask? Take it off and let me see.

"You should have gone to the cops."

Tell me something, Stephen. Tell me how it felt to wake up in the middle of the woods at the scene of a mass murder, left with the murder weapon and all those bodies for the cops and the press and the rest of the world to come down around you with their lights and their questions, demanding an explanation? Did you enjoy it when they hauled you away in an ambulance and filled you up with drugs to make the pain go away? I can tell you how it felt for me. But how did you like it?

They were our classmates. Cheryl and Scotty and Ash and Linda and Shelton. How could you forget about what happened to them?

"That wasn't real, Taylor."

Cheryl was real. Is that you under the mask? If so, you were always such a good friend to me. Always so brave. Both in my dreams and out. You knew I needed help after we met on the street that day. But you're not her, are you?

"No, I'm not. All I know about Cheryl is what you've told me."

Stephen, why didn't you arrest Hagari? When I first came to you and told you about losing my friends. If you knew that wasn't real, why didn't you look into what Hagari was doing to me? Why didn't you arrest him and throw him away to rot? Maybe if you had, we wouldn't be here now. But it's too late for all that, isn't it?

At least tell me this much. Tell me you're Stephen. Tell me you survived that night and Violetta didn't kill you with nothing more than a blow to the head from a shovel. Tell me you're alive so I know that we can be together.

"He's alive. But he's not here. I don't know if you can really go to him for help. Maybe. Not yet though. They're only beginning to uncover everything that was done to you."

Violetta? Violetta, if that's you, why'd you wait? Why'd you let them turn me into what I am before you lifted a finger? But it's too late for all that. That is you behind that mask, isn't it? You survived that night, just like you were still alive those times I found your head inside of my fridge. You're alive, so is Cheryl, so is Stephen, and so am I. Now all that matters is where we go from here. You said you knew everything. But everything is so much. So now, after everything has come and gone, after the cops came and hauled away the bodies, after their pathetic search for me, after they let Stephen out of the hospital, after they asked you what I'm sure had to be hours of endless questions, after a week of me hiding out in this abandoned hotel where Barb tried to bury me, do you understand now?

"I never wanted to be a part of this, Taylor. I sacrificed everything for you. Team Next in the Twin Cities is shut down. Does that surprise you? Do you really think I could run the whole thing by myself? Even if it seemed like I could, do you think they'd pay me what I'd be worth? No, Taylor. They shut down the Minneapolis branch and sold off the office space, never to be opened again. They covered up everything that happened and erased all the evidence of their own negligence. They laid me off. Threatened lawsuits against me if I said a thing. Smeared my good name so I'd never work a decent job again. You cost me everything. Can't you at least look me in the eyes and comprehend everything that I've sacrificed for you?"

Take off the mask.

"If I do, will you promise me you'll put it back on?"

The electrical tape you used came off easily. And when you handed it to me, there was still plenty of glue left on it to affix it back around my head. Inside the mask, with the cool porous clay resting on my skin, the sound my own inhales and exhales bouncing back to my ears was rhythmic and steady, like the waves of an ocean pushing in and pulling away from shore. For the first time in days, a fire returned to my eyes.

About the Author

Joe Prosit writes sci-fi, horror, and psycho fiction. His debut novel is "Bad Brains," followed by the "From Order Series" featuring the novels, "99 Town," "7 Androids," and "Zero City." "Machines Monsters and Maniacs" is a self-published collection of sixteen of his short stories. He has been published in various magazines and podcasts, most notably, in 365Tomorrow, The NoSleep Podcast, Metaphorosis Magazine, and Kaidankai Podcast. You can find it on Amazon or at his website, at www.JoeProsit.com. And if you're an adept stalker, you can find him on one of the many lakes and rivers or lost deep inside the Great North Woods. Or you can just follow him on X, @joeprosit.

Prefer to read on your device?

Go to this link and enter in the password: Ru@BadBrain? to download your free eBook version that is included in the purchase of this book.